Full Figured 10:

Carl Weber Presents

Full Figured 10:
Carl Weber Presents

Skyy and Anna Black

www.urbanbooks.net

Urban Books, LLC
300 Farmingdale Road NY-Route 109
Farmingdale, NY 11735

ISBN 13: 978-1-62286-456-0
ISBN 10: 1-62286-456-5

First Mass Market Printing May 2017
First Trade Paperback Printing May 2016
Printed in the United States of America

10 9 8 7 6 5 4 3 2 1

Distributed by Kensington Publishing Corp.
Submit orders to:
Customer Service
400 Hahn Road
Westminster, MD 21157-4627
Phone: 1-800-733-3000
Fax: 1-800-659-2436

This book is dedicated to the enigmatic
musician, known for his romantic exploits . . .

Special Thanks to:

Jill Robi for editing this book
and listening to my craziness.

The Birthday Girl

by

Skyy

Chapter 1

My whole life I was brought up to believe that good girls just didn't do certain things. I grew up in the Church of Memphis, and in accordance with church protocol, at the onset of adolescence all the girls were sent to a summer camp for a week to teach them all about how to be good young women. The main lesson was that you did not open your legs for anyone but your husband. Most of us laughed it off after the classes. We were at that age where the only things we thought about were celebrities and boys. Mostly celebrity boys. We dreamed of who we were going to marry when we grew up. For me, it was Ginuwine, while my friends concentrated on members of Immature, Boyz II Men, and Usher.

I knew at that point I was going to have it a little harder than my church friends. I had never been petite or even average. Although I was very cute in the face, I had always been a big girl. My size sixteen at sixteen years of age didn't make the boys run to try to hump me under the bleachers. So I developed a hard outer shell. I focused on school and graduation, and I conveyed the attitude that I had better things to do than to think about boys. My plan worked.

Even though I grew up in the church and loved it, I wouldn't call myself a "church girl." I enjoyed things outside of church, from music to movies, and I spent a lot of time traveling. Being the Cancer woman that I was, I was very observant. By my junior year in high school, the majority of the girls I grew up with in the church had their first babies, and by my freshman year of college, I was the only one who was not only without kids but was also still a virgin. I watched the other girls' stressed-out faces as they struggled to get their kids to act right, after they had had to deal with the early childhood stages of diapers, poop, and crying. I realized quickly that kids were something I had no interest in.

Luckily, I had decided early on that I wasn't going to partake in sexual activities until I was ready and had accomplished the goals I had set for myself. Out of the entire group of girls, I was the only one to go to college right after high school. I got to study abroad in Europe, I did a semester at sea, and I got my master's degree in business and finance. I bought and owned two of the most sought after wedding venues and a nice rental facility in the city. It was mostly used for private events, open mic nights, and salsa dancing.

Things in my life were going great until a bad bout with fibroids caused me to need a hysterectomy a few months after my twenty-ninth birthday. It started out as a blessing; I could finally not worry about birthing anyone's babies. I remembered the doctors asking me over and over if I was sure that I was all right with never having children. My answer was always the same. I didn't want any children, and if, by some miracle, I woke up one day wanting a child, I could always adopt.

The day of the surgery, I remembered feeling nervous, but I went through with what I thought was a simple operation. I woke up twenty-four hours later, strapped down to a bed, with a tube down my throat. Seems my simple operation had turned into a six-hour process.

Things only got worse from there. Three days after I got home from the hospital, I woke up in bed, filled with infection. Luckily, my housekeeper was able to get me back to the hospital. I stayed there for another week, only for them to send me home again against my better judgment. When the home health nurse arrived to check my wounds, she found *another* infection. I was rushed back to the hospital, where I endured another painful operation that ended with three months of healing and a scar that will never go away.

I had a lot of time to think during those months. While my housekeeper helped take care of me and a church friend or two stopped by, I didn't have anyone special to be with me. There were lots of late nights when I wished I had someone to help me to the bathroom or just hold me when the pain was more than I wanted to handle on my own. Although I had experienced a lot of amazing things in my life, I realized then that I could have died without ever experiencing true love or intimacy. I could have died alone.

I didn't want my life to turn into a cheesy movie; I didn't want to be the thirty-year-old virgin. About two months before my thirtieth birthday, it hit me that I didn't want to spend another birthday with people who worked for me or went to my church, with people who I just so happened to have known my whole life.

I just wanted something *more* and I was going to get it.

Chapter 2

The manager of my club called and informed me that he had the flu and couldn't open up the club. I figured that between myself and Honey, the long-running host of open mic and poetry night, we'd be okay. The night had become the biggest open mic night in Memphis, where poets and artist came to recite their pieces or debut new music or art. Honey texted me when she arrived at the club, and I headed over to open the door for her. She was an earthy chick with a thick Afro. She always smelled like incense with a small hint of weed.

"Coral, peace and blessings to you, sista," she said with a slight bow of her head when I opened the door.

I smiled and nodded as I opened the door wider and gave her room to walk in ahead of me. I turned on all the lights and dimmed them to create the mood that the patrons liked for the event. Within moments, the kitchen and bar staff came in. I made sure everything was set before I prepared to leave.

As I was walking out the door, I heard Honey call my name. I turned around to see her running toward me.

"Coral, why don't you stay for the night? We have a live band and everything. It's going to be really nice."

I winced. "I don't know. I really have things—"

"Oh, come on. I'd really like you to see what we have going on here." Honey smiled.

I thought about it. I really had nothing to do besides go home and catch up on *The Walking Dead* on Netflix.

"What the hell?" I smiled and headed over to the bar to take a seat.

Before long, members of a band started bringing their instruments into the building. They were setting up their equipment as early bird patrons started filing into the building. It didn't take long for the band to set up, and soon the sounds of instruments being tuned filled the room.

"Hey, can I get a water?" said a deep voice. The sound filled my ears. I turned to my left to see an attractive man standing next to me, talking to the bartender. He had an unusual accent, one I couldn't quite put my finger on. He looked up, and his eyes met mine. "Oh, hello. How are you, madam?"

"I'm fine." My voice trembled. As I looked at his face, I realized just how gorgeous the man was. His dark brown skin was smooth, and he had a manicured beard. He had long locks that hung down his back, and they were just as neat as the beard on his face. His eyes were very dark brown, almost black, with a few lighter brown speckles. And he smelled *amazing*.

"My name is Onyx. Might I ask your name?" He held his hand out toward mine. I hesitated but soon put my hand in his. A wave of energy shot through my body the moment his hand touched mine.

"My name is Coral."

"Coral. Nice. Well, it's a pleasure to meet you, Coral. I better get up there." He flashed his pearly white smile at me. A strange feeling filled my stomach.

I watched him walk through the tables until he made it to the stage. Onyx took a seat at the black-and-silver drum set. I turned my chair around, suddenly glad that I had stayed.

As soon as Onyx set his water down next to him, the band began to play "Say Yes" by Floetry. I didn't know what had come over me, but I couldn't take my eyes off of the beautiful drummer. Even though the band was playing a slow song, he was intense. He closed his eyes, feeling every beat. I swear I could feel each beat he played too.

As the song continued, the band's volume grew in intensity. Onyx nodded his head, his locks flying, as he pounded the drums with so much force, I wondered if he was going to break his set. At one point he brought his hand down so hard that a stick broke. He casually tossed it aside and produced another stick from the side, not missing a beat. I held on to every note as he killed his drum solo. When it was over, the rousing applause from the crowd broke me out of whatever trance he'd had me in.

I looked down at my legs and noticed they were trembling. I didn't know what had just happened, but my body was shaken, and my panties were soaking wet. I wanted to run out of the room; I felt so exposed. Had anyone noticed the effect this man had on me? Could people tell that I had just had some strange reaction to someone I didn't know? I felt like I was standing in front of everyone completely naked.

I needed to get out of there.

"Isn't the band amazing?"

I turned around to see Honey standing behind me. I just knew I was busted. She had to have noticed my episode.

"They are . . . good," I said cautiously.

"I know, right? Well, let me get up onstage." She patted me on my back before she walked off through the crowd.

I watched as she introduced the band before calling the first poet onto the stage. I couldn't concentrate on the poems. My mind was still occupied with the drummer, who was now sitting casually at his drum set, laughing with his bandmates. He wasn't paying me any attention, so why was I so focused on him?

Because I was a moth and he was my flame. That was why. I couldn't leave, even though I knew I needed to. Nothing good could come from my random, embarrassment-laden new obsession. This man was gorgeous, and I knew I couldn't be the only woman he was having an effect on in the room. Or maybe I just wished it. He was a hot drummer in a popular band, and he was gorgeous.

There was no way I stood a chance.

Even if I were a size six, I doubted I'd have a shot. Clearly, he could have any woman he wanted. I could tell just by the smiling people who were looking at him in the room. I was punishing myself at this point, but I couldn't stop looking.

Before I realized it, the night was over and the crowd was starting to disburse. I didn't know where the time had gone. It was like I had been in a time warp or the time had sped up. No, wait. I knew where the time had gone. With every song that was played, the man on the drums had affected me more. Each stroke of the drumsticks had sent more chills down my spine and had formed more butterflies in my stomach.

I watched from afar as he packed up his drum set while meeting and greeting different people. Fans. From my corner of the room, I watched as girls batted their eyelashes at him and flashed their smiles, each wanting to be the girl whom he took home for the night. To my surprise, he didn't seem interested in *any* of them. Still, he hugged each one the same way and laughed and joked with them before continuing to pack up his things.

"Hey, Coral. Do you need me to stay and lock up?" Dave, my head bartender, asked me after closing his register.

"No. I can do it. Not a problem at all," I said as I finally stood up from my chair. I noticed Honey walking toward me.

"So, what did you think?" She smiled.

"It was wonderful. I had a great time." I smiled, hoping she didn't ask any follow-up questions. There was nothing I could say about the night besides the fact that the drummer had made me moist.

"Good. We really love the spot and hope it can become a permanent place for us."

"I'm sure we can work on that," I said as I watched the drummer walk back inside to continue dismantling his drum set. His eyes met mine, but I quickly diverted my eyes back to Honey. I knew I was busted. I could feel his energy growing closer to me. Before I could figure out an exit strategy, he was standing right next to Honey, putting his arm around her.

"Coral, this is Onyx, the drummer of the band. Onyx, this is Coral. She actually owns this place," Honey said.

"*Oh*, damn. Really?" Onyx nodded his head, obviously impressed. "Your spot is great. The acoustics in this place are spot on."

I still couldn't place his accent, and it was driving me crazy. I wanted to ask him, but I couldn't make any words come out of my mouth. I just stood there with a goofy grin on my face.

"Well, I need to get out of here. Long day tomorrow. Onyx, you got all your things so Coral can close up?" Honey said.

"Yeah. Let me grab my last drum." He turned to me. "Wait, are you here alone?"

I nodded in response.

Onyx shook his head. "No way I'm letting you close up this late by yourself. Do what you have to do, and I will wait with you."

My heart skipped a beat. "I should be okay." My voice trembled again.

"No exceptions. Honey, you need me to walk you to your car?"

Honey shook her head. "I'm right out front. See you guys later."

Before he could object, she was out the front door.

The room was quiet. It was just me and the man who had mind fucked me with his drumming skills all night long. I had never felt this feeling before. Vivid images of him screwing me in the middle of my establishment flashed through my head. I tried to shake them off, but it wasn't working. The man had me gone.

"So this is really your spot? That is very cool," Onyx said as he grabbed his final bag.

I turned off the back lights and walked to the front of the building. He stood there, with just a single light illuminating his skin, giving him this ethereal glow.

"Yes, I own this and a couple of wedding spots."

"An entrepreneur. Very nice," he said, clearly impressed.

"Thank you." I blushed and felt my heart racing.

I turned the rest of the lights out, and we walked out the back door. I could feel his eyes on me. Why did he have to keep looking at me?

"Well, it was a pleasure meeting you, Ms. Coral. I hope this won't be our last time," he said when we reached my car.

"I'm sure it won't."

"Good. Make sure of that." Onyx winked his right eye as he opened my car door for me.

Once I was safely behind the wheel, he headed to his own car. I watched as he got in his car, and I let out a deep sigh. My womanhood was throbbing. I wanted him more than I had ever wanted anything before in my life. Why did I have to want someone so unobtainable? I decided to put him in my memory bank as a man to pleasure myself to in my dreams.

Suddenly, I noticed his car door open. He came rushing back over to my car. I rolled down my window, wondering what was wrong.

"So this might be a little forward of me, and you might want to curse me out since I'm some nigga you don't know, but I'm heading over to Denny's for some late-night breakfast. Would you like to join me?"

Was he serious? I let the words replay in my mind, because I knew I had to be dreaming. This gorgeous man didn't just ask me to go eat with him. Maybe he was just being nice, figuring the fat chick was probably hungry. I didn't really care about the reason, though.

I knew what my answer was going to be.

Chapter 3

I sat across from Onyx, watching him order a meal for two instead of one. He was naturally charming. He was making the old white waitress blush with his compliments and his unique accent. I watched quietly as he asked for eggs and pancakes and made sure that he would get turkey bacon instead of pork.

"Is there anything you want?" His voice brought me out of the trance he had me in. "I'm sorry. I am a fat boy at heart. I love to eat."

"It's cool." I smiled.

He smiled back. His deep dimples were too adorable.

I ordered a salad and a side of chicken strips. Onyx stared at me with a puzzled look on his face. As soon as the waitress walked off, he leaned across the table.

"So you gone have me looking like a greedy bastard while you eat a salad and some chicken?"

I smiled. "It's late, and I try not to eat a lot after a certain time."

"Yeah. I feel ya," Onyx said as he sat back in the booth. "That's good for a person with a regular schedule. This is my normal dinner or lunchtime."

"Night owl, huh?"

"You have no idea."

We sat in silence for a moment. Nervous, I acted like I was reading the dessert menu that had been left on the table. I snuck a peek at Onyx, who was tapping away on his iPhone. A few seconds later he laid it facedown on the table.

"So you own the spot. How come I've never seen you in there before?"

I shrugged my shoulders. "I usually leave it for Miguel to run."

"Oh, the salsa dancer. He's cool." Onyx took a sip of his water. I noticed the little pearl drops that dribbled on his beard. Onyx pressed his tongue against his lips, catching the drops of water. His tongue was long. I felt my stomach knotting up.

I was starting to regret my decision. As I sat across from him, things were starting to seem too real, and I was way too horny to be in such close vicinity to a man my body was craving but couldn't have. I didn't think I could handle him, anyway. Just from his outer appearance and the way he played those drums, he seemed like an aggressive guy. He was probably used to highly experienced girls, not some almost thirty-year-old virgin who wouldn't be able to tell him what she liked and didn't like.

"What's on your mind?"

I quickly realized I had zoned out again. Onyx was staring at me with an inquisitive look on his face. It was as if he was trying to read through my expression.

"Oh, nothing. I guess I am a little tired."

"Hey, sorry if I'm keeping you out past your bedtime. It's just always good to have someone to talk to when eating, ya dig?"

"I wish I was better company." I lowered my head.

"I think you would be amazing company if you would just relax a little." He smiled.

"Is it that obvious?" I blushed.

"Not to the untrained eye, but to me, you look like you are afraid of something. I promise I won't bite . . . well, unless you ask me to."

The devilish grin on his face made my stomach knot up more. I almost wanted to take that as flirting on his part, but I knew I had to be losing my mind.

"So, Miss Coral. Maybe this will be easier if I just ask you questions."

"That sounds like a good idea," I replied. "What would you like to know?"

"Let's start easy. What kind of things do you like to do?"

I replayed the question in my mind. I didn't really know what to say. Truth was, I didn't have much of a social life.

"I like to travel. I took myself on a trip to Mexico about a month ago, and it was really nice. People have no idea how beautiful the beaches are in the Riviera Maya."

Onyx stared at me, his expression not changing from a very straight face.

"So you took yourself? Was it like a girlfriend trip or something?"

"Oh no. I went by myself. I go most places by myself." I regretted the words the moment they came out of my mouth. I sounded pathetic. "What can I say? I'm a lone wolf." I smiled, hoping that I didn't sound so boring.

"So I guess that leads to my next question. If you are a lone wolf, I guess that means you are single, and no man is going to come in here and try to start no shit with me?"

I shook my head. "I'm very single." Again, I wanted to slap myself for sounding so desperate.

"How long have you been single?" Onyx asked.

"A long time," I replied as the waitress arrived with our food. I had never been so happy to see a waitress in my life.

Lucky for me, the subject of our conversation changed while we were eating. I laughed as he devoured his food like a man who hadn't eaten in weeks. He made jokes about being a fat boy when he was young, and about how he *still* had the mind of a fat boy.

"Well, at least you got rid of it. I'm still a work in progress." I laughed.

Onyx stared at me with jaws fat with food. He chewed his food and swallowed, then wiped his mouth before speaking. "I don't see anything wrong with your size. But, hey, it's whatever you're comfortable with." He didn't flinch or stutter when making this comment. He shrugged his shoulders before cutting another piece of his omelet and just continued eating his food.

I don't know why, but in that moment, it felt like weights were lifting off my shoulders. I could feel an unfamiliar sensation coming over my body. It was like someone was trying to break through to a side of me that I didn't know. I wasn't ready to unleash whatever it was, because I didn't know if I would be able to contain it if I did.

"So that's a big thing to you, huh? Is that why you are so scared?"

I looked up from my plate when I heard him speak. I was mortified; it was obvious I was wearing my fear on my sleeve.

"I'm not scared." My voice trembled.

"You are *terrified*. But I can tell you there is no reason to be. We are just two people having a late-night meal. Completely harmless." A grin appeared on his face, and it reminded me of the Cheshire cat's from *Alice in Wonderland*.

Nothing felt harmless. I knew I shouldn't feel so comfortable with this stranger, but I felt like I could tell him anything.

"So what are you so afraid of, Ms. Coral?" Onyx asked, staring directly at me.

I felt the butterflies again. I took a sip of my water and took a deep breath. "In the spirit of full disclosure, this isn't something that I do. I don't have late-night dinner dates with men, ever, especially not ones I just met."

Onyx nodded his head. "I feel ya. When was your last relationship?"

I stared at him with a straight face. He gave me an inquisitive stare, but then the meaning of my expression sank in. Both of his eyes bulged.

"Are you telling me that you have *never* been in a relationship? Okay. Well, when was the last time you went on a date?" Onyx asked.

I gave him the same expression.

"Coral, have you ever done anything?"

Embarrassed, I shook my head. "I always was just so busy. There was school and then work. You think I'm weird, don't you?"

I could feel his eyes on me. I couldn't look up. I didn't want to see the expression on his face. In my head I could hear my church friends laughing about my situation. Many times my inexperience had been the butt of a million jokes. I finally forced myself to look up. I was surprised at what I saw. He didn't look mortified. He looked concerned.

"Coral, I don't think you are weird. I think it's weird that no man has been man enough to approach the quiet but strong girl who probably always gives off the aura that she's too busy. You need someone to grab you by your arms, make you sit down, and make you relax. Tie yo' ass down, if need be."

Our eyes met. My legs were trembling. No one had ever said anything like that to me, and his serious, tight-lipped expression let me know he meant every word of it.

Our waitress appeared just then, breaking the intense moment. "How are y'all doing over here?" she asked. I had never been so happy to see a waitress in my life. She pulled our ticket out of her pocket. I held my hand out, and she handed it to me. Before I could do anything, Onyx snatched the bill from me and laughed.

"Girl, what am I going to do with you?" He chuckled while shaking his head.

"Sorry. It's a habit."

"Look, I know you might not ever want to see my black ass again, but if we are ever hanging out, your hands do not touch a door, a chair, or a check. You understand me?"

I couldn't speak. I just shook my head. Onyx handed the waitress a few bills and told her to keep the change. He stood up and walked up to my side. Onyx held his hand out to me. I put my palm in his, and he assisted me out of the booth. I wondered if he could feel the electric energy that I was feeling.

We headed outside. There was a distinct change in the air. There was an unusual breeze for a Memphis summer night. We walked to our cars, which were parked on the side of the building. We were the only two cars left. I pulled my keys out of my pocket and fumbled for the keyless entry.

"So I'd like to give you my num—"

Before I could finish my statement, I felt a strong hand grab my arm. With one quick jerk, Onyx had me pinned against the concrete building. He pushed my hands up over my head, then pinned them to the wall. My eyes bulged as his lips pressed against mine. My whole body tensed up at the feel of his soft lips.

Oh, God! My first kiss.

Oh, my God. I'm being kissed. What do I do?

Fuck! I'm sucking at this.

Stop thinking, Coral, and enjoy the moment!

I closed my eyes and slowly parted my lips. Onyx's tongue crept into my mouth, and he touched my tongue with the tip of his. My knees began to shake. He let go of one of my arms, only to put his now free arm around my waist, pulling me closer to him. I could feel his rock-hard body; it was calling my name, and I was more than willing to answer.

He pulled his lips away and pressed his forehead against mine. I looked at him. His eyes were closed.

"Give me your phone," Onyx commanded without taking his forehead off of mine. I pulled my phone out of my pocket and handed it to him. He finally pulled his head away from mine and pressed numbers on my phone before pressing SEND. I heard his phone start ringing. He pressed IGNORE and handed me back my phone.

"My number is in your phone. Text me and let me know you made it home. Do not forget," Onyx commanded.

I nodded, agreeing to his demand. I was so used to being in control and telling other people what to do. I had never had anyone demand anything of me. I felt like I was relinquishing my power to him, but crazily enough, I loved it. He pressed his lips against my forehead before walking over to my car door. I followed and allowed him to open the car door for me. I got in, and he closed the door.

I put my key in the ignition and waited so that I could watch him get in his car. I knew he wasn't going to move until I drove off. Reluctantly, I put my car in drive and took off, anxious to get home and to send the text he had asked of me.

Chapter 4

We texted for a few minutes before Onyx let me know he was going to call it a night. I climbed into bed. I knew I needed to sleep, but I couldn't stop thinking about him. I could feel his body still pressed against mine. I felt like his taste would forever be etched on my taste buds.

I ran my finger along my arm. My sense of touch was elevated, and it almost felt like an electric current was surging through my body. My nipples were so hard, they were sore to the touch. I gently thumbed my right nipple, and the sensation caused my pussy to throb.

I looked at my closet door. I stood up, then walked over to it and opened it. I searched in the bottom of the closet for a bag that I had buried deep in the back. I had always frowned at the idea of toys. It just didn't seem right, and I honestly didn't know how to use them. Still, there the bag was, hardly touched, with a light film of dust on it.

First, I pulled out the biggest box in the bag. A big black dildo with veins was inside the box. I was disgusted by the sight of it, just as I was the first time I saw it, on my birthday. I quickly put it back in the bag, as nothing about it seemed appealing. I opted for the smaller box, which contained an oval silver bullet. I opened it and pressed the ON button, but nothing happened.

Batteries.

I looked in the bag and realized that my friends hadn't been smart enough to provide batteries for the devices they bought me. I scanned my room for something I could grab some batteries from, and noticed the remote for my Blu-ray player. To my good luck, it took two AA batteries, which was just what the bullet needed. I removed the batteries from the remote, then placed the first battery in the bullet. As soon as I pressed the second one into place, the bullet started vibrating so fast, it fell out of my hands.

I turned it off and crawled back into my bed. Lying on my back, I stared at the device. I actually didn't know what I was supposed to do. I picked up my phone and Googled "how to use a bullet," but after getting a ton of porn sites, I decided just to wing it.

Still lying on my back, I spread my legs and held the bullet in my hand. I turned it on low and felt the slow vibration in my hand. I took a deep breath and bit my lip as I dangled the bullet on top of my lips. The sensation wasn't as intense as I expected, so I knew I needed to go a little farther. Using my index finger, I spread myself open a bit, allowing the bullet's vibrating ball inside. It touched something and sent a powerful surge of energy through my whole body, causing me to pull it out quickly and drop it.

So that must be my clitoris. It's real and very much alive.

I sat there, breathing heavy. My pussy was throbbing for more. I picked the bullet back up and this time held the actual ball with my fingers. I put it back where it was, allowing it to rest upon my clit.

I was soaking wet. I didn't know it was possible to get so wet. Now I understood why women talked about pleasing themselves so much. With my fingers holding on to the bullet, I massaged my throbbing knob with the cool metal-colored plastic. I pushed my legs together and held my hand in place as I started to grind against it. I had never felt anything so good before in my life. I noticed the little red button was on low, and wondered what would happen if I took it up a notch.

I pressed the button once, moving the speed to medium. The electric surge caused my toes to curl. I started breathing heavy as a knot formed in the pit of my stomach. I felt my legs trembling as they stiffened, and the knot in my stomach began to grow. My heart was racing as my entire body started to tremble. The sensation scared me, causing me to pull the bullet out and turn it off immediately. Within moments, whatever had been growing inside of me started to subside. I didn't know what was happening, but I was too afraid to find out.

I put the bullet on my nightstand and turned over on my side. Holding on to one of my pillows, I closed my eyes as the sensations in my body from the experience continued to subside. I could feel the wetness between my legs, and my womanhood was still calling out for more. The curious side of me wondered what would have happened if I had just held on for a little bit longer, but the rational side of me didn't like the idea of not knowing what was about to happen. My mind drifted back to Onyx. Could he make me feel those sensations? That felt amazing, and I hadn't even been penetrated. If I couldn't handle a small device, what made me think I was ready for a real man?

I took a deep breath and drifted off into my dreams. For now, they were all that I had.

Chapter 5

I sat in the youth office at the church, going over the budget for the upcoming Youth Day. I had recently assumed the job of ministry director, as my predecessor had moved into a different department. I could hear the choir rehearsing upstairs, and I mouthed the lyrics as I worked.

I looked up when I heard the squeaky knob turning on the office door. Tangie, the young women's mentor, walked in. We had known each other since childhood, and she was someone I would consider a friend, or at least a close acquaintance. I was always amazed by her state of dress. Her clothes were always a little tight for my comfort, at least in a church. Even her pant-suits left little to the imagination, as they held tight to her curves and to the round ass that she had had since childhood. The boys had always liked her because of her shape and beauty, and even as an adult, she had had an endless number of suitors attempting to get her in the wife position. She got pregnant her freshman year of college, but she managed to finish her education due to her large, supportive family. In fact, she was the only one in our age group besides me who had continued her education at all by becoming a medical lab assistant, even if it was a couple of years after high school.

"Hey, Coral. I need to grab the card to get supplies for the young women's sleep-in this weekend. Don't worry. I'm keeping it simple. Probably hot dogs and chips."

"Oh, it's fine. We did good this week on money for the young women's programs." I smiled as I pulled the credit card out of my desk and handed it to her. "What sort of subjects are you guys covering this time?"

Tangie shrugged her shoulders. "I usually just let it go and see what they want to ask. Heather and I like to make the girls feel real comfortable so they can come to us with anything."

"You guys do a great job." I smiled again, though I was a little envious of the relationship they had with the teen girls in our church. They were looked at as big sisters, whereas most of the girls barely spoke to me.

"It's all about trust. What we talk about doesn't leave the room. Girl, if you heard some of the things these girls talk about . . ." Tangie shook her head. "And I thought we were bad back in the day. Well, most of us. You were always a good girl."

I gave a somewhat regretful smile. She was right. When the girls had talked about sex, I had always sat in a corner, completely out of the conversation. When they had tried to include me, I had been so mortified by most of what they were saying that they had eventually just stopped trying. After a while, I believed, they had feared I would rat them out, so they had just stopped talking about things around me altogether. I could remember countless times when I walked into a room, and the conversation stop immediately.

"Tangie, I really was a square, wasn't I?"

Tangie stared back at me. Her facial expression confirmed everything I already knew. I lowered my head as she sat down.

"Coral, it wasn't that you were a square. You just weren't into the things that we were into. It wasn't a bad thing. Hell, it was a great thing, actually. You didn't get caught up like the rest of us."

"But what do I really have to show for it? I have no real friends, no love life. I just have jobs."

Tangie scooted her chair closer to my desk. She put her hands on top of my hands on the desk. "Coral, girl, you just don't know how good you have it. You are single, with no kids, and financially independent. And you are in the prime of your life. You literally have the world at your feet. You don't have anyone to answer to or to coordinate anything with . . . well, except God."

We both laughed.

Tangie went on. "What I'm saying is, if you want to get out there and find your groove, you are well within your rights to."

"I don't even know where to start," I replied softly.

"Why don't you come to the lock in tomorrow? Maybe being around some younger people will help you loosen up a bit. And you can give some advice on college and things of that sort," Tangie said as she stood up. "I'm not taking no for an answer."

I thought about the offer and wanted to say no. The idea of being in a room with a bunch of teenagers who didn't even like me didn't seem appealing at all. But I could tell by the look on Tangie's face that she meant business.

"I'll be here." I smiled.

***

I stared at my phone as I sat in my car, in the church parking lot. It had been over twenty-four hours, and I hadn't heard from Onyx. I knew it was my fault. I came off as too inexperienced, and probably no man wanted to deal with someone like that. I wanted to cry. The first guy I had ever truly liked was gone before anything could even start.

I grabbed my overnight bag and headed toward the church. I saw two of our older girls, Precious and Caitlyn, walking ahead of me.

"Hi, girls," I called out.

They turned around and looked at me as if I had the plague.

"Ms. Coral, what are you doing here?" Heather asked with a bit of an attitude.

"Tangie asked me to come. You guys don't mind me crashing your party, right?" I replied, trying to sound as hip as possible. They both looked completely uninterested as they shrugged their shoulders and gave each other a look of complete disapproval as we walked into the church.

The other young women were already settled in the large room in the basement. A phone sat connected to a little blue speaker that looked like a pill, and it was playing music I had never heard before. I knew it wasn't gospel. I suddenly realized that all eyes were on me. The looks ranged from confused to mortified at the sight of an outsider.

"Hey, girl." I felt a hand touch my shoulder. I turned to see Tangie, who was wearing a pair of cotton yoga pants and a tight tank top.

"Coral, so cool that you came. This is going to be nice," Heather said, walking in right behind Tangie. Heather and Tangie had been best friends since birth. They tolerated me, but I had never been one of the girls, and I definitely was not as close to one of them as they were to each other. Heather had had her first child when she was a senior in high school. Now she had two boys and was married to her church sweetheart.

"Okay, ladies. So Ms. Coral has been gracious enough to come and party with us. She's just like us. You can talk to her about anything, and the same rules apply," Tangie said, addressing the group.

Immediately, Precious raised her hand. "I'm sorry, and I don't want to sound rude, but how do we know we can trust her like that?" Precious asked with her arms folded.

From the heads nodding, I knew the other girls felt the same way.

"Because Coral knows the rules. The moment this bell rings, this is an open space for anyone to talk about anything. Nothing leaves this room. Those are the rules," Tangie assured them.

I could tell my presence was going to take some getting used to, but most of the girls seemed to lighten up with Tangie's words. I knew I needed to say something to reassure them.

"I know that you guys don't talk to me, but I promise you that I do not want to do anything to harm the bond you guys have formed here. I just hope that I can be a part of it and will offer any advice that I can," I said, finishing with a smile.

To my surprise, the rest of the girls quickly lightened up. Some even gave me a smile in return.

We unpacked our sleeping bags and created a circle. I sat on the little bed I had made out of a comforter I had brought from home. I watched the girls laugh and show Tangie and Heather how to do new dances they had learned. Soon Tangie called for the circle of trust. All the girls sat down on their individual sleeping bags.

"All right, ladies. So I am about to ring the bell. As you know, once the bell rings, we are in an open environment. We are able to talk about anything you would like. Please understand that with some things, we might not be able to give the advice that you want. But we will do all that we can to be as open as you are."

Within moments I felt like I was sixteen again. I wanted to run and hide in a corner. The girls talked about all types of things I had no grasp on. I sat on my bed, trying to keep a straight face and to not look as mortified as I felt. Plenty of times I had overhead adults talking badly about the youth of today, but never had I thought they were really as sexually charged as they were. When I was young, the idea of giving a blow job was taboo. Now girls were talking about giving blow jobs as if it were a natural day-to-day thing.

I had to commend Heather and Tangie, who were both able to talk openly but did not cross the line with the girls. They gave good advice but never agreed that the girls should be having sex so early.

"Ladies, we can sit up here and talk about sex all day and all night, but this is not what this group is about. You are young women, and I know that the subject is important. But the thing we want you to understand is that there is so much more out there than just sex. That's really why I wanted Coral to be here."

I turned my head to see Tangie looking at me.

"Coral, do you mind if I share a little with the group?"

I nodded my head, scared about what Tangie was about to say.

"When we were your age, Heather and I were just like you guys. Boys and dating were the only things on our minds. Heather was with her boyfriend, and well, I had a few boyfriends myself. Coral, on the other hand, was more focused on school and put her energy into that. Now Coral owns multiple successful businesses and can literally do whatever she wants in life. Heather and I have families we have to support. We don't have the freedom that we could have had if we had just buckled down."

The young women were all ears. I listened as Tangie and Heather continued to sing my praises. I wished I felt the same way about myself.

Finally, I spoke up. "Thanks, Tangie, but I would like to add that you need to have a healthy medium. I was far left. I didn't do anything. I didn't go to school dances, football games, and I missed my prom. I never had a boyfriend and never got to experience young love. Even now, most of you didn't even realize I was the same age as Tangie and Heather."

"So are you saying you think we should be dating and stuff?" Precious asked.

I couldn't believe they were actually listening to me. "I just wish that I would have been more of a teenager when I was young. There are some things you just can't undo. But I'm not saying you should be having sex," I explained. "I think that sex is something that you really need to be mentally and financially ready to handle. What if you did get pregnant? If your boyfriend refused to help, would you be able to take care of things on your own?"

I was relieved when the open session was finally over. The girls went back to dancing and joking among themselves. I headed to the kitchen with Tangie and Heather to grab more supplies.

"I'm really glad you came, Coral. The girls really listened," Heather said with a smile.

"I'm glad I came too. It was a little intense, but informative."

"Girl, sometimes we find it hard to listen to what they are saying. Some of those girls are more experienced than we are," Tangie said, and we all laughed.

For the first time I felt like one of the girls. I didn't know why, but I suddenly felt completely comfortable with them.

"I haven't done anything that those girls were talking about. I feel like I'm missing out," I said as I grabbed a bag of chips. I looked up to see Heather and Tangie looking at me.

"Wait a minute. Coral, girl, are you saying you still haven't lost your virginity?" Tangie's mouth dropped open as I shook my head. "How on earth is that even possible?" "Right. Shit, I would die. Are you, like, seriously waiting for marriage?" Heather asked.

"No. I mean, I just never did it. But now it's like I want to experience things, and I don't know where to start," I revealed.

"You should try online dating," Tangie said.

I thought about Onyx. "I met this guy, and he blew my mind. But I think that my experience level might have scared him off."

"When was the last time you talked?" Heather asked.

I told them about the other night with Onyx. They listened to me, hanging on to each word. I could almost feel him again as I relived the moment. I wanted to touch him, or at least hug him and feel his lips one more time.

"Okay. So why haven't you texted him?" Tangie asked.

"Because I'm not trying to look desperate." I frowned.

"Girl, it's not about looking desperate. It's about showing interest. Maybe he's waiting on you to make the first move. Where is your phone?" Heather held her hand out.

I pulled my cell out of my pocket and handed it to her. I watched as she started texting something on my phone. My body started to tense up.

"Wait. What are you doing?" I said.

"I'm sending him a message. Something flirty and fun, but also serious." She pressed SEND and handed me back my phone. I immediately read the message.

> Drinking wine and thinking about the other night. that meal was really tasty. What did you think?

I didn't know what was flirty about the message, but before I could ask, my phone buzzed.

> The food wasn't the tastiest part. WYD?

"He responded back," I yelled excitedly, handing the phone back to Heather. She and Tangie read the message.

"Okay, good. Let me." Tangie took the phone from Heather and started to type. I waited, biting my nail. Finally, Tangie pressed SEND and gave me back the phone. I read her message.

> Nothing. Trying to decide what to get into tonight. And you?

It took only a second for him to respond.

>   No need to decide. Meet me in the Harbor
>   Town Riverfront parking lot in an hour.

"What am I supposed to do?" I screeched.

"Get your stuff and go," Tangie and Heather replied in unison.

"But wait." Tangie took my phone, wrote a text, and sent it. "There. It says 'See you in two hours.' That way you have time to go home and get cute."

"I can't do this."

"Yes you can. Now, get yo' ass out of here and go get that man!" Tangie ordered.

I looked at the two women, who were now both yelling at me not to pass up this opportunity. I knew they were right. I had my chance, and I was going to take it.

Chapter 6

I held my hands at ten and two o'clock on my steering wheel. I had to focus, or I knew I was going to drive right off the small bridge and into the Mississippi River. Mud Island, where the upscale neighborhood of Harbor Town was situated, was home to some of the most expensive houses and apartments in Memphis. Although it was considered pretty remote, many people used the small riverfront area for romantic rendezvous or late-night make-out sessions.

I glanced at my reflection in my rearview mirror. I had done the best I could. I didn't own "date" clothes. I had taken my friends' advice and had kept it simple with a colorful maxi dress that I'd purchased a few months ago from Ashley Stewart but that I had never worn. When I'd tried it on, all the saleswomen in the store had gushed about how good I looked in it, so much so that I'd actually bought it. Up till now, I had left it in the store bag.

I finally had a reason to wear it.

I pulled into the parking lot and saw his truck facing the river. I popped a mint in my mouth as I drove forward. I watched him get out of his truck when I pulled into the space next to his. It was late, and only three other cars were in the lot. I noticed one couple sitting out on the rocks under the streetlights. Onyx walked over to my car door, wearing his cute, but devilish grin.

"Hey, you," Onyx said as he opened my car door. "You look beautiful." He held my hand as I stepped out of the car. Onyx wrapped his arms around me. I accepted the embrace, wrapping my arms around his muscular torso.

"You look nice too. I totally forgot to bring mosquito repellent." I frowned as I swatted a bug off my arm. I knew this was supposed to be romantic, but the idea of sitting by the river in the Memphis heat while getting attacked by mosquitoes had never sounded romantic to me.

"Oh, we aren't staying here. I just wanted to meet you at a well-known place so you wouldn't get lost," Onyx said as he motioned for me to get back in my car.

"Oh, okay. So where are we going?" I replied as I got back in my car.

"My place." Onyx closed my door before I could object. I watched him, my mouth agape, as he got in his car and backed out of the parking lot.

We took a curvy street and drove deeper onto the island until we made it to a set of apartment buildings I didn't even know were there. My hands were becoming clammy as I yet again pulled into a parking space next to his. I tried to steady my breathing as I watched him get out of his car and come over to mine. He opened my car door and helped me out—a true gentleman. He led me toward his apartment.

"Now remember, I'm a bachelor, so my place isn't all fancy and shit," Onyx said, laughing, as he opened the door to his place.

He didn't have to worry, though, because I was more than impressed. He had a large studio apartment, and he'd done a lot with the open space. His king-size bed was the main focal point, with its massive headboard that covered the whole back wall. The headboard was also a bookshelf, and its various shelves were filled with hundreds of books. In the opposite corner, his drum set sat next to a small table and a futon. An abstract painting of musical instruments hung on the wall next to his fifty-inch flat-screen TV. Underneath the TV was a small entertainment center that was big enough only for his PlayStation 4 and some video games.

"Would you like something to drink? I don't have much, but I got some apple juice, Merlot, and some water. I really should have prepared better for company," Onyx said with a shrug of his shoulders.

"Water is fine," I said as casually as possible, trying to wrap my mind around the fact that I was standing in a man's apartment. I stood in the middle of the room, unsure of what I was supposed to do while he was in the kitchen. I didn't know if sitting on the bed would send the wrong signal or if sitting on the futon would send no signal at all.

A minute later Onyx appeared at my side, holding a wineglass filled with water. He handed it to me and laughed.

"Girl, if you don't relax . . . Get comfortable. Kick those sandals off and have a seat somewhere."

"I didn't know where you wanted me to sit." I blushed. He sat down on the futon and patted it for me to sit next to him.

"Coral, you have nothing to be nervous about. We are two adults sitting here, about to enjoy each other's company. You want to watch something on TV? You like *Game of Thrones* or *Spartacus*?"

My eyes widened, and I gasped. He liked my two favorite television shows.

"Do you really like *Spartacus*?" I asked.

"Hell, yeah, girl," Onyx said as he stood up and walked over to his entertainment center. He pulled out a box set of *Spartacus*. "What season you want?"

"I like *Gods of the Arena*." My inner geek had appeared, and I felt myself relaxing a bit.

Hours passed, and the geek in me took over completely as we discussed our favorite episodes of the season. Onyx talked passionately about everything. I found myself hanging on to every word. I knew he would make an excellent salesperson, because I was ready to buy anything he talked about.

As we moved on to the fourth episode, I glanced at the clock on his cable box and saw that four hours had passed. It was almost two in the morning, and I was still sitting in this man's house, right next to him. I didn't know the protocol, but I did know about booty-call hours, and we were way into those hours. I let the reality set in that nothing was going to happen that night, which actually lifted the little bit of weight I had left off on my shoulders.

"What are you thinking about?" Onyx said suddenly.

I turned my head to see him staring at me. My nerves instantly took over, causing my right leg to tremble. I shrugged my shoulders. "Nothing really. I didn't realize it was so late," I replied as I focused on the television.

"Oh, my bad. Do you have something to do or someplace to be in the morning?" Onyx said, sitting up straight on the futon.

I shook my head. "No. I am fine." My voice trembled a bit.

"Are you sure? I really want you to be comfortable around me, Coral," Onyx said with sincerity in his voice, which helped to ease my nerves again.

"Well, I just . . . Well, this is just a bit new for me."

"What? Kicking it and watching *Spartacus*?" Onyx joked.

I hit him playfully. "No. Just this." I waved my hands in the air. "The only place I have ever been at two in the morning is in my bed or in a hotel room's bed."

"Ah." Onyx nodded his head. "So I have you out past your bedtime. But tell me, is it the being out that's the issue, or is it being here with me, on my futon, that's the problem?"

I thought about the question for a moment, even though I knew the answer. Inexperienced or not, I didn't want to come off as a complete square.

"I will be thirty soon, and I own my own businesses. Therefore, I do not have a bedtime, sir." I rolled my neck, causing Onyx to laugh.

"Okay, Ms. Independent. Well, since it's not the late thing, I guess it's safe for me to bet on the latter. So you aren't used to being out this late with a man. That's just so hard to believe."

"What is hard to believe?" I questioned. "You don't believe what I told you the other day?"

Onyx shook his head. "No, I one hundred percent believe that you aren't that experienced. I just find it had to believe that no man has ever tried to claim that prize for himself."

I shrugged my shoulders. "To be completely honest, I can't put it all on them. I haven't been very approachable. I keep to myself. I go to church, work, and home. I've had a guy or two stop me at, like, a gas station or something, but of course, I didn't pay them any attention. So maybe if I made myself more available . . ."

"Nah," Onyx interjected. "First off, if a man wants something, just because a woman isn't that approachable isn't going to stop him. A man is going to go for what he wants. The problem is a lot of men don't pay attention. Take the other night. I'm a drummer, so I'm sure you know girls make themselves readily available for me. But I saw you, I noticed you, and even with you being somewhat standoffish, there was something about you. I needed to know more, so I did what I needed to do. I thought for half a second about not asking you out to eat, just because it was late and that's not the way I normally want to make an impression. But then I realized I might not see you again, so I acted on the opportunity in front of me." Onyx patted his chest with his right hand.

I felt my body betraying me again. I wanted his arms wrapped around me and his mouth anywhere. He seemed so far away from my lips. I studied the lines in his face—he was serious, and I knew it.

"I just . . . I don't get it, Onyx. Why me? I mean, you are right. You are a drummer and a very, very attractive man. I know I can't be the only chick you saw that night."

"No, I saw a lot of chicks. But there was only one woman who caught my eye."

I wanted him to stop looking at me. I could feel his eyes on me, and they were causing a fire to ignite in the depths of my soul. My toes tingled, and my womanhood pulsed with an unknown desire. And the sex happening on the television wasn't helping the situation.

"Why are you so nervous, Coral?" Onyx's deep voice echoed through my ears.

"You make me nervous."

"I don't want you to be nervous," he said softly.

"I can't help it."

"Then it's up to me to make you feel at ease." Onyx stood up. He held his hand out to me. I placed my palm in his hand, and he helped me stand up. Hand in hand, we walked toward the door.

I began to panic. I knew I had done something wrong, but I didn't know what to do to fix it. I didn't want to leave. I wanted to spend a lifetime in his arms. I wanted him to show me what I had seen only in television shows and movies. I wanted to do anything besides leave him.

"Am I getting kicked out?" I said with a laugh, hoping it sounded like I was joking, when I really meant it.

We stood by the door. Onyx put his hands on the sides of my arms. He stared at me with a sweet grin on his face that showed off his deep dimples.

"It's late, and like I said, I need to make you a little more comfortable."

"I'm okay."

Onyx shook his head and pulled me into his arms. He placed a kiss on my right cheek.

"Coral, you are something special, and with special things, you don't rush it. When the time is right, things will happen. I want you to be one hundred percent comfortable and sure. Because when I do taste you, I need you to know that it's because you are my favorite meal."

I felt a flood rush into my panties. I held on to Onyx, afraid that if he let go, my legs would give out. He kissed me on my left cheek before planting a seductive but romantic peck on my lips. My body no longer belonged to me; in that moment, it wanted only Onyx.

I didn't know how I made it to my car without my legs giving out, but somehow I did. Before parting, we had made plans to see each other the next night, but this time, my house would be the destination. I drove home with my eyes on the prize.

I had some planning to do.

Chapter 7

I walked into Torrid with a whole new look on life. I didn't want a pair of jeans or a simple shirt; I wanted some of the formfitting, sexy clothes I had seen on the models on the store's Web site. The moment I started perusing, my nerves set in. I was lucky to have weight that was well distributed, but as a big girl, I was always cautious about what I put on. The last thing I wanted to do was wear something that wasn't flattering or become a joke in a Facebook meme.

I asked one of the associates to help me. She asked me what I was looking for. I didn't really know the answer—I just knew I wanted something that I couldn't wear in church. She laughed as she guided me around the store, picking out various pants, skirts, and tops.

I opted to keep it cute, but not over the top. I bought three pairs of jeans, two of which were distressed and had holes in various parts. The shirts I chose were sexy and hip. One of them hung off my shoulder, as if I were in *Flashdance*.

I bought a pair of black wedges and a few different pieces of jewelry. I had never really worn jewelry. The most would be a pair of studs, just to keep my ears from closing, so the chunky statement pieces were definitely something new. After leaving Torrid, I headed back to Ashley Stewart and purchased another maxi dress to wear that night. I wanted to look nice and also to offer easy access, which my new formfitting jeans wouldn't allow. And to finish my shopping spree off, I purchased two lace bras and a few pairs of matching lace underwear, just in case something happened.

I arrived home to find my maid, Helena, finishing up in the living room. She was more excited about my night than I was. I had been using her once a week for years, and she had become almost as close as a friend as anyone. She always questioned me about when I was going to have some company, and so she'd jumped at the opportunity to help me set up for the night. By the time she left, there wasn't a single thing out of place in my house.

I had hit Pottery Barn and had purchased a bunch of new candles in various sizes. I wanted to create the right ambiance for the night without overdoing things. I lit a few of my big candles and sat them inside of my fireplace. I'd just made a homemade lasagna, and the smell of garlic and spices filled my house. I added a few toppings to the house salad and brought out ranch and Italian dressing.

I jumped when I heard my phone ringing. I answered, and Onyx's smooth voice asked me to open the gate to my gated community. I pressed the buttons on my phone and could hear the buzzer for the gate in the background. I stayed on the phone as I guided him through the winding streets of Collierville. My house was small in comparison to many of the mini mansions located there, but it was good in that it was easy to spot. Instead of going for a big two- or three-story house, I'd opted for a spacious one-story ranch with large rooms and open spaces.

I stayed on the line with Onyx and laughed as he admired all the large houses he passed while I checked myself in my full-length mirror. I fixed a few flyaway strands of hair while he joked about possibly getting pulled over for being a black man in my neighborhood. I assured him that he was safe as I walked back into my living room. I looked out the window and could see his headlights turn off, which meant he had finally made it to the back of my driveway. I took a deep breath and unlocked the door.

"See? No cops," I said and laughed as I met Onyx outside. He was staring at the landscaping of my home. I had already turned on my outside lights, which had illuminated the lush bushes and the front of my house.

"This place is beautiful. I almost forgot I was in Memphis," Onyx said as he walked up to me. He wrapped his arms around me, hugging me tight. "You look beautiful."

"Thank you. Come on in."

We walked down the dimly lit pathway to my side door. He held my hand as I guided him, all the while joking about the possibility of a frog appearing at any moment. Onyx let out a sigh when he walked into my house. I could tell he was impressed. My hardwood floors shined from the good buffing I had done earlier.

My living room was huge, with nothing on the back wall but windows, which showed off my backyard, my pride and joy. My swimming pool had been made to look like a lagoon, complete with a grotto. I had covered the backyard with green plants and had built a patio that included a custom fire pit. I spent most of my nights sitting out on my patio, just listening to the crickets chirping and the sound of my waterfall.

"This is insane. Seriously, if I lived here, I would never leave." He admired the living room for just a moment before deeply inhaling the Italian aroma. "Girl, I don't know what you are trying to do to me, but that shit smells delicious."

"I made lasagna. I did it with turkey. I hope that's okay. I don't eat pork," I said as we walked into my kitchen.

"Turkey is great. I try to limit my pork intake to when I'm at my mom's house. She's never gonna stop cooking with it, and I'm never going to stop eating her ribs."

We both laughed.

I motioned for him to have a seat at the kitchen table and open the wine. I pulled the deep pan of lasagna out of the oven and set it on my kitchen island. Onyx walked over to look at my creation. He rubbed his belly while humming and shaking his head.

"Girl, the fat boy in me is about to kill that."

"Do you want a separate plate for your bread?"

"Baby, there is no need for presentation. In the end it's going in my stomach. Put it all on a plate, and I will be just fine," Onyx said, smiling.

I blushed. I fixed a plate with lasagna, salad, and Italian bread and set it in front of him. I put a smaller portion of lasagna and salad on a plate for myself and joined him at the table.

He poured wine in my glass before grabbing my hand and closing his eyes. "Lord, thank you for this blessing we are about to receive and for the amazing hands that made it. Amen." Onyx opened his eyes and picked up his fork.

I watched him as he took his first bite, which was quickly followed by moans of pleasure. We talked quite easily. I was much more comfortable now than I'd been the night before, and we laughed and got to know each other on a more personal level. I found out that his family was spread out between New Orleans and Texas. I told him about my family, including the fact that I had grown up with my aunt and cousin due to my mother's drug problem. Like most families, his had a few members who had fallen prey to drugs as well.

Onyx refused to let me wash the dishes alone and assisted me after dinner. Once we were finished, he asked if he could check out my backyard, which I was more than happy to do. As we walked outside, I used a control panel to turn on the waterfall and the pool lights, illuminating the backyard and making the waterfall look like it was shining.

"Is that a grotto?" he asked as he pointed to the waterfall.

"Yes, it is. But you can also get in down there," I said, pointing to a cobblestone pathway.

"Let's go. I've always wanted to act like I was at the Playboy mansion."

We took the pathway to the entrance to the grotto. The lights from the waterfall were just enough to create beautiful moving light in the grotto. We sat on the rock bench that was right in front of the bubbling spa water inside the grotto.

"Your house is amazing," Onyx said, putting his arm around me and pulling me to him.

"Thank you," I said as I rested my head on his chest. We sat quietly, staring into the waterfall.

"Is the water cold?" he whispered after a while.

I shook my head as I pointed to a little electronic thermostat on the wall. "I can make it as warm as you like, actually."

"Really? Let's get in, then." Onyx pulled his shoes and socks off.

I watched as he stood up and pulled his shirt over his head. I admired his chiseled chest and the six-pack on him.

"You coming?" He looked at me as he started to unbutton his pants.

My heart skipped a beat. I was nervous, but something in me began to push the nerves down. I stood up, walked over to the thermostat, and turned it up just a little bit. I pulled my sandals off as I watched him step into the water with just his boxer briefs on. He praised how warm the water was. I stood there wondering what I was supposed to do. I didn't want to be naked in the light.

"Coral, take that dress off, or I will take it off of you myself," Onyx demanded.

"Onyx, I don't think I'm comfortable with that. It's okay. I can get the dress wet."

"Coral, I don't give a damn about your size."

"That's just one thing." My voice trembled. "I have this scar from a surgery. . . . It's something I don't think anyone would want to see." I looked away.

But Onyx wouldn't take his eyes off me. I watched in my peripheral vision as he stepped out of the water and walked over to me. He gently turned my head till our eyes met.

"Coral, I am not a weak-ass nigga. You had surgery, and you have a scar. So the fuck what? I don't want to see you in a dress. I want to see you, *all* of you."

I took a deep breath and closed my eyes. I felt his hands pulling my dress up. I raised my arms as he pulled the dress over my head. I opened my eyes and watched him drop the dress on top of his clothes. I stood there and attempted to cover the unattractive, large scar with my hands.

Onyx took both my hands, kissed them, and walked me to the steps of the grotto. He really didn't seem to care at all, and that allowed me to loosen up. By the time the water covered most of our bodies, I was completely relaxed.

"You are really something special, Coral." He grinned, causing me to blush. "But I think we need to talk about something."

I felt my body tense up. "What's wrong?"

He shook his head. "I really like you, but I also know that since you are new to this, I want to make sure you understand that I don't want to rush anything. I'm not really looking for a relationship, but I do love the time we are spending together, and I do want to spend as much time as we can together."

I didn't know how to respond. In the time I'd spent thinking about what might happen between us, the idea of a boyfriend hadn't crossed my mind. I had been too worried about the first time we had sex to even think about the long-term situation we might be facing.

Or maybe I just hadn't been that optimistic.

"Oh, I totally agree. I haven't had a boyfriend for this long, and I'm in no rush to have one now."

"That's easy to say, but you also haven't been intimate. That can change a lot of things."

"Onyx, I really understand. I do. I am fine. I just really like spending time with you."

"I just want to make sure we are on the same page. I want nothing more than to show you so many things and to make you feel the way you deserve to feel. I just want to make sure that you are okay in the end."

I didn't know what came over me, but I leaned in and pressed my lips against his. Onyx's wet hand gripped the back of my hair. My pussy began to throb as he kissed his passion into me. He wrapped his left arm around me and guided me out of the water and to the edge of the grotto. Then he pulled me down to the ground, on top of him. I straddled his body and felt his hard manhood pressing against me. I could feel how large it was through his boxer briefs, and it both excited and terrified me.

Onyx's fingertips traced up and down my spine. He kissed me on my neck, then moved slowly down to my chest. I felt my bra unsnap with one touch, causing my large breasts to fall from underneath the lace and underwire. He pulled the bra off and threw it over near my dress. Our eyes met. I had never been so exposed to a man before. My body was trembling.

"You are very beautiful, Coral," Onyx whispered in his deep, raspy voice. "I can't wait to taste you."

I could feel the wetness filling my panties. I closed my eyes as his lips pressed against my hard, swollen right nipple. He licked around it with his tongue, then took turns nibbling and licking it. I felt my body twitching. It felt so good, I didn't know how much of it I would be able to take. He held me close as he devoured my breasts, going from one to the other, growling as he claimed his territory, and wouldn't let me move.

His left hand moved down my side until it rested on a piece of the thin lace on my panties. He moved the fabric and allowed his index finger to enter me. Onyx massaged my clit with his finger, making my mouth drop open. My head fell back as I let out a moan of pure pleasure. This was what I had been missing, and my body was ready to make up for lost time.

Onyx's finger slowly slid into my softest spot. My body jerked as his thick finger moved back and forth inside of me. I couldn't close my mouth. I opened my eyes to see Onyx staring directly at me. His face didn't change; he stared at me with his lips pressed firmly together. Suddenly, I felt his right hand on the back of my head again. He pulled me closer and sucked on my bottom lip before allowing his tongue to dance the forbidden dance with my tongue. I let my head drop to the crook of his neck, panting heavily as he finger fucked me. I felt another finger entering me. My body jumped from the slight twinge of pain.

"It's okay. Take it, baby," he growled as he slowly moved both fingers. I closed my eyes tight, biting my bottom lip. The pain quickly turned into pleasure as he moved deeper inside, pressing against something that made my whole body jerk hard. I felt a familiar feeling; it was the same feeling from the night before with the bullet. An intense pressure formed in my toes and moved up my body until it landed in the pit of my stomach. He continued to move his fingers, each time hitting that spot and causing my body to jerk over and over. I felt the pressure in my stomach growing. I hit his shoulder, but he ignored me. I continued to hit him over and over again, hoping he would stop.

I didn't have control of my body. Moans escaped my lips, which remained parted. I couldn't seem to close them. I grabbed his shoulders and dug my fingertips into his flesh. My head began shaking from side to side.

"No. Take it," his deep, raspy voice demanded.

I didn't think I was going to make it.

Suddenly, my body froze, and my toes straightened out completely. I knew I had to be in some kind of shock as an eruption came, causing a rush through my body. My body went limp against him, and my head fell against his chest. My heart was racing, and I struggled to catch my breath. Onyx held on to me as he pulled his fingers out and placed them in his mouth.

Onyx grinned after sucking my essence off his fingertips. "I knew you would taste good. . . ."

He held me, kissing my forehead. Then he helped me stand and led me back to the water. It was an effort, as my legs felt like jelly. He stroked my hair as we sat in the bubbling water. I couldn't move. Onyx held me as I attempted to process what in the hell had just happened.

"Are you all right?" he asked after a while, finally breaking the silence.

I nodded my head.

"We should dry off," he said.

Onyx got out of the water and helped me out. I turned the water temperature down in the grotto before we grabbed our clothes and headed back into the house. I went to my linen closet and grabbed two bath towels.

"Would you like to take a shower? I can put your stuff in my washer and have it clean and dry for you in a little while," I said as I handed him one of the towels.

"That sounds good. But I'm not taking a shower by myself." Onyx looked at me with a devilish grin. "Don't worry about my clothes. I'm going to go outside and get some dry clothes, and we are going to shower when I come back in."

My eyes widened. I had just been mostly naked in front of him, and *now* he wanted me to go fully nude?

It took him only a minute or two to retrieve a small duffel bag from his car. He grabbed my hand and began to walk toward the back of my house, as if he knew where he was going. Taking the lead, I guided him to my master bedroom. He nodded his head, impressed by my California king bed, which sat in the middle of the big room. We walked into my bathroom, and he turned the light on. I watched as Onyx turned on the shower. Within moments, steam began to fill the room. He pulled his underwear off, allowing me to check out the amazing ass he had on him. I watched him climb in the shower. His arm reached out for me.

I took a deep breath and pulled off my underwear. I stepped in the shower and allowed the water to hit my hair. My flat-ironed hair quickly curled, returning to its natural state. We took turns washing the chlorine from the grotto off our bodies. He didn't try anything sexual; this was purely sensual and sincere.

After the shower, we dried each other off. Onyx ran his hands through my long, curly hair.

"I love your natural curl. You should wear it sometimes," he said as he massaged my scalp with his hands.

I could feel myself blushing. I didn't know what was going to happen next. I washed our wet underwear in the sink and then put it in the dryer. I didn't want him to leave, but I didn't know what the protocol was for situations like this.

"It should be dry soon," I said as I walked back into my bedroom to find Onyx sitting on the side of my bed and rubbing the ends of his wet locks with a towel. He looked amazing. He was shirtless and had a pair of jogging pants on.

"Oh? What? Are you putting me out now?" he questioned while staring at me.

"No, of course not. You can stay. I want you to stay. Wait. Do you want to stay?"

Onyx laughed. He patted the spot next to him on the bed. I walked closer to him, allowing him to put his arms around me and pull me between his legs.

"I'm not going anywhere," he replied as he kissed me right above my belly button. Those were the best words he had ever spoken to me.

We lay back on the bed, and Onyx held me in his arms as he quickly fell asleep. I listened to the sound of his breathing as his chest moved up and down. I watched him sleep for a moment, still in awe that this incredible creature was in my bed. I knew I had to accept that something amazing had happened and I had loved every moment. I turned over and closed my eyes, hoping the night wouldn't end.

Chapter 8

The light coming in my windows blinded me when I woke up. I stretched for a moment, before remembering what had occurred the night before. I turned over to see Onyx's back turned toward me. He was still sleeping. I smiled. It wasn't a dream—he was there, and everything had happened the way I remembered.

I tiptoed into the bathroom to freshen up. I put conditioner in my hair to loosen up the tight curls, brushed my teeth, and sprayed on a little body splash. I wanted to cook for him, so I headed to the kitchen. I pulled out my Rubbermaid containers filled with precut veggies that I used to make my omelets most mornings. I grabbed the turkey bacon and sausage, and within minutes, my house smelled like breakfast goodness.

It didn't take long for the aroma to alert Onyx's senses. I heard him walking sluggishly into the room. I turned around and smiled when I saw he was still shirtless. I couldn't help but notice the large print his dick made in his pants. He sat on one of my bar stools.

"Girl, I woke up thinking I was at IHOP or something. What are you in here making?" Onyx said, rubbing his eyes.

"I have turkey bacon and sausage cooking, and I was going to make you an omelet, but I didn't know what you wanted in it."

"I told you before, I'm a fat boy. I'll eat anything you put in front of me." He gave me a wink.

I finished making the breakfast, and we sat down to eat. I stole glimpses of him as he devoured his meal. He was starting to cloud my mind inadvertently with every moan or shake of the head. He seemed to really be enjoying the food.

"So, how are you feeling?" Onyx asked, though he had a mouth full of bacon.

"I feel fine. Why?"

He shrugged his shoulders. "I just want to do a check-in, see if you are all right."

I smiled. "I'm cool. How about you? Are you all right?"

"Oh, I'm in heaven right now. I'm eating this fly-ass breakfast, so things are rather perfect."

We sat in silence as we both continued to eat. The events from the night before ran through my mind. I felt amazing, and I had yet to be penetrated by him. I thought about the pain I had felt when he first entered me with his two fingers. I wondered how painful things would be when something bigger replaced them.

"What's on your mind?" Onyx asked, obviously noticing my daydreaming.

"Can I ask one question?" I asked him.

Onyx nodded his head.

"Why did you use only your fingers yesterday?" I put my elbow on the table.

Onyx giggled. "Look at Speedy Gonzalez over here. I already told you, I am not going to do more until I feel like you are completely comfortable."

"I was—"

"No you weren't," Onyx said, cutting me off. "Even in the water you still tried to put your hand over your scar. And when we were taking a shower, you did it again. I think it was subconsciously, but you still did it. I want you to get to the point where you can walk around this bitch buck naked and know that I still crave only you."

The familiar knots formed in my stomach. I knew he was right. Even with him sitting directly in front of me, my mind still couldn't completely grasp the fact that this beautiful man wanted to be here with me. I had never thought I had a self-esteem issue, but having an Adonis who could have any woman he wanted tell me how he craved me just was hard to comprehend.

"So when is your birthday again?" Onyx asked me.

"July sixth."

He shook his head. "You damn Cancers, with your crazy asses." He laughed.

We finished eating and headed back to the bedroom. I made the bed, while he took a shower. He came out of the bathroom completely dressed, with his locks pulled back in a ponytail.

"I gotta roll out. Gotta get to work. And I have rehearsal tonight," he said as he threw his sleep clothes back in his bag.

"Yeah, I should probably get some work done too," I said, trying to hide my disappointment. I wanted nothing more than to spend the rest of the day in his arms.

I walked him to the door. We hugged for a while before finally letting go. Onyx planted a kiss on my cheek before walking out the door. I closed the door behind him. The room instantly felt cold and lonely.

Chapter 9

I was in a self-inflicted tug-of-war. On the one hand, I was spending a lot of time with Onyx, and I was loving every moment of it. He was unique and always kept me guessing. We went to some of the best galleries in the city. He talked about art and music with more passion than most people talked about anything. We took a dinner cruise on the Mississippi, danced during a salsa night at my club, and tried some of the new restaurants that were opening up all over Midtown and Downtown Memphis.

We spoke of things in the future tense. We both talked about spending a weekend in New Orleans and New York. I brought up going out of the country, even if it was somewhere simple, like Mexico or Jamaica. I loved thinking of a future with him in it.

Yet, even with things going so well, he had yet to touch me again since the first incident in the grotto. Besides heavy kissing and cuddling, he hadn't made a move on me. I had tried little things to entice him, like wearing new, scanty sleepwear or sexy underwear, but nothing had worked. I couldn't even get the finger action that had driven me crazy the first time.

Now we sat on my couch, watching television. Onyx was into the nature channel, especially any program that showed hunters versus prey. While watching a tiger about to pounce on an unsuspecting herd of gazelle, I wondered if maybe I was the problem. Maybe he was waiting on me to make the first move, to show him that I was ready for another step.

I rested my head against his broad shoulder. He smiled, then kissed me on my forehead before turning back to the television. I peered up at him and put my hand on his thigh. I caressed it up and down until he shook his head.

"What are you doing, Coral? Trying to wake the snake?" Onyx snickered.

"Maybe," I said as I moved my hand closer to his crotch. "Maybe I'm a tiger about to pounce."

"A tiger wouldn't tell the prey she was about to pounce on them." He smiled.

"Well, I'm a new tiger, and not sure of all the rules yet," I said as my hand made it to the bulge in his pants.

Onyx put his hand on my hand. "Coral, baby . . ."

"Onyx, why haven't you touched me since, well, you know?"

Onyx turned his body toward me. "I told you already, we aren't doing anything until I feel you are completely comfortable."

"I am." I slouched down on the couch. "See? This is comfortable."

Onyx laughed.

I sat back up and put my hand back on his knee. He looked so good, even when he had a serious expression on his face.

"Babe, you know the crazy thing about mouths is that they can say a lot of stuff. That doesn't necessarily make it true." Onyx winked his right eye at me.

My body was heating up. I didn't know if I was just horny or if I was frustrated by the fact that he wouldn't give me what I really wanted.

"Look, I don't know how comfortable you expect me to get. But I do know that I like you, I want you, and I want to do it with you." I folded my arms in protest.

"You want to do it with me," Onyx repeated. "You saying that lets me know you aren't ready." He chuckled again. His laugh was sexy and annoying.

I sat back on the couch, knowing that I was arguing with a brick wall. My body was craving

Onyx, and he simply sat there, watching a movie, ignoring the vibrations I was sending his way. A minute later Onyx put his arm around me and pulled me back into his arms.

"Check this out, Coral. I dig you. You are a phenomenal chick. Under many circumstances I would love nothing more than to knock you off right. But because I do like you, I'm not trying to break something that I'm not in the position to purchase."

His words replayed in my head. I wanted to scream.

"How can you be more concerned about my virginity than I am?" I questioned.

"Because I care about you, and I know what comes with the whole thing, Coral. You are special. And that mouth of yours might say you don't want a relationship, but in the end, once that transfer of energy happens, you don't know that you are going to feel the same way."

I stood up and stood in front of him, blocking his view of the television. I didn't want anything to distract him from me.

"Look, I completely appreciate the fact that you care. Actually, that's one of the reasons why I want to give it to you to begin with. But you know what? This is reminding me of when I had my surgery. Those nurses and doctors asked me a million times if I ever wanted children. Most of them couldn't believe that I was a young woman who didn't want kids. But I've always known kids were not in my cards. I am not a person who goes back on what she knows she wants. It's part of what makes me such a successful entrepreneur. I'm decisive. I know that I am totally happy being single, and I know that a long-term relationship is something that I just don't care about, unlike most women. So no matter what energy shifts, I know in the end I will be perfectly fine with kicking it with you the way we are now."

"Again—"

"Again nothing," I said, cutting Onyx off in mid-sentence. "There is one thing I want, and I want you to be the one. So stop treating me like I'm some lovesick seventeen-year-old."

I didn't move from where I stood. He stared at me as I stood there, arms folded, as serious as I could be. Onyx ran his hands through his dreads. I could almost see the wheels turning in his head. His agonized expression worried me. Was I pushing too hard?

"How about a middle ground?" I said as I unfolded my arms, trying not to be as combative.

"What would that be?" Onyx folded his arms. I acted as if I hadn't noticed.

"You want to take it slow. I get it. But there is one thing that I've always wanted to try that would be a win-win for both of us. I want to try giving you head."

Onyx raised a quizzical eyebrow. "And how is that a win-win for both of us if you don't know what you are doing?"

"Because, Professor, you get to teach me."

I wasn't sure what was coming over me, but I felt flirty and seductive. Onyx shifted his position on the couch, obviously enjoying the playful banter. He continued to look at me, until the right side of his mouth curled upward, causing his dimple to appear.

Nerves started to settle in, but I refused to let them take over the moment. I sucked my fears up when Onyx grasped my hands, and I got down on my knees. Onyx raised his arms and rested his head on them. My furrowed eyebrows made him laugh.

"You gotta go get what you want, Coral." Onyx's expression didn't change as he continued to watch me with a cheeky smile on his face.

I rolled my eyes as I placed my hands on the button on his jeans. My nerves were now taking over again. My hands were trembling as I unbuttoned the button and slowly unzipped his pants. I knew it was now or never. I inhaled as

I reached inside the opening in his briefs. The hardness startled me.

Onyx put his hand on my shoulder. "Don't be nervous. Just pull it out," his raspy voice whispered.

I did as I was told. I pulled it out and was face-to-face with his penis. He filled my hand; it felt even bigger in my hand than when I saw it in the shower. It was much bigger this close up. My terror didn't suppress the desire that I had. I wanted to do this.

I licked my lips and slowly parted them. I closed my eyes and leaned in to his crotch, then took his tip in my mouth. I pressed my lips together, allowing them to wrap around the thickness. I thought about the pornos that I had watched recently. The one thing I always noticed was there was no hesitation. I began to mimic what I'd seen in the movies, bobbing up and down his shaft. I was impressing myself. I had had no idea I could get so deep.

"Coral," Onyx called. "Babe."

I stopped, opened my eyes, and saw a peculiar look on Onyx's face. His forehead was crinkled between his eyes.

"What's wrong?" I asked.

"Babe, you gotta stop watching porn." He patted my shoulder. "You are doing way too much."

I glanced down at his penis. I was shocked. While I had thought I had his whole penis in my mouth, the glistening of my saliva showed me that I had barely gotten past the tip. I wanted to run into my bedroom and never come out. I felt Onyx's hand on my face. He grasped my chin and raised my head. Our eyes met.

"Coral, that shit on TV is fake, and I don't want you to try to be someone else. I want you to do what you feel is comfortable for you. This isn't a race. Take your time, relax, and just go for it."

His words comforted me. Even though I was still highly embarrassed, I didn't want to give up before really trying. And looking at him, seeing the sincerity on his face only made me want to succeed even more.

So I went for it. I closed my eyes and thought about all the things I wanted him to do to me. I craved his kisses as I kissed his tip. Picturing his arms around me fueled the passion that I had as my lips gently pressed his erection. I took my time, slowly sucking, allowing the tip of my tongue to dance around his thickness. With each stroke, I furthered the deepness, testing my own limits and abilities.

I didn't know what it was, but something about having him in my mouth was liberating.

The soft moans that escaped his mouth aroused me, each one fueling the carnal desire that was consuming me. Holding his most cherished part in my hands made me feel a power I had never felt before.

I was in control in that moment, and I loved it.

Adrenaline coursed through my body, and my pussy pulsated with its own rhythm. The familiar fire was pooling in my abdomen, the same feeling he had given me in the grotto. I was close; I could feel the waves of energy forming in my toes and creeping slowly up my body, seeking a release. I didn't stop; I wanted more. I wanted nothing more in that moment than for him to experience his own version of what I was feeling right then. There, on my knees, I discovered a new love in my life. I loved giving this man head.

I could hear Onyx's stifled breathing after the moans stopped. I felt Onyx's hand grip my shoulder. I frowned when he asked me to stop while pushing me away from the thing giving me so much pleasure. My hand was still wrapped around his dick, and he placed his hand on top of mine and moved it back and forth in a steady motion. A deep moan escaped his mouth as he came. I felt the warmth as his cum trickled onto my hand. I usually stopped videos right here, since I was grossed out by cum shots. But

Onyx was right. This wasn't the movies; this was beautiful.

He sat there, head resting back on my couch. I smiled as he incoherently applauded my work. The curious part of me wanted details.

"Was it okay? What do you want me to do differently?" I babbled.

"Shh." Onyx put his finger on his lips. After a moment of silence, he leaned down and planted a kiss on my lips. "Perfect."

Chapter 10

I was living in a constant state of bliss. I wanted to kick myself daily for denying myself this feeling for so long. I now knew what it was like to truly feel happy. Onyx had come in and turned my world upside down, and all I wanted to do was thank him for it.

I watched him drum at my club on Mondays. Watching him work was better than anything else. I loved the emotion he put into his art. I couldn't watch him for long without my whole body betraying me. Even when he wasn't around, I could just think of him on his drums and be back in the moment.

After my first experience in oral territory, things didn't change as much as I wanted them to. He still refused to have sex with me. One oral experience had turned me into a junkie for head. I wanted to give it to him all the time and had to fight back the urge to just wake up and take him into my mouth. But he wouldn't let me do it like I wanted to.

"There's no rush, Coral," Onyx would say to me when I was about to have a childlike tantrum. He would smile or shake his head at my attitude. There was no rush to him, but as for me, I had been waiting almost thirty years to experience the pleasures that he was giving me a taste of. How could he blame me for wanting to experience it all?

I headed over to the church to do my weekly work. I was surprised to see Tangie sitting in the office, opening a bunch of large boxes.

"Hey, girl. The shirts came in for the Fourth of July family day. They look good too." Tangie held up one of the purple shirts. I had no idea why they had picked purple for a Fourth of July event.

"Looks nice," I said as plopped myself down at my desk. I checked my phone just to make sure I hadn't missed a call or a text. I looked up to see Tangie staring at me, with an inquisitive look on her face. "What?"

"Don't what me. You have been walking in here with all this pep in your step lately. I'm guessing it has to do with the guy."

I blushed. "It's nice. He is rather perfect."

"Perfect?" Tangie pressed her lips together. "No man is perfect. Tell me more."

I told her about our encounters. I found myself gushing about my time with Onyx. Tangie sat quietly as I spoke. I paused when I noticed her concerned expression.

"Coral, I don't want to be a Debbie Downer, but I really hope you are taking your time. You are sitting up here, about to bust over a man you have known for only a little while. I know things seem amazing, but take the time to get to know him."

I was a little upset that she was casting a cloud over my happy moment, but deep down I had the same reservations that she had. He did seem too good to be true, and at the moment he had me wide open. I was going to have to find a way to control my feelings.

"Don't worry. We are taking it slow. We haven't actually had sex. He said he wants to wait until I'm completely comfortable."

"Well, that is different," Tangie said, folding her arms. "Most niggas don't give a damn about comfort. All they care about is their nut."

We both laughed.

I spent the day helping Tangie with preparations for the family day. Being that my birthday was on the sixth, I usually had only the family day to look forward to. Things were going to be very different this year. We laughed and joked about different things, from church members to reality TV. I had to admit that it was refreshing to have someone to talk about things with. Now I understood why women had girlfriends.

"So are you going to bring this mystery man to church?" Tangie asked.

I shook my head. "No, I don't think we are on that level. Maybe one day, but right now we are just having fun."

"All right. Just make sure you remember that. Don't go catching feelings for a man who has said he's not looking for a relationship. That will only lead to heartache for you. Trust me. Been there, done that."

At the end of the day I made it home a lot later than I expected. I was worn out and was actually ready to climb into my bed. I hadn't heard from Onyx all day, and I was working hard not to focus on that fact. Thankfully, work and Tangie had kept my mind occupied all day, but now I was home, in my big space, by myself.

I knew I shouldn't care, but the energy in my house had shifted. Now that I knew what it was like to have someone lying with me, I hated the nights when he wasn't in my bed with me. I contemplated calling him, but knowing that he already feared me getting clingy, I resisted.

I decided to just go to sleep and hope that when morning came, there would be a text or a phone call from him.

Sleep didn't come easy. I tossed and turned all over my bed. I finally decided that it was going to take pharmaceutical help for me to get the rest that I needed. I popped an Ambien and crawled back into my California king. My bed had never felt so big. I knew I was tripping. There was no reason for me to miss him this bad after just a few days. I felt like a junkie.

Chapter 11

I was now becoming restless. Three days had passed, and I hadn't heard from Onyx. I finally broke down and sent a text, saying hello, but I got no response. I was finding it hard to concentrate on my work because of my feelings. I knew I shouldn't care, but I did. How could you do something so amazing to a person and just never call back?

I tried to remain positive, but my mind was going straight to the worst-case scenarios. Maybe the thought of a virgin had scared him away. I had heard many times that men didn't want the responsibility of deflowering a woman. Or maybe I had made it too easy. Was I too willing to give it up, and therefore, had I taken the fun out of it? Then there was always the distinct possibility that he was just a whore and an asshole who fucked with girls' emotions and left them high and dry. He was an artist, after all.

Maybe he had tons of other girls he needed to give time to outside of me.

I sat in my office at my largest wedding facility. I could hear the hustle and bustle of preparations being made for a wedding that was about to take place. This was my most expensive and most sought-after property. Venetian Estate offered three different wedding areas, including the garden, which was covered with flowers and featured Roman-style columns; and the lake, which had a beautiful gazebo inside a pavilion. For my most expensive weddings, clients rented the full facility, just to be able to treat their guests to different experiences. I had never realized how much old money there was in Memphis until I purchased the estate. Everyone from those wanting beautiful million-dollar weddings to spoiled sixteen-year-olds wanting to have lavish parties booked the large mansion for their events.

I walked out of my office to watch the setup for another million-dollar affair. The pavilion was being transformed into a winter wonderland in the summertime. White was everywhere, with hints of powder blue. Large centerpieces sat in the middle of the ten-person round tables. I couldn't help but be moved by the romantic feel of the venue.

My mind drifted to thoughts of a wedding of my own. Rome being my favorite city, I envisioned a destination wedding or a Roman-themed wedding. I could see the dress I would wear. It would definitely have a Roman column, draped feel to it—maybe one shoulder with a long train.

I gasped at the thoughts I was having. I had never thought about marriage before and had always filed myself in the "never getting married" folder, convinced that I was a lone wolf destined to spend her life living luxuriously and traveling the world. I had never wanted children, but the thought of a child with the right man didn't mortify me at this moment. My brief encounters with Onyx had opened Pandora's box.

I didn't want to be alone forever, after all.

I walked into my house with three bags of groceries. I heard my phone start to buzz in my pocket. I ran to the counter and dropped the groceries so I could pick up my phone. Across my screen was Onyx's name. I let the phone ring until it stopped. I wanted to answer, but I was angry. I wanted to make him wait, the way he had made me wait. It took only a few seconds for my phone to ring again.

"Hello?" I said with attitude as I put the phone on speaker.

"Hey, you. I'm in your neighborhood. Are you home or busy?"

I grinned but quickly wiped the smile off my face. *How dare he think that he can just show up when he wants, without a call or a text in days?*

"Yeah, I'm home."

And yet I told him I was home.

It didn't take long for him to show up. I opened the front door, hoping he could feel the angry energy coming out of me. Onyx hugged me, but I didn't hug him back. This made him take two steps back.

"What's wrong with you?" he questioned.

"Nothing," I said as I stepped away from the door and walked farther into my house. "What's up?"

"What's up? You tell me. You the one walking away with the sassy attitude. What's going on?"

I gave a loud sigh. "I texted you, and you never responded. Now you show up here, as if days haven't gone by and I haven't heard from you."

Onyx lowered his head as he sat on one of my bar stools. "Coral, I have been really busy. But it's been a couple of days. Didn't we have a talk the other day about expectations?" Onyx responded calmly.

"That's not the point, Onyx. I'm not asking you to call me every hour on the hour, but you spent the night at my house, and then I didn't hear anything at all."

I watched Onyx as he shook his head. He stood up and pushed the stool back under the bar. "See, this is why we had the talk we had. I am not trying to be your boyfriend—"

"I'm not asking you to be!" I felt myself getting frustrated. "I am just asking for common courtesy, for you to return a simple text."

"This was a bad idea. This is why I'm glad we didn't go all the way. You aren't going to be able to handle me, Coral. You want more than I'm able to give."

There he was, Mr. Brick Wall. I replayed my words in my head. I didn't think what I was asking for was unreasonable or warranted the response I was getting from him.

"Why are you acting like I'm asking for your hand in marriage? I asked you to return a text. Do you have any idea how I felt these past few days? I felt like I did something wrong. Like you weren't happy with what happened between us. I was starting to think I was never going to hear from you again."

We stood in silence, staring at each other like two cowboys at high noon. Even with his mood, he was gorgeous. He stood there with his hair hanging down on his shoulders, his cotton tee tight around his biceps as his muscles flexed.

"Coral, I have a lot going on in my life, and I can't guarantee that I am going to call or text you every day. When I'm going in for rehearsals or anything, I might not even have my phone on me. But the bottom line is, I shouldn't have to explain this to you. We just started talking."

"So because we just started talking, that means I can't ask for simple common courtesy, like you returning a text message just to let me know you are okay? I didn't ask you to come to see me. I didn't tell you to tell me you loved me. My text said hello. A simple, one-second text back was all that I asked for."

"I came over here because I wanted to see you. I wanted to spend some time with you. I wanted to give you time that I honestly could put somewhere else."

I didn't know how to respond. As angry as I was, I also understood where he was coming from. But mentioning that he could give his time to someone else felt like a slap in the face. I didn't sign up to be insulted.

"If you have other places you want to be, then go and be there."

"Fuck, Coral! Didn't I just say that I want to be here? Don't start this bullshit, or you are going to ruin a good thing before it even happens." Onyx fell silent and paced the floor.

The silence in the room was maddening. I didn't want to say anything else that could upset him. And the look on his face made me believe that if he walked out the door, it would be the final time. How did we get to this point? All I had wanted was a simple text.

"Onyx, I don't want you to leave. I just want you to understand that, well, I missed you. I know that's not what you want to hear, but since I'm not good at any of this, I think honesty is the best thing for me."

Onyx stopped pacing and looked at me. He walked closer to me and put his hands on my shoulders.

"I think we might have made a mistake here," he said. "I like you. Honestly, I like you a lot, but you are in a space where what you need is someone who can give you all the time you need. I can't take care of you like that."

I felt the walls closing in. I wanted to cry, but my pride wouldn't allow me to shed a tear in front of him. I pulled away from him and walked over to my front door. I opened it without looking at him.

"I hope that we can be friends. I really think you are an amazing woman," Onyx said as he tried to touch me, but I pulled away before he could. He walked out the door, and I closed it behind him, knowing it would be the last time he entered my house.

Chapter 12

Restless nights and days fell upon me. I spent the next few days in the solitude of my house. I even missed church on Sunday. I spent my time drinking wine, watching television, and replaying events with Onyx in my head. My birthday was creeping up on me, and what I thought was going to be the best birthday ever had quickly turned into something I wanted to come and go as quickly as possible.

I spent my time trying to understand where I'd gone wrong. How had we gone from zero to one hundred that fast? I knew it wasn't that irrational of me to request that he contact me after a few days, so why had he flipped out? Maybe things were done differently than I imagined. Maybe I wasn't cut out for a casual thing with anyone. But Onyx had never felt casual. No matter what he'd said, we were more than just something casual, or at least I thought so.

By Sunday afternoon, my phone was blowing up from Tangie and other members of the church. I made my voice sound as horrible as possible and blamed my absence on being under the weather. I knew that I couldn't say I was too sick, or people would show up at my doorstep with all types of soups and homemade remedies.

By late Sunday night, I knew I had to get a grip on reality. I had businesses to run, and no person was ever supposed to come between me and work. But I couldn't help but miss him. I battled with thoughts of whether I missed him or whether I missed only the possibilities that he presented to me. Onyx had given me a look into the way my life could be if I had a mate next to me. And as much as I wanted finally to lose my virginity, the idea of having someone by my side was more important than any sexual act.

I knew there was one place where I could see him. On Monday he would be playing at my venue. I contemplated the pros and cons of attending. He could see me and realize that he had overreacted, and things could get back to status quo, or he could see me and feel like I was only there for him—which would totally be true. What if I got there and he was with another woman? That would break me, and I knew it.

But maybe seeing him would be better than driving myself insane from thinking about him all day and night.

I arrived at my venue Monday night and was surprised by the huge turnout. There was a line to get in, something I had never seen before. I parked and came in through the back door. My heart dropped the moment I saw him sitting onstage, performing with the band. He was in his element and was moving his head to his beat. He didn't see me come in, and I managed to sneak into the back without him noticing my presence.

"Hey, boss," Miguel, my manager, said when I walked into the office. "I didn't expect to see you here."

"What's going on? It's a serious crowd out there." I took a seat in one of the office chairs.

"It's someone's birthday. I think one of the band members. Yeah, it's insane out there. I just came back here to do a drop. The bar is making a killing tonight."

Miguel excused himself, leaving me in the office alone. I could hear the crowd cheering over the number the band was playing. When the band finished the last note, I decided it was now or never. I walked out into the main room and stood in the corner, behind the bar. One of the waitresses was holding a tray full of shots on the stage. The band was giving toasts to the birthday boy, who turned out to be the saxophonist.

I smiled at how happy Onyx looked as he and his bandmates took the round of shots. Afterward, they headed back to their instruments and began playing a round of old-school classics. The crowd was grooving; many couples filled the dance floor and danced to their songs. I couldn't take my eyes off of Onyx. He was so intense, he had a big smile on his face, and he played the drums with so much passion. I couldn't help but feel the energy coming from him.

I stayed in the corner, watching as the band played and continued to consume various drinks. Finally, they had their last set and allowed a DJ to take over. Then they headed to the VIP area of the club, where a birthday cake was waiting, along with a lot of women. I tried to hide in the shadows, in hopes of seeing who Onyx might be hugged up with. To my surprise, he mingled like he had the first time I met him. He hugged a few women but also gave handshakes to some of the men and conversed with groups of people. I didn't see anyone who looked a little too comfortable with him.

The night went on, and the crowd thinned out rather quickly due to it being a workday for most people. Because there was such a large crowd, I decided to help Miguel with counting down. Once we pulled and sorted all the registers and the front door and then settled everything in the office, I headed back out. I saw Onyx lying down on one of the couches in the VIP area. The other band members were packing up their instruments while he slept.

"Hey, is he okay?" I asked one of the band-mates.

"My man had one too many drinks. We will get him after we get all the instruments packed up," the keyboard player said, winking at me.

Still concerned, I walked over to the VIP area and attempted to wake Onyx up. He didn't budge. I shook him until finally he opened his eyes for a moment.

"Coral. Baby," he uttered before falling back asleep.

"Aye, who's going to drive Onyx home?" one of the band members asked, loud enough that I overhead him. I listened as they all debated about who should be responsible for their friend. Finally, the decision was made.

I wanted to take him home myself, but I knew they would think it odd for a woman they didn't know to take their friend home. I would check on him in the morning. I knew there was nothing else I could do that night. I said my good-byes to Miguel and headed home.

I was exhausted when I got home. I climbed in bed and fell asleep the moment my head hit the pillow. I was awakened by the sound of my doorbell. I looked at my clock and saw it was two in the morning. I was pissed. Whoever was at my door was about to experience the wrath of a sleepy and angry black woman.

I stumbled to the front door and glanced through my peephole to see Onyx standing there. My body immediately perked up. I rubbed my hand against my hair, hoping that I didn't look too crazy.

"Onyx?" I said as I opened the door.

"Why did you leave?" he asked, slurring, as he leaned against my wall. I could smell the tequila on him.

I helped him into the house as he questioned me again about why I had left the club. He plopped down on my couch and kept losing and regaining consciousness

"I'm going to get you some aspirin and water," I said as I headed to my bathroom to get the aspirin, a cup of water, and a cool, wet towel.

When I got back to my living room, Onyx was sleeping, though he was sitting straight up.

"Onyx, you need to take this. And you can come and get in the bed," I said, attempting to wake him up. I put the cold towel on his forehead, which woke him back up.

"Baby, Coral, I am sorry for showing up here," he said, slurring. "I couldn't make it home. Had my boy drop me off. Your place was close."

"It's okay. Now let's get you into the bed."

Onyx finally stood up, and I assisted him in walking back to the bedroom. He pulled his shirt over his head, fell down on the side of the bed, and lay on his back, with his feet still on the floor. I pulled his tennis shoes off and placed them against the wall. I struggled but was able to get his legs onto the bed. I unbuckled his pants, pulled them off, and laid them neatly on the chaise in my bedroom. I walked out to my linen closet and grabbed an extra blanket, as I knew there was no way I was going to be able move his body from on top of the covers.

I walked back into the bedroom to see Onyx still lying down, with his eyes closed. I tried not to stare at the bulge in his Ralph Lauren briefs. I covered him with the blanket, causing him to open his eyes.

"You are great. So great," he said, slurring. "I'm going to keep you."

"Onyx, just get some rest."

"Omar."

I paused. "What?"

"My name . . . it's Omar," Onyx said before he drifted off into a deep slumber. I stared at him for a moment, realizing he was out for the count.

I crawled over to my side of the bed. The moment I lay down, Onyx turned over and placed his arm around me. I could feel his manhood against my ass. He fell asleep with me in his arms. Even though he was in a drunken state, I couldn't help but smile. I didn't know if he would remember telling me his name in the morning, so I would enjoy the moment for tonight. Anything was better than nothing.

Chapter 13

Unfamiliar with having a hangover, as it was something I'd never experienced, the next morning I Googled "morning hangover remedies" just to be safe. I kept it simple. I mixed up my personal pancake batter and made my strawberry-banana smoothies.

Sluggishly, Onyx walked into the kitchen, with his hand on his forehead, the moment I turned off the blender. "That thing is loud." His raspy voice filled the room. "What time is it?"

"Ten," I said as I used my perfect pancake batter dispenser to pour batter onto my griddle. I pour some of the smoothie in a glass. "Here." I handed him the smoothie.

Onyx drank half of it in one gulp. "Man, this is just what I needed. I have no idea what I was thinking last night, drinking so much. I don't remember what happened. I woke up and didn't know where I was for a moment. Then I remembered I knew only one person with such a heavenly bed." He smiled.

"You don't remember, huh?"

"Not really. I know it was my brother's birth-day, so we turned up at the club last night. You should have been there."

"I was," I said, shaking my head. "Well, I came to help Miguel. I saw you for a moment. I figured that's why you came over here afterward."

"Babe, I was so out of it. . . ." Onyx drank more of the smoothie while staring at me. "Thank you for last night. I'm pretty sure I didn't take my own clothes off."

"I just gave you a little help. No big deal."

"No." Onyx reached his hand out and touched my arm. His eyes were locked on me. "It's a big deal, a very big deal. After the way we ended things, you could have left my black ass outside. But you took care of me. I need you to under-stand how much I appreciate you for that."

I felt an overwhelming feeling coming over me. I felt like I was going to cry, but tears were not forming. I didn't know the feeling that I felt for him, but I had never felt anything like it before. I was scared, ecstatic, anxious, and nervous all at one time. I knew this wasn't some crush or a feeling of lust that I had. It had to be more. I started to question whether there was really love at first sight, because if there was, I was now a victim.

"Onyx, I'm sorry about what happened. I didn't want to come off as clingy or anything like that. I just wanted to hear from you," I said softly.

"I get it, and I overreacted. I apologize for that as well. I just . . . I still feel like you need something that I'm not going to be able to give you. You don't deserve to get fucked, Coral. You need someone to truly make love to you, and as much as I wish that could be me, I'm just not in that place right now."

Now the tears were starting to form. I walked over to my refrigerator, just so he didn't have to see me. I stuck my head in, hoping the cool air would dry up the water forming in the ducts of my eyes. A few tears fell, but I was able to dry them and regain my composure.

"Coral, are you all right?" Onyx asked in his beautiful, sincere voice.

"I will be fine. I understand what you are saying, and maybe you are right. I do want something more. I want someone who knows that I am there for them and who is there in return for me. I thought I wanted sex, but the truth is, I want intimacy. Real intimacy."

"I really hope we can be friends. I don't want to lose you out of my life, Coral." Onyx looked directly at me.

The truth was, I didn't want to lose him, either.

We ate pancakes, laughed, and drank smoothies. Although I was hurting inside, a big piece of me was just happy to spend the time with him. I cleaned up while Onyx got dressed. When he walked back out, he looked as gorgeous as ever, even though he was still a little hung over.

We hugged for an unusually long time. I knew the reason for it. Even though he wanted to be friends, I had this overwhelming feeling that I wasn't going to hear from him again, except in passing at my club or if I saw him on the streets. I held on to him, hoping that my feelings would transfer to him. I wanted him to realize what he was walking out on, but it didn't work. He planted a sweet kiss on my forehead and walked out the door.

Once again he was gone, and I was alone.

Chapter 14

Brokenhearted or not, I had businesses to take care of that day. I wasn't going to lie in bed, mourning a relationship that had ended before it had even begun. I checked on my facilities and made sure all the wedding details were in order with my planners and managers.

Driving to my club, I passed a building for sale in Downtown Memphis that caught my eye. It needed a lot of work, but it had an amazing rooftop that overlooked the Mississippi River and the Memphis Bridge and would be perfect for contemporary city weddings. I talked to the owners, who were more than happy with the amount that I was willing to offer as long as the building passed inspection. It was perfect; and a new rental facility was just the distraction that I needed. After speaking to my attorneys and contractors, I made appointments for the building to be inspected.

After my busy morning, I headed over to church to catch up on business there that I was a little bit behind on. Choir rehearsal was in full swing when I got there, and I sat in my office, nodding my head to the music coming from the chapel. It sounded so good, I wanted to take a close look.

I made my way to the chapel, sat in a pew, and listened to the young adult choir rehearse a song for the family day event. There were more young adults in the choir than I remembered. I noticed a guy named Vernon smiling at me from the choir stand. I almost wanted to turn around, just to make sure no one had come in behind me, but I remembered the main doors were locked. I was the only one sitting on that side; there was no way he was looking at anyone else.

Soon the choir was dismissed for a break. I stood up to meet Heather, who was heading toward me. I couldn't help but notice that Vernon was still looking at me. I felt strangely uncomfortable.

"Hey, girl. How did we sound?" Heather asked as she approached me.

"Amazing, as usual. You guys always sound amazing."

"You really should join the choir. We have a ball, girl." She patted my shoulder.

Out of my peripheral vision I noticed Vernon was headed our way. Before I could get away, he joined us.

"Hey, Coral. How are you doing?" Vernon asked with the same smile on his face.

He wasn't an unattractive guy by any means. He was very tall and toned, but not very muscular. The one thing I had always admired about him was his silky smooth dark brown skin and his sparkling white teeth. His hair was cut well, with just a few waves, and he obviously kept it manicured. He had played basketball all through high school and some in college, before he'd injured himself his sophomore year. I admired the fact that he had still finished college and now was a coach and a teacher at a local high school.

"I'm good. How are you, Vernon?" I responded politely. I noticed a very big grin on Heather's face.

"Well, I'm going to go get some water and leave you two alone," Heather said. She continued to grin as she walked off.

I wanted to kill her.

"So, Coral, how have you been lately? I heard you were sick for a minute."

"Yes, I had a cold, but I'm all right. Been doing just fine," I said as we started walking toward the door.

"There is just something about you lately. It's like there's a light around you or something. You have been looking really good. I mean, really good." Vernon nodded his head in appreciation.

"Um, thanks. I don't know what the 'light' may be. Just been the same ole me."

"Na," Vernon said. "There is a difference. Whatever it is, it suits you well."

I knew there could only be one thing he was speaking about. Onyx obviously had had a bigger impact on me than I had ever imagined.

"So I am going to go ahead and try something I have wanted to do for a long time but haven't had the courage to do. Coral, if you aren't busy one day soon, I would love to take you out for a bite to eat or something. I mean, it doesn't have to be a date. It can be two church friends having some food together," he said with a smile.

My eyes widened. I had known Vernon for years, and he had never once shown any interest in me, at least that I could remember. I couldn't fathom why he was asking me out now.

"Vernon, why now?"

"I mean, truthfully, I told you there is something different about you lately. Not to mention that normally, you have a look on your face that essentially says 'Screw off.'" He laughed.

I couldn't deny the fact that I wasn't the easiest person to approach. But lately, I had let my guard down. And it was because of Onyx.

"I just—"

"Coral, before you say no, just think about it. No pressure. But I really would like the opportunity to spend a little time with you. Just think about it." Vernon smiled as the rest of the choir started to make their way back to the choir stand. He walked off before I could object.

I sat back down in the pew and listened as they started working on harmonies for another song. I glanced up at Vernon, who quickly winked at me. I couldn't help but blush. I thought about his invitation. Maybe that was what I needed, after all. Vernon was very different from Onyx. He was deeply rooted in our church, which was a great thing. And the fact that he was a teacher, and not a musician, meant no late nights, no nighttime gigs, and no groupies to worry about. Onyx had said I deserved someone who could give me more; maybe Vernon was that type of guy.

While the choir was still practicing, I headed back to the office to finish up my work. By the time I finished cataloging all the receipts and balancing my books, the choir rehearsal was ending. I packed up my things so that I could leave with everyone else. As I was locking my drawers, I heard a knock on my door. I looked up to see Vernon standing in the doorway.

"Just wondering if I could walk you to your car."

I hesitated, but then I realized there could be no harm in walking me to my car.

"Sure. Why not?"

It was darker outside than I had expected. Vernon wasted no time and started pleading his case on why we should go out. He made some good points. We were both single and childless, and there weren't many single, independent younger women in our church. Most of the women my age had children or were married, something that wasn't appealing to him.

"Come on, Coral. You gotta know how bad you are. I'm not the only one who thinks so. A few of the fellas have talked about attempting to take you out, but they are intimidated by you."

"Intimidated?" I questioned.

"Coral, you aren't like the other sisters. You have major shit going on for yourself. You are very well off, and that in itself can be very intimidating to a man, especially one who knows there is no way he is going to ever make more than you."

"Okay. So I make a little more than most, but that still shouldn't be a reason to be intimidated by me."

"You're right, which is why I decided to step to you. You gotta give me some brownie points for not being a punk." A goofy grin covered his face. I couldn't help but laugh.

"All right. You get some brownie points for that."

"Thank you. So can I cash those points in for a meal? We can go out, or I will even cook if you want me to."

"You cook?" I asked.

Vernon looked guilty for a moment. "No, but I can order some amazing food."

We both laughed. I had to admit that making me laugh was a good start. As I looked at the adorable smile on Vernon's face, I couldn't help but think about Onyx. I knew there was only one thing I could do.

"Fine. One meal."

Chapter 15

This felt completely different from my first dating experience. I was unusually calm. I decided to wear one of the pairs of jeans and a shirt I had bought from Torrid. I didn't feel the need to get too dressed up; it was just dinner, after all.

I arrived at Vernon's home and climbed out of my car. He had a decent-size town house in the Hickory Hill area of Memphis. Like most areas, Hickory Hill used to be amazing, but due to migrations, it had gone downhill a lot. Still, it had plenty of well-kept streets and nice houses.

Vernon greeted me at the door. He looked nice in a simple pair of dark denim jeans and a blue and white cotton tee that was a bit oversize. His bright smile was welcoming as I walked up to the door.

"You look amazing," he said while looking me up and down.

"Thank you," I replied, even though he was making me feel a bit objectified due to the lustful expression on his face.

As we walked into his house, I was instantly hit by a musty smell. It was obvious he had tried to mask the smell with a sweet fragrance, but it hadn't worked. He had a true bachelor pad. It was neat, but not clean. I could see dust, which had obviously been forming for months, on top of the fan blades and on the entertainment center. I noticed the pairs of gym shoes sitting against the wall next to his old sectional, which had obviously seen better days. I knew I was being judgmental. He was a man and a basketball coach. I wondered if I was supposed to expect anything better.

He led me into his kitchen. Sitting on his kitchen table was a bag full of Chinese take-out boxes. He had also purchased a cheap bottle of passion fruit Moscato. I didn't really care for the fruity wine but decided to grin and bear it.

"So I ordered your sesame chicken and veggie fried rice. This place is amazing. Probably the best ghetto Chinese food in Memphis." He smiled and handed me two cartons and chopsticks. I smiled back as I took the two cartons and the chopsticks and followed him into the living room.

I set the cartons of food on the small table and attempted to sit down, only to sink into the oversize sectional, which was very low to the floor. He sat next to me and turned on his massive entertainment center. That was the one thing he obviously hadn't skimped on. He had a sixty-inch 4K television. Vernon also owned both PlayStation 4 and Xbox One, along with the earlier versions of the gaming systems. Along the wall were two large DVD racks, one filled with over one hundred DVDs and the other with almost the same number of video games. Each gaming system had a row of games that were perfectly organized.

Vernon picked up a remote and pressed a button that turned on the television and sound system. He had the latest installment of *The Fast and the Furious* films queued up and ready to play. I opened my fried rice box and began to eat with my chopsticks. The rice was greasy. I opened the sesame chicken box, took a bite, and discovered that the chicken was even worse. I forced myself to eat a few more bites, but then I couldn't have any more.

"So, Coral, when was the last time you dated someone? I've never seen you with anyone at the church, and I've asked around. No one seems to know if you date or not."

"People actually wonder about that?"

"Yeah. The word *lesbian* came up a few times."

I jerked my head around to look at him.

He shrugged his shoulders as he laughed. "Well, you know how people are."

I was mortified. "Truth is, I really don't date. I just recently was seeing someone, but it ended. It wasn't anything serious, though. Casual dating."

Onyx's face flashed in my mind. I could vividly see him sitting across from me at Denny's on our first date. I wondered if I should be completely honest with Vernon and tell him that I was a virgin. Would that scare him away too?

"So you don't date? Why not?"

"Busy. I have my businesses, which take up a lot of my time, and my church obligations."

"Yeah, but everyone has to have time for a personal life. Even busy Coral." Vernon's eyes were burning into the side of my face.

"That's true. I'm now starting to make more time for things. I realized I need to put myself out there more."

Vernon put his hand on my thigh. "Well, I am just happy you decided to take some time with me."

I smiled. Maybe he wasn't that bad, after all.

We quickly found ourselves involved in the movie. Vernon put his arm around me, and after a while I allowed my body to sink down closer to his. He rubbed my shoulder with his thumb, which was actually soothing.

I didn't know if it was because I was so comfortable, but I soon felt Vernon's breath against my ear. His nose touched my earlobe. Vernon pressed his lips against my neck, right below my ear, causing my body to shiver. I pulled away.

"You okay?" His voice was deeper than usual.

"I'm okay," I responded as I sat up straight.

"I'm sorry. Did that make you feel uncomfortable? You just smelled really good, and I just really wanted to kiss you. Please forgive me."

"It's cool," I replied. "Let's just finish the movie."

The rest of the night went by without another problem. The energy in the room shifted. Vernon was on alert now, trying to be on his best behavior. He made sure his arm stayed in a safe spot until the movie was over.

Afterward, Vernon walked me to my car. He wrapped his long arms around me and held me tight. I hugged him back and waited for him to let me go. He smiled at me, but I knew he was lingering because he wanted to share a good-bye kiss.

"So is it all right if I kiss you?" Vernon asked in a boyish voice.

I felt so awkward. It felt strange that he had actually asked for my permission to kiss me. I knew it was probably because of the incident in the house, but it still made the moment uncomfortable and strange. I stood on my tiptoes and planted a kiss on his cheek.

"Have a good night, Vernon." I smiled as I got inside my car. I could tell he was displeased but was attempting to keep on a good face.

"Please call me and let me know you made it home," he requested.

I nodded as he closed my door behind me.

I drove home with the radio off. I had to digest the night in my mind. There was no reason for me not to like him. He was, for the most part, a perfect gentleman. He had respected my wishes and hadn't tried to do anything more. Outside of his terrible taste in wine and Chinese food, and the smell in his house, the night wasn't bad. I knew I was being overly critical. I wondered if I had the right to be so critical. I was still a newbie to dating, and just because my first attempt had blown my mind, it didn't mean that every date was going to be a home run.

I thought about the good qualities that Vernon had to offer. The main one was his interest in me. He was very much at that stage in his life where he wanted to settle down and get married.

And from the looks of his house, he was badly in need of some female assistance.

We could be a good match. He was settled; he had a career and insurance. He could offer stability, even though I didn't need him for that. Looks-wise, he was attractive, and although his house needed work, he kept himself polished. The fact that he was in the church was a major plus. I started to think that I had been way too hard on him. He was a good guy. Why had I looked for negative things so that I could push him away?

Traffic was light, so the drive to my house was a breeze. When I got settled in my house, I picked up my cell phone and dialed Vernon's number. He answered on the first ring, which made me smile. We talked for an hour, just getting to know each other a little better. He was so much more interesting over the phone than in person. I decided to give it a shot, and I allowed myself to accept his offer for a proper date to the movies the next night. I might as well see where this was going, I thought. Maybe it would help me forget about Onyx.

Chapter 16

Vernon and I walked out of the movie theater, amped. Marvel's latest creation had brought out the geeks in both of us. We walked from the Paradiso movie theater to the ice cream shop that was across the street. Vernon tried to show off, telling me to order anything on the menu. I opted for a double scoop of cookies 'n cream, while he did three scoops of rocky road.

After the ice cream, we headed back to his car. He had insisted on a proper date, one where he picked me up from my house and everything. We drove back to my house, and when we were almost there, I gave him the code to open the gate to my community.

"Man, you know when I pulled up here, I was not expecting you to be living like this. I mean, I know you got a lot going on with your businesses, but damn." Vernon's eyes widened as he drove slowly and admired the different houses.

"My house isn't nearly as big as the majority of these."

"Yeah, but it isn't small, either." We both laughed at his comment.

Once we were through the gate, Vernon pulled into my driveway. He hopped out of the car. I had learned when he picked me up that he wasn't the overly chivalrous kind. He held the door to my house and the doors at the movies, but he didn't open my car door before I got in or come over to open it when I was getting out.

Vernon walked me to my door. I fumbled in my purse for my keys. He stood there, watching me, until I finally grabbed the small key ring. I made a mental note to buy a lanyard so it wouldn't be so difficult next time.

"Thanks again. I had a good time," I said with a smile.

"I'm glad you did," Vernon said while gazing down at me. "So do I get to see the inside of this mini mansion?"

I looked up to see him staring directly at me. I hadn't thought about inviting him in. Why hadn't I realized this might happen? "Normally, I would say sure, but it's a mess. But I promise the next time we go out, you totally can."

Vernon's frowned but nodded. "All right. I'm going to hold you to that, Ms. Coral."

Rather than heading to his car, Vernon lingered on my doorstep. We stood there, feeling as awkward as ever. Finally, he took two steps closer to me, bent his head, and planted a kiss on my lips. His lips were softer than I expected. He opened his lips slightly, but I kept my lips pressed closed. I wasn't ready for tongue, not yet.

Vernon finally pulled away, with a smile on his face. I couldn't believe he was actually happy with the kiss.

"Until next time, beautiful." He bowed like a gentleman.

"Until next time." I blushed.

I walked into my empty home. I didn't want to turn the lights on until I knew that Vernon was out of the driveway. I headed back to my bedroom and pulled off the tight pants I was wearing. Wearing my T-shirt and panties, I walked into my kitchen and grabbed a bottle of wine. There was no need for a glass; it was a "drink out of the bottle" type of night.

I headed to my bedroom closet and grabbed the bag of goodies I had. The other day I had bought packs of batteries in all sizes to use in the various contraptions. I hadn't tried any of the bigger items; the silver bullet was my friend. But tonight I wanted to try something new.

I opened a blue vibrator. It was long, thin, and smooth, with a slanted tip. It didn't look like an actual penis, though the biggest toy I had been given did. This looked rather harmless. I put two C batteries inside it and screwed the base on until it started vibrating in my hand. I played with the twist control for a moment, getting it to a speed I thought I could handle.

I laid my head on the pile of decorative pillows on my bed. My hand rested against my leg, which was bent, allowing my foot to lie flat on my bed. After bending my other knee, I opened my legs and closed my eyes. I could see him in my mind.

The heat began to rise as I allowed the tip to move up and down between my moist lips. I bit my lip as I allowed the tip to enter me. A twinge of pain shot through my body, causing me to pull the small piece out. I sat there for a moment, wondering if I was doing it right. To my surprise, my body continued to respond favorably, as my pussy throbbed for more. I obliged, allowing the smooth tip to enter me again. The pain evaporated and turned into a pleasurable feeling. I slowly allowed it to go deeper as the vibration massaged me, causing my body to tremble.

I pulled it out slowly and pushed it back in until I got into a rhythm. I could feel his hands on me, holding me tight, as I moved up and down in a steady pattern. I could feel him kissing me, touching me, his fingers inside of me. We were back in the grotto. I could feel the tip of his tongue circling around my hard brown nipples. With my free hand, I rubbed my nipple with my hand. It was hard. I pinched it, giving myself a surge of pleasurable pain. I needed more; I craved more. I pushed the vibe deeper inside, until it hit the spot.

My body jerked each time the vibe hit this spot. I moaned, arching my back to get more. My hand was moving faster. I turned the vibe on high as I continued to fuck myself rapidly. I felt the familiar pressure forming in my stomach. The feeling grew and grew until I reached the height of pleasure. I could feel the pressure intensifying to the point where I could no longer take it. I pulled the vibe out and threw it on the floor. The sensation had taken my breath away.

I turned on my side and balled my body up in the fetal position. I felt tears forming in my eyes. I could make myself feel pleasure, but I couldn't hold myself afterward. I grabbed a pillow from where he used to lay and held it, rocking my body. I didn't want to sleep in my bed alone.

I picked up my phone. In less than thirty minutes Vernon was at my house. We enjoyed a glass of wine before getting into bed. I allowed him to fill the void. He held me until I fell asleep in his arms.

Chapter 17

Vernon and I were the talk of the church. Against my better judgment, I allowed him to sit with me during service. By the end of the service, everyone wanted to know what was happening and when we had started dating. No matter how many times I said we were just friends, people ignored it.

"We are just happy to see you dating, Coral," one of the older women of the church said to me after service. I heard the same thing from most of the usher board on my walk out of the church.

By the time I made it out of the church, I was exhausted. I was putting my shades on when Vernon rushed up to me after speaking to some of his friends. He put his hand on my back as we walked down the steps.

I didn't want his hand there.

"Man, today was insane," Vernon boasted as we got into his truck.

"Yeah, insane," I replied, staring out the window.

"Well, at least we know that people approve of this. I think every usher told me to marry you." He laughed.

I didn't find it funny. "I knew we shouldn't have sat together. They are relentless."

"Well, I mean, it was going to happen one day."

"It just shouldn't have been this soon."

We pulled out of the church parking lot and stopped at a red light. I could feel Vernon looking at me. I turned my head to find him staring at me with his lips pressed firmly together.

"Coral, are we on the same page here?" Vernon's voice filled the car.

"What do you mean?" I asked, sitting up straight.

"Coral, I am crazy about you, and I just feel like you are not opening up to me. I wanted to sit with you at church because I want to be seen with you. I don't care what people think, because, yes, I do want to be with you, and I do plan on making you my girlfriend. But sometimes I feel like you aren't trying to move toward the same thing."

The light turned green, and Vernon turned his gaze back to the traffic. I stared at him and the concerned expression etched on his face. I was being selfish, and I knew it. He was doing everything right, but I just couldn't connect to him. I wanted to feel that instant attraction I had had with Onyx, but that intense feeling wasn't there. It was probably a good thing. I didn't want to feel the way I had felt when Onyx left. Onyx was dangerous; Vernon was safe.

"I'm sorry. This is all just so new to me. I want to go slow, because I want to make sure I am making the right choices in life." I rested my hand on Vernon's thigh.

He let out a sigh of relief. "I am willing to take things as slow as you want to. I just want to make sure you are feeling me the way I am feeling you."

I smiled. Vernon's expression changed the moment I smiled. A massive grin covered his face. He leaned in and planted a wet peck on my lips. Then we both turned back and focused on the traffic ahead of us. I knew he was a good catch, and I wanted more than anything to get over Onyx. I could only hope that the feelings Vernon had would grow in time within me.

We arrived at my house. We went inside, and I headed to the kitchen, turned on the oven, and pulled out the pan of ravioli I had prepared the night before and some shredded mozzarella. Standing at the counter, I sprinkled the mozzarella on top of the ravioli and then placed the pan in the oven. I felt Vernon's hands grip my sides from behind, and I turned around. Vernon's lips pressed against mine.

I was caught off guard. He forced the kiss on me. I knew if I backed off, it could mean another uncomfortable talk, which I didn't want to have. I closed my eyes and slowly opened my lips, allowing his tongue to enter my mouth. He let out a growl as he wrapped his arms around me.

With no effort at all, he picked me up and sat me on top of the counter. Vernon's hands roamed up and down my back before making their way to my front. I opened my eyes when his left hand gripped my breast and his right hand tried to find its way under my dress. I quickly grabbed his hands and pulled my head away.

"Um, what are you doing?" I asked.

"You just looked so good just now, I had to have you. I need you, Coral. Let me please you," Vernon begged.

"I'm not ready to have sex, Vernon. We discussed this." I pushed him away and jumped down from the counter. He followed me into the living room.

"I'm not asking to have sex. I said, 'Let me please you.' As good as that ravioli smells, that's not what I want to eat right now."

I was confused. It took me a moment to realize what he was asking me. He stared at me and laughed at the blank expression on my face. He wanted to give me oral sex. Onyx had never given me head, saying it was something I would get when we had sex together for the first time. I remembered him telling me that once he tasted me, I would belong to him. I wanted to belong to him so bad.

I snapped out of my Onyx daze to find Vernon still staring at me. I was curious. I knew how much I enjoyed giving Onyx head. Could it feel as good as I felt giving him head? Vernon took my hand and led me to the couch.

"I want to show you how much I care about you," Vernon whispered in my ear as he held my hands and I lay on the couch. "I can't wait to taste you," he cooed.

I closed my eyes. I felt his hands hiking my dress up. His hands were hard from calluses from working out without gloves. He pulled my underwear down. I felt embarrassed that I didn't have on cute underwear. I hadn't worn the cute ones since Onyx left.

Vernon raised my right leg and put it on his shoulder. I bit my lip as he used his fingers to spread my lips. The prickly feeling from his beard felt weird as he dived in. His tongue ferociously licked my clit. My eyes popped open.

He was lapping me like a dog drinking water after playing outside in the heat for hours. This couldn't be what this was supposed to feel like.

I lay there, listening to his moans as he continued to devour me. A big piece of me wanted him to stop. I couldn't feel anything but discomfort. It wasn't sexy or erotic; it felt gross and sloppy.

"Oh, you taste so good," Vernon said when he came up for air. "I could live inside you."

I rolled my eyes. I wanted this to be over. If I never had to get head again, I would be all right with it. My mind raced as I wondered what I was supposed to do. He was working hard down there, and I couldn't feel anything pleasurable at all. How could one man make me feel ultimate pleasure just by looking at me and another make me feel nothing, even when he was trying very hard?

I wondered if this was what it would be like with Onyx. I could see him vividly in my mind. My mind went back to our first sexual encounter. I hadn't been back in my pool since he christened it. I could almost feel his hands on me. I bit my bottom lip and closed my eyes as tight as they would go. I wanted him there. I wanted to smell him, breathe in his energy and essence. I craved his touch and his kiss; I missed everything about him.

My body ached for Onyx. Just thinking about him brought back that familiar tingling in my toes, and it danced its way through my body. All I wanted was to have him near me again. I was addicted, and nothing was going to change that fact.

"Shit, girl." Vernon pulled up. "You really liked Daddy, didn't you?"

My eyes popped open. I was back in my living room, lying on my couch. I shifted my blurry eyes until they focused on Vernon, who was smiling at me, his mouth wet with my essence. It dawned on me that he was smiling because of my thoughts of Onyx.

I sat up on the couch, hoping the guilt I felt didn't show on my face. Vernon moved in closer to me and put his arms around me as he planted a kiss on my cheek.

"Baby, when you are ready, I am going to make love to you ten times better than what I just gave you." He stood up and walked to the back of my house.

The thought of losing my virginity to him turned my stomach. There was only one person whom I wanted to give it to, and it was the one person I couldn't have.

Chapter 18

It was becoming painfully obvious that Vernon was not the one I wanted to experience my first time with, so I had to figure out a way to end things with him.

I was not accustomed to ending things with anyone, and he had done nothing wrong. I had spent my nights thinking of Onyx while he gave me head, something he just couldn't get enough of. I had hoped and prayed that I would eventually like it. Vernon was wonderful in many aspects, and the most important thing was that he truly wanted to be with me. That was something that I couldn't say about the man who consumed my mind on a regular basis.

Things were out of control. We were being invited to couples' dinners by people who usually spoke to me only in passing. People wanted to know how we met, and praised the idea of us being together. I hadn't realized how many people were concerned about my love life until then.

I was stuck in limbo. On the one hand, I did enjoy the companionship that Vernon was offering. He was very sweet and did things I had only imagined or seen on TV. I had had flowers delivered to my house. I would wake up to cute notes or small trinkets from him. He cooked for me almost as much as I cooked for him, and he did things that I hated doing, like fixing stuff in my house or taking the trash out. But on the other hand, there were things I could not stand. The oral was awful, and he wanted to do it all the time. He was messy, and I found myself picking up after him every time he spent the night at my house. I didn't want to sleep at his house, as his old mattress was unbearable, and the manly stench just didn't seem to go away.

I had talked to Tangie about it, and she had reassured me that I was overreacting. She'd said that most men needed to be trained, and it was up to me to do it. The problem was that I was still in a state of learning myself. How could I train someone if I didn't know what I really wanted or needed myself?

My birthday was approaching, and I wasn't happy in the situation that I was in. I had a man who adored me, but it wasn't the man I wanted. I found myself staring at Onyx's number in my phone. Calling would only hurt me in the end.

If he didn't answer or call me back, I would be devastated.

That was something I didn't want to risk.

Vernon insisted we have lunch together, so I finally gave in and met him. We sat across from each other at Applebee's, a place he loved, but I wasn't particularly fond of it. He had ordered his usual ribs, while I had settled on Cajun pasta.

I had a lot on my mind.

The deal for the new downtown space I wanted went through, but I realized quickly the building was going to cost more than I wanted to spend to renovate, and there was no way around it. I sat there crunching numbers in my head, completely ignoring Vernon.

"Earth to Coral," Vernon finally said, snapping his fingers in front of my face.

"I'm sorry. I have a lot on my mind," I replied with a small smile. "What's going on?"

"I asked you if you wanted to eat with the Pattersons after church next Sunday. They invited us."

I frowned. The last thing I wanted to do was eat with more couples. We hadn't made any-thing official, but I felt like I was one step away from walking down the aisle. By the look on

Vernon's face, I could tell he wasn't happy with my response.

"I actually wanted to prepare something special for us. We haven't had much time together lately." I stared into his eyes and watched as his frown turned into a smile.

"That sounds like an excellent idea." Vernon took a bite of a rib.

We finished dinner and headed back to my house. I grabbed my mail, and we headed inside. Vernon was already making himself comfortable on my couch as I thumbed through the various letters. I sat down on the couch next to him when a blue envelope caught my eye. I opened it and pulled out a postcard.

My heart dropped as I read the postcard, which was a flyer for a special Fourth of July night at my club. There was going to be a concert by Onyx's band. On the front of the postcard, in the middle of four other men, stood Onyx with a serious expression, holding his drumstick out toward the camera. I couldn't take my eyes off of him. He looked even better than I remembered.

"What is that?" Vernon asked, taking the postcard out of my hand. "Oh, this is at your spot. Looks like fun. We should go."

"No!" I took the postcard back. Vernon's face twisted with concern due to my protest. "That's

the same night as the family day, and I know we
are going to be super tired after that."

"Oh, we shouldn't be too tired. And it's your
birthday week. You are supposed to turn up
every night."

I stood up. "I'm not really the 'turn up' type
of gal," I replied as I noticed a lustful gaze on
Vernon's face. "Why are you looking at me like
that?"

"I want to run something by you. Feel free to
say no, but I think that it's time we move a little
further in this relationship."

"What do you mean?" I folded my arms. I
didn't know why his referring to whatever this
was as a relationship got under my skin.

"You know how much I love tasting you. Well,
I was wondering if maybe you wanted to try
doing something yourself." He grinned as he
grabbed his dick through his pants.

"Are you asking me to suck your dick?" I
gasped.

"I just think that you might like it. I'm not
asking for sex, but I love pleasing you, and I
just hoped that maybe you would want to do
something to please me in return."

I knew he was right. Vernon spent almost
every night we were together trying to give me
what he thought was amazing head. Up until

this point he had never asked for anything in return. I didn't want to do it, but I knew it was incredibly selfish of me not to.

So I gave in. I played it off, making it seem as if I had never done it before. He talked me through what he wanted me to do. I got on my knees in front of him. I thought about Onyx and how much I loved pleasuring him. Maybe I just enjoyed giving head and would enjoy it with Vernon as well.

Vernon pulled his hard manhood out. He wasn't nearly as big as I had expected. He was such a tall man, and I had expected something similar in his pants. Instead, it was rather thin and much shorter than I'd expected. I closed my eyes as I wrapped my mouth around him. I sucked as he moaned, grabbed my shoulders, and ran his fingers through my hair. This wasn't the same as with Onyx. I wanted Onyx and craved him. With Vernon, it felt more like a job.

It didn't take long for him to tell me he was about to cum. I pulled back as he jerked himself off until he erupted. He was breathing heavily as I stood up. I walked to the linen closet and grabbed a hand towel to give to him.

"Baby, you are really trying to make me fall in love with you?" he muttered in between deep breaths when I gave him the towel.

I sat down on the couch and turned the TV on. I wanted to know why I was so void of emotion. Vernon sat there, singing my praises while begging to take me into the bedroom so he could taste me. I just wasn't in the mood. After a few more moments of begging, he finally retreated to my bedroom. I just sat back on my couch, staring at my television. Moments later I heard the stomping of feet headed toward me.

"You know what, Coral? Fuck this shit!" Vernon shouted as he stood in the doorway, fuming.

"What?" I sat up, startled by his tone.

"I fucking bend over backward for you, because I really care about you. I am trying to make this work on your terms, and you still just don't seem like you care at all. I don't get it. You need to give me some answers."

I sat there, speechless, as he continued to stare at me. I knew he was giving me the perfect moment to tell him that I didn't want to be with him. I just couldn't. There were things I liked about him, but I just didn't have the feeling that I had had when I was with Onyx.

"Hello?" he yelled, arms spread wide as he waited for an explanation.

"I don't know, Vernon," I said, standing up. "I don't have an answer for you. I like you. I really do. But there is something that is just pulling me back, and I don't have an answer about what it is."

"It's gotta be something." Vernon walked closer to me. "Just tell me what to do, Coral."

"I don't know," I sighed. "I wish I had a better answer, but I don't."

We stood in silence for a few minutes. Vernon exhaled and walked toward me until he was close enough to place his hand on my shoulder. Our eyes met. I could see the sincerity in his eyes. He really did care about me, and I was treating him like crap. I wanted to kick myself.

"Well, how about I give you some time to figure that out? When you are ready, you know my number." Vernon removed his hand from my shoulder and walked back to my bedroom. He emerged a few moments later with his duffel bag, then headed to the front door.

I didn't stop him. I knew that it wouldn't be right for me to. I needed to get myself together, and having him there wasn't going to help my situation. I had to figure out what I wanted, and the only person who could help me with that was me.

Chapter 19

I tossed and turned until I finally woke up. I was restless. I stared into the darkness in my room until my eyes finally adjusted. It had been four days since Vernon left, and I had that feeling of loneliness all over again. I didn't know if it was sleeping alone or if I really missed him. The only thing I did know was that my bed didn't feel the same when I was in it alone.

My feet touched the cold hardwood, sending shivers through my body, as I got out of the bed. I slowly walked through my house, headed to the kitchen. I hoped that maybe some wine would calm my nerves. I could see the blue light coming in through my back door. My pool guy must have turned the auto timer on while cleaning the pool. I walked over to the door. I stared out at the water; it looked amazing. I didn't know what came over me, but I opened the door and headed outside.

I bent down next to the pool and felt the water with my hand. Even with the hot weather, the water was cold. I hadn't been back in my pool since the experience with Onyx. I glanced over at the pool entrance to the grotto. I could vividly remember the things he had done to me in that small cave-like area. Flashbacks filled my head—I couldn't shake them. Without thinking, I closed my eyes and jumped into the water with my sleep shirt still on.

The cold water awakened all my senses. Submerged, I opened my eyes. All I could see was blue. Holding my breath, I swam to the underwater entrance to the grotto, then came up for air when I got inside. It was dark. I swam over to the same place I had sat when I was with Onyx, on the small edge, in the water. Leaning back, I closed my eyes. I could see him.

I felt his hands on my skin as I touched my thighs. I ran the tips of my fingers up and down my legs, allowing the magnetic energy to consume me. Sliding my right hand between my legs, I inched my ass up just enough to take my panties off, then threw them on the dry ground.

My fingers felt like lightning bolts, jolting energy into me. I could feel the magnetism coursing through my veins as my right hand found sanctuary between my thighs. I wanted to feel the way he had made me feel that night. I had to wonder, could my fingers be enough?

I entered myself. Even in the cold water, I was warm inside. I touched my clit; it was sensitive to the slightest touch. With two fingers, I massage myself as I thought about my body against Onyx's. I could feel his hands gripping my ass as I bit my bottom lip. Eyes closed shut, I let my fingers slowly move farther south, finding their way to my softest place.

He was there with me. I could picture his face, his right dimple visible as he bit his bottom lip. I could feel his locks between my fingers, taste the saltiness of his sweat as I kissed his neck and face. My body tensed as my fingers worked my innermost depths while my thumb tickled my clit with figure eights. My stomach tightened as a familiar feeling took over, a feeling I had almost forgotten. A falsetto moan escaped my mouth as I climaxed. Tears began to fall, as I could no longer control my emotions. I couldn't stop crying as all my pent-up emotions came flooding out.

I suddenly began to laugh. I was hysterical. Crying and laughing, I didn't know what had come over me. But for the first time in a long time, I didn't feel numb.

I felt relieved, and I liked it.

Chapter 20

It was insanely hot. We were all in the park across from our church on the Fourth of July. Our members and the community had all come out for our celebration. I sat under one of the large tents set up for people to keep cool. This year we had added misting fans for a cooling effect, but it only seemed to make me feel sweaty.

I watched as Tangie and Heather finished a round of double Dutch with some of the girls. They headed over toward me. I glanced over at Vernon, who was assisting some of the men with the industrial grills and arguing over who had the best barbecue sauce.

"I swear, every day I'm reminded of how old I am," Heather said as she plopped down on the bench next to me.

"I know. We used to be the queens of double Dutch. Now I can't hang at all," Tangie uttered while trying to catch her breath. I handed her a water.

I caught myself looking at Vernon again. He did look nice in his basketball shorts and cotton jersey. I could see the definition in his arms more, for some reason. He seemed a lot more buff today than usual.

"So how is that going for you?" Tangie asked, alerting me that I'd been caught. She and Heather had goofy grins on their faces.

"Truthfully, it's not. We haven't talked in almost a week and a half."

"Why?" they asked in unison.

Tangie and Heather listened to my story, hanging on to each and every detail. When I was finally finished, I noticed the straight faces they had. I didn't know what that meant.

"So let me get this straight." Tangie held her index finger up. "You had a man who just really wanted to please you however he could, who was giving up the head at the drop of a dime, and you let him go?"

"The head wasn't good." I winced.

"Girl!" Heather hit the table with her hand. "It never is. You have to teach them what you like. If you didn't like something, you should have said it."

"I didn't want to hurt his feelings," I explained, but the explanation sounded hollow even to me.

"Well, looks like you did that, anyway, so might as well have done it in the bedroom, where things could be fixed." Heather rolled her eyes.

"I have a question." Tangie's index finger flew in the air again. "I want you to be really honest with me. Was this because you just weren't attracted to him? Are you still thinking about the musician?"

Onyx entered my mind. I didn't want to answer the question, but from the look on my face, they already knew the truth.

"Coral, Vernon is a good man, and I personally think you two would make a great couple. But I will say that you need to deal with whatever lingering feelings you have for the musician before anything. It's not fair to you or Vernon." Tangie patted me on my shoulder.

But it didn't make me feel any better.

We all headed into our gym for the annual old-school vs new-school basketball game. We cheered as the older men played the high school boys. I watched Vernon in his element. He was still an amazing basketball player, although not as fast as he was back in high school. I found myself getting excited each time he got the ball.

Our eyes met. I was caught staring by Vernon.
He cracked a smile in my direction right before
taking a shot. I blushed. On the next play, he
stole the ball from one of the younger guys. The
crowd yelled as he ran down the court. He went
up for a layup, but when he came back down, he
slipped on some sweat on the floor. There was a
unanimous gasp from the crowd as he held his
knee. I grabbed Tangie's hand as we watched
the other men surround him. A member of our
congregation who was also a doctor rushed to
assist.

"I need to get down there," I blurted out.

"Let's go." Tangie held my trembling hand as
we made our way to the court.

I was truly worried.

Hours later I stood outside of Vernon's hospital room. I didn't know what I was going to
say to him, so I continued to pace the floor. Our
pastor came out of the room and smiled at me.

"Coral, he's going to be just fine. But he tore
his ACL again. They are going to perform surgery on him in the morning, but he will be fine."
My pastor gave me a reassuring smile. I let out a
sigh of relief as I hugged him. "I'm sure he would
want to see you. Go on in."

I nodded, and then he walked down the hallway to let everyone else know. I went into the room and found Vernon staring at the ceiling.

"I didn't think you were going to come," he mumbled while still staring at the ceiling.

"Of course I was going to be here, Vernon," I said as I walked up to his bed. "You scared the hell out of me."

"Guess my attempt at impressing you didn't go over the way I had expected." Vernon turned his head to look at me, cracking a smile. I grabbed his hand and held it.

"You didn't need to impress me. I'm already impressed by you."

The words surprised me just as much as they did Vernon. I hadn't realize how much I liked him until he was no longer there. Vernon rubbed the palm of my hand with his thumb.

"I've really missed you, woman," Vernon declared.

I smiled. Even when he was in pain, he was catering to me. I had missed him. I'd missed him a lot more than I had ever imagined I would.

"You are having surgery tomorrow on your knee. Do you need me to go pick up anything for you?"

I wrote down a list of things that Vernon wanted from his house. I jotted down a few things I felt he would need that he had forgotten about. If there was one thing I was good at, it was organizing and planning.

"Coral, your birthday is this week. I don't want you dealing with me on your day."

In all the craziness, I had completely forgotten about that. I shrugged my shoulders. My birthday no longer mattered to me. The one thing I really wanted was completely out of the question now.

"Don't worry about my birthday. It's just a day. Now, let me go get your stuff, and I will be back first thing in the morning."

Chapter 21

The eve of my birthday came a lot faster than I had expected. Between Vernon and the remodeling of my new venue, I could barely think straight. I had wanted to spend the night at the hospital with Vernon, but he had insisted that I go home. I was happy, as sleeping in my own bed was what I really needed.

The comfort of my bed caused me to oversleep. When I woke up, I was still drowsy. I rushed to my bathroom and took a long hot shower. I let the water hit my hair, not caring about the flat iron that I had gotten a few days earlier. It wasn't like I had any reason to look good.

Vernon's best friend was on hospital duty today so that I could have the full day to do whatever I needed to do. I decided to adhere to my usual birthday customs. I ordered a cake from my favorite bakery. I went all out, spending over one hundred dollars on a pineapple cake. I usually cooked myself a birthday meal, but this year I decided I was going to order a meal from my favorite Italian restaurant.

I stopped by my club to pick up a deposit. Daytime at the club was so different from nighttime. I couldn't help but look at the stage. I could almost picture Onyx up there. I felt as if I could feel him in the room. Poetry night had been the night before, so I knew he had been there recently.

"So, boss, your birthday is tomorrow, isn't it?" Miguel asked with a grin when I stepped into the office.

"Yeah, it is."

"You should come by tonight. We are trying something new, something called Island Fever. Salsa plus reggae equals a hot, sweaty night of fun." Miguel showed off a few of his salsa moves while speaking.

"Sounds nice, but I think I'm just going to chill at the house."

"Oh, no. No chilling at the house. At least stop by for a few minutes. I have a present for you," Miguel pleaded, holding his palms together.

I sighed. I knew he wasn't going to stop asking, and the idea of at least being out for an hour sounded like a good one. "I will stop by, but I can't stay long."

"Excellent. I'm saving you a VIP booth, anyway, just in case." Miguel hugged me before walking away, shaking his hips the entire time.

After squaring things away at the club, I decided to take a walk down the street. The street on which the club was situated was home to a lot of galleries and small, trendy boutiques. A GRAND OPENING sign in the window of a nearby boutique caught my eye. I peeked inside and saw large posters featuring thick women next to some mirrors. I realized it was a new plus-size boutique and decided to go inside.

The moment I walked in, the dresses caught my attention. Everything was hip. Nothing looked old-fashioned, like in many of the other full-figured stores. A black maxi dress caught my attention immediately.

"That would look good on you, but I would suggest something with a lot more color."

I turned around to see a thick, brown-skinned woman emerge from behind some beaded curtains. She walked over to a rack and picked out a dress before approaching me.

"Now, this . . . this would look stunning on you," she said, holding up a tangerine and white print dress.

"That is beautiful. I've never seen dresses so nice in these sizes before."

The woman smiled. "That's because I make them."

"Oh, wow." I admired the dress. It was of a very high quality, which made me not mind the one-hundred-fifty-dollar price tag on it.

We talked as I tried on a few different styles. I found out that her name was Gina, and that she was new to Memphis. She had designed more than three collections and had finally been able to open her own small store. She truly had a gift. Each dress that she picked out for me looked better than the one before it. We talked about business and shared tips on owning property. I could tell she was going to need help; she was an artist, and artists often didn't make the best businesspeople.

"Gina, why on earth would you come to Memphis to open this store?" I asked her while trying on another beautiful dress. "Though I am kind of glad you did," I added, staring at the mirror and marveling at my form in her unique piece of clothing.

"Because I've always loved this city, and I think that it's something that could blossom here. Atlanta has tons of plus-size boutiques, and so do a lot of other big cities. Not to mention the cost of living is a lot cheaper here. With e-commerce, I can essentially be set up anywhere and sell. I get tons of orders through my Etsy site alone."

She gave my latest try—a colorful, long maxi dress—an appraising glance. "I think that is the one," she said. It was the type of dress that could be worn for a few different occasions.

"It's beautiful, so beautiful. Like the perfect birthday dress." I suddenly felt sad.

"Wait. It's your birthday?"

"No. Tomorrow. But I'm not doing anything. My guy friend is in the hospital, so I'll just be with him."

"Oh, I'm sorry to hear that. My birthday is next week, so as a fellow Cancer, I just feel like birthdays are supposed to be celebrated and big. But I can't talk. I'm new, and I haven't met that many people, so it will probably be a quiet birthday for me as well," Gina said as she tied the back of the dress for me. "Now, that is perfect."

I looked at myself in the three-way mirror. I could see Gina smiling at me, admiring her design. She was right—I looked beautiful. This dress was better than any outfit I owned. I wanted to buy it, even if it meant staring at myself in the mirror at home.

"Hey, I own the club right down the way. We are having this salsa-reggae night tonight. Would you like to come?" I said.

I could tell Gina was shocked by the invitation. She hesitated but finally said yes after I told her I wasn't taking no for an answer. I bought the dress; she gave me half off for my birthday. I told her I would meet her at the club at eight. I left the store, feeling renewed. I called Tangie and Heather and told them to come out with me. They both were happy to get away from their normal lives for a night. It was the eve of my birthday, and suddenly, celebrating early seemed like a good idea.

Chapter 22

"I cannot believe I've never been to your house," Tangie said as she and Heather admired my living room. "This is fucking gorgeous."

"Thanks," I yelled as I walked out of my bedroom. "So what do you guys think?"

I walked into the living room. Heather's and Tangie's mouths dropped open when they saw me in my new dress. I had decided to go natural, with my curls in my hair. I had added a cute small feather clip to my tresses to give myself a little bit of an island feel. They both praised the look, telling me how great I looked.

"FYI, I'm coming over to hit that pool one of these days," Heather said, finishing her glass of wine. "Like, seriously."

"Anytime. I'm really glad we have connected so much lately, guys." I hugged both girls. I was happy to have actual friends to spend my birthday with. Well, it was Saturday night, and my birthday was Sunday, but tonight still counted as a birthday celebration.

Tangie picked up my birthday cake on the counter in the kitchen, and we headed to my car. We pulled up to the club and saw a line wrapped around the corner. I saw Gina standing on the sidewalk. I honked the horn and waved her over, and she got in my car. I pulled into my personal spot at the back of the club.

"Man, it is so cool knowing the owner, 'cause that line was something else," Gina said and chuckled as we got out of the car.

We walked in the back door. The salsa music was going. The floor was packed with couples dancing. I saw Miguel in the middle, dancing with a petite woman. They looked amazing as they tore up the floor. When I caught Miguel's attention, he quickly rushed over to me.

"So glad you are here. Happy birthday! I see you need the VIP section, after all," Miguel said, and then he ushered us to our table.

The night was just getting started, and people continued to pack the club. I sat in my seat, grooving to the beat while I watched Tangie and Heather dance with two cute Latino men. One of my bartenders brought over a pitcher of a frozen concoction he'd made for my birthday. I took a sip of the potent, fruity beverage. Before I knew it, I had drunk two cups and was really starting to feel it.

"This night is amazing," Tangie said as she sat down and grabbed her cup. "Girl, these little Puerto Rican men are about to make me forget I'm married."

We both laughed.

A few minutes later Gina and Heather joined us at the table. The music stopped in the club.

Miguel, soaking wet from dancing, took the microphone on the stage. "I want to welcome everyone to Island Fever."

The crowd cheered.

"I am Miguel, the manager of this fine establishment. I wanted to take a moment to thank someone very special. This has been our home for salsa for the past two years, and it's all because of my boss, the beautiful Coral, who is sitting right up there." Miguel pointed at me, and the spotlight hit my table.

The crowd cheered, and I waved shyly.

"And in"—Miguel paused to glance at his watch—"one minute it will be her birthday. So on the count of three, I want us all to sing 'Happy Birthday' to Coral."

I shook my head to dissuade them, but the crowd began to sing "Happy Birthday" while staring at me. Heather and Tangie made me stand up when one of the waitresses brought out my cake, which had three long sparkler candles twinkling on it. The shy part of me was mortified, but another part of me loved feeling special in that moment. Everyone clapped as Tangie snapped photos.

"Now, we have loved all this amazing Spanish music, but it's time to visit another island," Miguel announced. "The island of Jamaica. And we have a special band that is going to bring the flavor to us. Introducing our house band for poetry night, the Bluff City Ensemble!"

I froze as I watched Onyx's bandmates take the stage. My heart started to race when he appeared. His locks were braided back into two big cornrows, the bottoms of which hung down. He looked amazing, better than I remembered. The tight black shirt he had on hugged his arms, which looked even bigger than before.

"Coral, what's wrong?" Tangie asked, noticing the look of horror on my face.

I couldn't speak. Onyx's eyes turned straight to me. The right side of his mouth curled upward, allowing his right dimple to appear. I quickly looked away as the band began to play.

"It's one of them, isn't it? The musician you were involved with?" Heather questioned as she sat next to me.

I nodded my head.

"It's okay, girl. Just ignore him," Heather told me.

"Maybe we should leave," I muttered.

"And let him have the upper hand?" Heather said. "Girl, you look amazing, and we are all having a good time. Fuck him! Let him eat his heart out. Just have another drink, and let's go dance."

I didn't know if it was the liquor in my system or my girls egging me on, but a burst of confidence came over me. I followed my friends down to the dance floor, where we danced to the band's rendition of a Bob Marley classic. A few men joined us as we danced together. I allowed a guy to hold me close as our bodies moved to the beat. I, however, quickly moved his hands up when they found their way to my butt.

I didn't know if Onyx was looking at me, but I had a feeling that he was. So I took the moment to turn up the heat. I slow danced with the guy, grinding my ass against his pelvis. I allowed myself to get lost in the music. I wouldn't turn toward the stage; I couldn't look at him when he drummed. Even when I wasn't looking, I could feel Onyx's beats affecting every part of my body.

But I was enjoying myself.

I was happy when the band took its first break. The DJ began playing reggae music as the girls and I left the dance floor. Before I made it all the way, the man I'd been dancing with grabbed my arm.

"Oh, don't tell me you are leaving me now." The guy was taller than I'd realized, but very thin.

"Yeah, but thanks for the dances." I smiled.

He held on to my arm and pulled me closer to him. "Come on. Just one more," he begged while pushing his pelvis against me.

"Um, no thanks." I tried to pull away, but his grip tightened.

"You are too hot." He pulled me closer. "Let me get a little more."

"Please let go of my arm," I said, starting to get a little nervous.

"I can take it from here, brother," a familiar voice said, sending chills down my spine. I turned around to see Onyx with his hand on the guy's shoulder.

"Nah. I wasn't finished," the guy objected.

"Yeah, you are," Onyx growled, staring the man in the eye. The man looked at me, then at Onyx, and decided it was a risk he didn't want to take.

I felt like my heart was going to fall out of my chest. Onyx's cologne excited my senses. I was too close to him. There was no way I was going to be able to play it cool.

"You okay, Coral?" Onyx questioned.

"I'm fine. Thanks." I forced a smile as I turned to walk away. Onyx gently grabbed my arm.

"Come on now, babe. Don't just walk away like that." Onyx's voice was causing my knees to shake.

"I'm sorry, but my friends are waiting on me," I replied, looking up at the VIP area to see Tangie, Heather, and Gina all watching, just in case they needed to step in. "But it was nice seeing you." I began to walk away.

"Happy birthday," Onyx yelled over the loud music.

I paused in my tracks.

"I didn't forget," he called.

I turned around to see Onyx staring directly at me. His face was strong; there was no smile, just a tight-lipped expression. He almost looked concerned.

"Thank you, Onyx. I appreciate that."

And with those words, I walked away. I joined my friends back in the VIP area, and we continued to party. It was easier than I had expected to ignore Onyx, especially since I knew his eyes were on me.

It was almost two in the morning, and the club was still going strong. The band leader announced it would be their final set. I looked at

Onyx. Our eyes met just as he hit his drumsticks together. He began to stroke the drums, closing his eyes. I knew what that meant: he was in his zone.

Onyx's solo came somewhere in the middle of the set. He stroked the drums as if it was the last time he would ever play. The crowd and his bandmates all went wild as he killed his solo. Sweat fell from his face as the intensity of the moment took over his whole body. I couldn't take my eyes off him. No one could. I was in sync with him. I could feel each note; each stroke was like he was in me. And with his final stroke, he dropped the drumsticks, causing the crowd to lose it. Onyx looked directly at me.

I knew that this was meant for me. Every beat was meant to affect me. He wasn't playing for anyone but me in that moment, and I could feel him just like he wanted me to. My body was trembling. I couldn't get a grip on myself. Tangie looked at me.

"I think it's time for us to go," she told me. She alerted the other girls. They quickly grabbed our stuff, and we headed out of the club.

Chapter 23

"Tonight was amazing. I really needed it," Heather said as she hugged me.

"Yes, girl, amazing. Thank you again, and happy birthday," Tangie declared as she pulled her body off of my comfortable couch. "We must do this again soon."

"Thank you, guys. You made my birthday memorable."

I walked them to the door and hugged both of them again before they left. I closed the door behind them and locked it. I leaned against the door. The night replayed in my head. I couldn't help but smile. Although Onyx had had the upper hand, I had been able to hold my own in the room with him. It had been a great game of cat and mouse, and I had essentially gotten away unscathed.

I pulled my shoes off and threw them to the side of my door. I walked into my kitchen and grabbed a bottle of smartwater. I was still very tipsy and wanted to fend off the hangover I could see coming in the morning. I took two aspirin and swallowed the cold water. I could feel the liquid trickling down my throat, and it gave me a second wind. I wasn't sleepy. I was still on a high, something I hadn't felt in a long time. I figured some television would help me unwind.

My doorbell startled me mid-drink. I noticed the extra pair of heels Tangie had brought with her sitting next to my couch. I picked the shoes up and walked to my door.

I cracked open the door just enough to hold the shoes out and stood behind it. "Forget something?" I said with a laugh.

"I did."

I froze. The voice with the familiar accent made the little hairs on my arms stand up. I couldn't move. My body wouldn't allow me to open the door so that I could actually see him standing there. I just stood behind the door, holding the pair of shoes out like a crazy person.

I felt his hand touch my hand. He took the shoes from me, grazing my palm with his fingers. The touch sent his electric energy through my body, bringing me back to my senses. He slowly pushed the door open enough so that he could get inside. I didn't move as he closed the door behind him. Our eyes met.

There was nothing to think about; nothing mattered in that moment. He was in my house, standing in front of me. I didn't think. I knew what I wanted, and I wanted him.

Before he could say anything, I walked up to him, threw my arms around his neck. Our lips were pressed tightly together. His tongue found mine easily, earnestly. Onyx didn't hesitate. He wrapped his arms around my thighs and gripped my butt with his hands. I jumped, and he took me in his arms, I wrapped my legs around his waist.

I kissed him hungrily, holding him tight, just in case he changed his mind and wanted to leave. My right hand held on to his locks, gently pulling them. Onyx pushed my back against the front door. Our passion was well matched. My desire for him only intensified as he kissed me. I didn't want to let him go. I needed to feel him, and so I ran my hands under his sleeves just so I could feel his muscles. I had to feel his flesh against my skin.

Onyx slowly moved his hands so that my feet touched the floor. He pulled his face away. I looked at him, concerned. His eyes were fixated on me, staring directly into my eyes.

"I'm sweaty, and you had that other dude's hands on you," he muttered.

"What? You act like he actually touched something."

"He touched you. That's more than enough. Let's take a shower." Onyx didn't allow me to respond. He took my hand and guided me back to my bedroom.

I looked at Onyx's reflection in my large bathroom mirror as he prepared the shower. Steam began to fill the bathroom. I watched as he walked up behind me and kissed the nape of my neck.

"Did I get to tell you how beautiful you looked tonight? This dress, your hair, everything. You were stunning," Onyx said, his deep voice echoed in the room as he ran his hands through my curls.

His fingertips touched my right shoulder as his left hand unzipped the back of my dress. He slowly pulled each strap off my shoulders, allowing the dress to fall to the floor. I stood there in my black lace bra and panties. I silently sent up a thanks for my having thought to wear a matching set. He unhooked my bra, then repeated the steps employed for the dress, taking each strap down before pulling my bra completely off. We stared at my body in the mirror as the steam began to settle on it.

"Beautiful," Onyx breathed as he kissed my neck.

I turned around as Onyx pulled his shirt over his head. I unbuckled his belt and unzipped his jeans. His jeans hit the floor. My mouth watered at the large print in his gray briefs. We walked over to the shower. I pulled my panties off as he pulled his briefs off. The water was perfect as it hit my skin.

We cleaned each other slowly, exchanging kisses during the act. I couldn't resist the urge to take him into my hand. I wanted to taste him again. I started to go down on my knees, but he stopped me.

Onyx shook his head. "It's your birthday."

Onyx got closer to me, until I was firmly against the shower wall. He slowly fell to his knees. Onyx raised my left leg and rested it on his broad shoulder. I bit my lip as I felt his tongue slide between my lips. My bottom lip fell as he tasted me. My body trembled as he kissed and licked my inner thighs. His tongue danced circuitously from one side to the other side, completely skipping over my throbbing clit. I couldn't wait. My voice quivered as I begged him to touch it.

"I got this," he mumbled, then resumed his attack on me.

My nails dug into his shoulders as he continued his assault on my noni. I couldn't take it.

Flashbacks of our previous encounters filled my head. The familiar feelings tugged at the desire I had deep inside for him, while creating new feelings I had yet to discover until this very moment. My hands instinctively grabbed his locks as a spasm shot through my stomach. A deep moan escaped his mouth, sending vibrations through me. I was going to cum. I could feel it coming.

He pulled away.

I whimpered.

"Not yet," Onyx said as he stood up.

He turned off the shower and helped me out. We dried each other off in silence. I wanted to know what he was thinking. I wanted to know what was coming next.

Chapter 24

Onyx led me into my bedroom. The cool air in the room caused my nipples to harden.

"Lie on your stomach," he commanded.

I quickly obeyed.

He retreated to the bathroom, and I could hear him walking around in there, but I didn't turn my head to find out what he was doing. I wanted to be surprised. I let my ears be my guide, and soon I heard his footsteps growing closer. His knees made the mattress sink down just a little as he straddled my butt. I felt a cold liquid hit my back. Onyx's strong hands began massaging oil into my skin.

I moaned as he massaged my back. This was a pleasant surprise. I could feel all the tension releasing as he worked his way down my spine, stopping only to kiss the small of my back. The heat coming from his body radiated to his hands, causing my body to become a full inferno. He rubbed my lower back, then made his way to my ass. He pressed firmly against my cheeks with his left hand, while his right hand was between my legs as he massaged my pussy.

"Damn, Coral. I gotta have you," Onyx taunted, causing me to moisten even more.

I wanted him to have me. Onyx commanded me to get on my back, and he helped turn me over. But fear quickly filled me. It was really about to happen. I was about to lose something I had hung on to for thirty years. Reality started to creep into my brain. I hadn't talked to Onyx in months, and now he was about to take something that I didn't know if he truly deserved. I looked at his lust-filled face. The light from my lamp touched his face just right; he was beautiful.

"Coral, baby, are you sure about this?" Onyx asked.

I knew he could sense the change in my mood. Suddenly, I didn't know if I was sure or not.

Onyx sat on the side of the bed, and I sat up. I put my arms around my knees and gently rocked myself. Onyx put his hands on top my knees.

"We don't have to go any further. In fact, how about we just stop?" Onyx sighed as he stood up. He kissed me on my forehead.

As I watched him walk into the bathroom, another reality hit me. He was the one. For months, I couldn't focus, because of how much

I missed and craved him. I was allowing fear to ruin a moment I had dreamed about nonstop since the moment we met. When he walked out of the bathroom, holding his clothes in his hands, I knew it for sure. He was the one.

"Onyx," I whispered.

"Coral?"

"Take me."

Onyx didn't hesitate. He reached into a pocket of his jeans before dropping them back on the floor. He slowly walked closer to the bed as I scooted my body back down until I was lying flat on my back. He didn't take his eyes off of me. Onyx climbed on top of me. Our flesh was pressed together. He bit the condom wrapper with his teeth and pulled the piece of latex out of the package. He didn't take his eyes off of me as he protected us.

I was nervous. My body trembled as he lifted my left leg and propped it on his shoulder. My body continued to tremble, and then I felt it fluttering, as if I had a thousand hummingbirds inside of me. My nerves didn't trump the desire throbbing deep inside of me. I wanted him; I needed it.

Onyx positioned himself, his weight on top of me, but it didn't hurt. As he placed his manhood at my entrance, I closed my eyes. I gasped, then held my breath, anticipating what was about to come next.

"Coral," Onyx whispered. "Look at me."

I opened my eyes to see his beautiful face staring directly at me. Our eyes were fixated on each other. In that moment it was just us—no music, no noise of any kind. The only sound was of our hearts beating in perfect sync. I exhaled as he pressed his lips against mine. He kissed passion into my mouth as he slowly pressed his tip inside. Pain shot through my body. My nails dug into his arms as I gasped. He bit my bottom lip.

"Breathe, baby." Onyx's voice soothed me as he kissed me over and over. "Breathe."

I did as I was told. We stared at each other as he inched his way in me. It was painful, but as I moistened, the pain became more pleasurable. I closed my eyes. Onyx kissed the few tears that rolled down my cheeks.

"Coral," he moaned. "Baby."

I opened my eyes and saw that Onyx had his eyes closed tight. His lips were pressed tightly together. He let out another moan. The sight of his face brought me even more pleasure. I felt a tidal wave coming down, which only allowed him to go deeper. I held on to him as I felt each inch. Each stroke was more pleasurable than the one before. I began to roll my hips in a steady rhythm with him. Onyx moaned again, thrusting deeper until he reached that spot that had been touched only by fingers. A spasm hit me, causing my body to jerk and making me let out a high-pitched squeal.

He didn't stop. My squeal turned into short screams that couldn't quite come out of my mouth. I hit his chest, which only enticed him. He held me close as his thrusts went long and deep. I couldn't take it. I hit the bed repeatedly, trying to get out of this. I attempted to move my butt so that he couldn't continue, but he held me so I couldn't.

I made the decision to stop fighting it. I let go and allowed him to deliver the most exquisite torture to my body. It didn't make me want to stop—it only heightened my arousal. I moved my hips as he worked me. We moaned some more, both of us unable to form actual words. Spasms continued to shoot through my stomach, forming a volcano of energy that was going to erupt at any moment.

"Not yet," Onyx demanded. "Not y-yet," he stuttered as he continued his assault. He cupped my breasts, pinched my hard nipples. He leaned in, pressed his lips against my right nipple, allowed his teeth to nibble gently before he sucked it hard and rough.

I couldn't hold it anymore. My body no longer belonged to me. I began to tremble as I hit his chest. I whimpered; short breaths escaped me. I opened my eyes. Onyx lifted his head. His eyes met mine.

"Now!" he yelled.

And with his command, I let go. My body shook as I grabbed him, pulled him as close to me as I could. My body shook as he continued to thrust until my nectar covered him. He tensed up as he let out a deep and loud moan that made his body vibrate. Onyx dropped his head on my chest as his orgasm consumed his body, until he finally fell down on top of me.

"Fuck!" Onyx yelled as he gasped for air. Even with our bodies sweaty and sticking together, I wanted to live in the moment a little longer. I held on to him, felt his chest rise and fall as he caught his breath. Finally gaining composure, Onyx rolled over to his side of the bed. He put his arm around me as I turned over on my side. We stared at each other as he rubbed my hair.

"Are you okay?" The aggression in his voice was gone, replaced with a soft, low tone.

I nodded. I was more than all right. My body ached, but it was a pleasurable ache.

"Are you sure?" Onyx asked. He was really concerned about my well-being. This only made me feel better.

"I'm great. Perfect." I smiled.

He pressed his lips against mine as he pulled his body closer to mine. We lay there, soaking in our essence, before he retreated to the bathroom. I slowly forced myself out of the bed. I grabbed a bedpost as my legs almost gave in. Once I was steady, I pulled my comforter back. I was afraid of what I would find. I remembered hearing horror stories as a teen. To my surprise, there were only a few traces of blood, but the sheets were soaking wet.

Onyx came back into the bedroom. "Yeah, that's all you," he joked as he looked at the massive wet spot on my sheets. He kissed me on my neck and took my hand, then led me to the guest room. We climbed in bed. Onyx held me tight, and we spooned until we fell asleep in each other's arms. I couldn't help but think that this was the best birthday ever.

Chapter 25

The sound of my phone ringing woke me out of my sleep. I didn't open my eyes but instead fumbled around the nightstand with one hand. I couldn't find the phone. I finally forced my eyes open. I squinted. Nothing looked familiar. Suddenly it hit me—I was in my guest room and not in my bedroom.

The night's activities flooded through my mind. I turned over to see Onyx's back to me. He was sleeping peacefully on his side. I slowly climbed out of the bed. The moment I stood up, I felt the ache from the hurting he had put on me. I tiptoed out of the room.

I went into my bedroom, pulled the sheets off my bed, and put them in the washer. I then walked back into my bedroom with a fresh pair of sheets and put them on the bed.

I walked into my bathroom and studied myself in the mirror. I didn't look any different, but I felt like a completely new woman. My fingertips traced the outline of my jaw as memories from the night played in my head. I got in the shower, only to remember how Onyx had had me as his meal in there just a few hours earlier. Onyx and that night would forever be etched on my brain.

After a hot shower, I felt renewed and refreshed. I grabbed a maxi dress and threw it on. My hair was wild and curly, but I didn't care. It was still my birthday, and I could do whatever I wanted.

In the distance, I heard my phone ringing again. I skipped into the kitchen and picked my phone up off the counter. As soon as I looked at the screen, my giddy feeling left me. Vernon's face flashed on the screen. I composed myself before pressing the green button.

"Hey," I said. I tried to sound as innocent as possible. "How are you?"

"Happy birthday, baby. I wanted to be the first to wish you happy birthday, but you didn't answer your phone last night." Vernon sounded a bit disappointed.

"Oh, yeah. I was out last night."

"Out?" Vernon questioned.

"Yeah. The manager of my club wanted me to come there for my birthday, so Tangie and Heather went with me. It was fun." I sat on one of the bar stools.

"Oh, okay. Well, I'm glad you had a good time. When am I going to get to see you?"

Onyx walked into the kitchen just then. He wrapped his arms around me, kissed me on my neck, and nibbled on my ear. I motioned for him to stop. He looked at me, his gaze inquisitive. He sat down on the stool next to me while I tried not to sound guilty.

"I will be headed that way soon. Okay?"

"Great. Can't wait to see my birthday girl."

I smiled. I could hear the excitement in Vernon's voice. I hung up the phone. I didn't feel the way I thought I would. I wasn't sad, and I didn't feel guilty. An overwhelming feeling of happiness filled me.

"What was that about?" Onyx questioned.

"Nothing," I said, standing up. "So, I gotta get ready to go. Did you want to take a shower?"

Onyx stood up as well. "Hold up. Are you trying to get rid of me already?"

I couldn't stop smiling. Even with the confused look on his face, I continued to grin from ear to ear. "Yeah. I have to go. Sorry, but—"

"It's the other dude, huh?" Onyx folded his arms.

I turned my head and looked at him closely. How did he know?

Somehow he read my thoughts. "Come on, Coral. I saw the gym shoes in your bedroom. I know they don't belong to you. So you got a dude now?" Onyx said.

I stood staring at the man whom I had lusted over since the day I met him. He stood there with his arms crossed over his bare chest, his biceps protruding, all the things that I loved about him on display in front of me. But it didn't matter.

I nodded my head. "Yeah, yeah, I have a man." I laughed. "I have a man who is crazy about me."

I didn't know what had come over me, but after that night, a dark cloud had disappeared. I wrapped my arms around Onyx, hugging him tight.

"Thank you. Thank you for everything," I said as I held on to him. I soon felt his arms gripping me in return.

"You are something special, Coral." He kissed me on my cheek.

Onyx got dressed, and I finished getting ready to go see Vernon. We stood in my living room for what I knew would be the last time. Onyx had a purpose in my life, and now that purpose had been fulfilled. He was the one who was supposed to prepare me for the next step in my life. Now his job was done, and I could move forward in life with someone whom I could truly be with.

I knew it wouldn't be the last time I saw him. I knew the day would come when we saw each other at the club or on a street. We would be cordial; we'd exchange pleasantries before going on our way. He would have a new woman by the end of the day, and I would always have the memories of what we'd had. I would take the memories of us to my grave. It was special, and everything I had wanted it to be.

Once Vernon's knee got better, we had our first time. I didn't have thoughts of Onyx consuming me anymore, and consequently, I realized that Vernon was actually an incredible lover. I was able to vocalize what I liked and didn't like, which made things even better. He would forever believe that he was my first, which might not be right, but a girl was allowed to have her secrets.

Life went into full swing. I got my new business opened, and it was an immediate success. Bookings for weddings and events flooded in. Before I knew it, a year had passed, and it was almost my birthday again. Vernon had moved in with me, and our relationship was going very strong.

One night, while Vernon was on an overnight trip with his basketball team, I decided to meet

Gina at the club for open mic night. I didn't know if Onyx's band was still playing there, but I knew there was a chance I would see him for the first time since he left my house on my birthday last year. We walked into the club, and I saw him standing next to the stage. There was a cute girl standing next to him, and by the way she was draped on him, I could only guess she was his new squeeze. We made eye contact as he joined the band on the stage.

After his set, he came up to me where I sat, hugged me, and asked me how I had been doing. I showed him the ring on my finger. He took two steps back, grinning and showing off his deep dimples.

"So someone is taking my Coral off the market. Congratulations," he said as he wrapped his arms around me again. He put his lips near my ear. "You know that pussy still belongs to me." He pulled away, with the same grin on his face.

I could feel my heat starting to rise.

"Whatever. You probably wouldn't know what to do with me now. You should probably stick to li'l mama over there," I joked.

"Oh, trust me, I *always* will know. And it doesn't take nothing but a word from you to find out. July sixth, right?" Onyx winked at me.

I shook my head as he walked back to the stage. As I sat there, my panties moist from just contemplating the possibilities, I could only think to myself, *It will soon be my birthday. And doesn't a girl deserve whatever she wants on her birthday?*

Part One

Chapter One

Lynn

"Stop it. Just stop it, okay!" I yelled.

Nothing he could say or do at that moment would make me feel better. He had broken my heart for the final time. I was tired of begging, tired of pleading, more than tired of longing for love. It had been an eight-year waste of time. Eight years of my fucking life that I couldn't take back, and I was sitting there, trying to keep myself from jumping across the table and taking his ass down.

He frowned like he was irritated. "What do you want me to say, Lynn?" he asked.

I twisted my neck and exhaled before I answered. Softly, I said, "The truth, Chez."

Chester was the pilot who had spent the past six years of our marriage flying the friendly skies and neglecting me. The first two years had been okay, not steamy or hot, but I had convinced myself that things would get better, only for them to get worse. He had had his moments where he played the role of a husband, but the rest of the time he had played the part of my homeboy, my part-time roomie, when he was in town.

"I've given you the truth," he countered.

"No you haven't. How can you say you love me, Chez, when we haven't made love in over a year? You come home, and . . . and . . . and you are in this zone, this 'no romance for Lynn' zone. The zone of friendship and maid service. I do everything for you. I cook. I clean. I wash your drawers. I fix you a drink whenever you ask. I pick up your pile of funky clothes from the bathroom floor. Fix your plate, serve you, and take up your plate, even after you've eaten the meal I cooked.

"How long did you think I'd just play this role of a fool for you, Chez? I mean, all I ask of you is a little affection. A little romance, a little time spent. And some dick. If not on a regular, just sometimes. I mean, you are my husband, my only source and means of getting it, yet you refuse to share yourself with me. You are cold, a cold-ass bastard."

"I've never mistreated you," he said, refuting my allegations.

"You're right. You don't whip my ass, cuss me out, or call me names, but you're not a gentleman, either. I want to be held, loved, complimented, or just made to feel like a woman. You never hold me. You never touch me."

"I'm not a lovey-dovey guy, Lynn. I'm not a romantic."

"Who cares about the romance, Chez? There is still no intimacy."

"Maybe if you'd stop hounding me and let me do it on my own, instead of always trying to force me . . ."

"And then what? Huh? You'll devour me? You'll take me to a level where my thighs shake? Tell me, Chez. I mean, I've done everything I can to turn you on, to pique your interest, and all you do is push me away, and I'm fucking fed up with this bullshit."

"See, that's one of the reasons. Your attitude. You're like a ticking time bomb. If your food is wrong, you snap. If I forget to pick up something or do something you asked, you go off, and that is a turnoff. No man wants to deal with that shit."

"And no woman wants a man who would rather play with a PS3 than her. Have you ever stopped to think that my attitude, my short fuse, or my demeanor is because of your lack of interest? Maybe if I had an orgasm on a regular basis,

I'd be a little less stressed or more relaxed. You act as if you don't care, Chez, and this relationship has run its course. I'm done with begging. You've ruined my self-esteem and my confidence in myself. I've asked you, are you turned off by the weight I've gained? You say no, and still you won't love me. I want a man to love me. I want to be touched. I want to be wanted. I want to be with a man who wants to be with me."

Silence fell upon the room. I knew then that he didn't love me. I knew he didn't desire me or even want me. Not touching me in over a year was the physical evidence of this, and now the silence was the forensic evidence for me.

"Okay then, I guess this conversation is done," I said and stood. I headed for the kitchen, and he just sat there. "What do you want for dinner?" I called. I knew after asking this that I was foolish, but I was an oven whore. As a professional baker, I was also a chef at heart. Baking and cooking were my thing. Food was my enemy: I was a size eighteen because I ate as much as I cooked and baked.

Finally he spoke. "That stuffed poblano chicken dish with the Spanish rice and the refried beans you make would be perfect."

"Yes, it would be," I said.

I grabbed my keys and headed to the store. I had everything for that dish but the poblanos, and I had to make a run to get them. After grabbing a few things that were not on my list, I hurried home to cook.

Later we ate in silence, like we normally did, but before I could eat my last bite, he spoke.

"I'm moving out."

I almost choked. I coughed and then took a sip of my water and then guzzled my white wine. I moved the last few grains of Spanish rice around on my plate with my fork and then said, "When?"

Without looking at me, he focused on his plate. "At the end of next week. I got a place, and I was waiting for the right time to tell you."

"And now is the right time?" I yelled. My blood boiled over. I had never hated anyone in my life, not even my first husband, as much as I hated the man sitting before me. "You had this planned, you son of a bitch, and I . . . I . . . I . . ." I stood. "Fine. Get your shit, Chez. I know you've never loved me. Why you married me, I have no clue, but fuck us, okay? I'm tired of waiting on us. Hoping for us," I shot at him. "As a matter of fact, don't wait. Please get your shit and leave tonight. Seeing your face until the end of next week is not the move."

"My place won't be ready for almost two weeks."

"So fucking what!" I barked.

"This is exactly the reason why I'm leaving your evil ass."

"No, baby. I'm not evil. I'm just lashing out. Lashing out from how my pussy aches to be touched. Lashing out from how I want to share a deep, passionate kiss. Lashing out because not one fucking time in this entire marriage have you ever sent me flowers. Lashing out because I've never been your babe, bae, darling, sugar, honey, baby, love, muffin, dumpling, or even boo. I've been Lynn or Lynniah this entire marriage. I know people who treat their pets with more love and affection than you treat me.

"Let's be real. When I met you, I thought you were a little weird, as you were not full of flattery. I was thinking, 'This guy is genuine. He's not saying things that most men say to get between my legs. He's being him, and I like that.' Somehow realness turned into coldness, and I was thinking, 'Once we are married, he'll loosen up.' I married you, knowing you didn't eat pussy, Chez. Yes, I compromised."

I went on. "I married you, knowing you had a thing about washing your clothes with mine.

Yes, I adapted to your ways. Oh, and the toilet seat cover. We were raised different. I was raised with it up, and apparently, you were raised with it down, and you'd have a mini heart attack if I forgot, even after I said to you, 'A learned behavior is hard to break. If I grew up with a different kind of upbringing and am not accustomed to yours, don't be mad.' Yet it irritated the fuck out of you when I'd forget to put the cover down, something so small.

"I have endured all I can, Chez. So fine. Move out. I'm good," I said. I got up and began to clear the table.

Wanting an argument, he said, "So you gon' let me leave."

"*Let* you?" I laughed. "I can't stop you, baby. You got a place, remember? You didn't discuss it with me, nor did you tell me sooner, and I'm tired of holding on. This thing is over. As much as it hurts, I will admit it was over a long time ago. You're no longer welcome here, so please, go pack what you can take and move around. I'm past foolish. I'd be stupid as hell if I begged you to stay. So please do us both a favor and get your things and leave."

He stood and watched me clear the table with no response. Of course he had nothing.

There was nothing left to say. I hummed a tune in my brain—Melanie Fiona's "It Kills Me"—as I cleaned, and I wiped the tears that graced my face. I just wanted him gone so I could go through the heartbreak period alone.

Hell, I knew he didn't love me . . . well, not the way I wanted him to, so it was a done deal.

After cleaning the kitchen, I sat down on a staircase step with a refilled glass of pinot. He passed me on his third trip from our master to his SUV.

"That's all I need for now," he announced.

"Bye, Chez," I said, not looking up.

"You know this hurts me too."

I laughed. "That I don't believe, but you are forgiven. Just go." I needed no condolences, no apologies, and definitely no lies.

"I do love you, Lynn."

"I'm sure you do in your mind. I know people who love their dogs more than you love me. Mrs. Warren across the street literally kisses that Maltese more than you've ever kissed me. And if I was weird, I'd say Sammie, her Maltese, would love to lick her cat before you'd lick mine."

"And you wonder why I have issues with you."

"No, you got issues with yourself, minute man."

He shot me a look. "Don't, Lynn."

"No, let's just be real, Mr. Eruption. This right here . . . ," I said, waving a hand over all my big sexiness. "You couldn't hang with this. You couldn't deal with a real woman, and the sooner you leave, the sooner I'll be free to find someone who will."

He gave a grunt and frowned. "Whatever. I'll be in touch." He stormed out of the house.

I knew I'd hit a button, and that made me smile. He was no more than a pain in my ass at that point. Lovers, we weren't. Couldn't call us even that. In my good years, my sexy years, before all these pounds from overdrinking and being undersexed had taken over my body, I was a dime. Over the years I'd become a half-dollar piece. Yes, that was largest coin that made the cut, but at the end of the day, it's still money.

"That's right. Run, you limp-dick bastard," I yelled at the door. Even if it was me, even if I was the reason he was no longer excited about sex, I didn't give a damn. I had suffered more than long enough.

I worked ten to twelve hours a day and still managed to keep a clean home and cook and do laundry and, to top it off, run errands. Chester had no responsibilities, because I had foolishly stepped up and spoiled his unromantic ass. I can honestly admit to myself that I had gone in doing it big, because I had had this high expectation that I'd get doing it big back. Ha! To my unfortunate surprise, Chester had been and still was a limp dick, a selfish, self-absorbed asshole.

I had let him get me to this point.

Yes, Lynn, you had, I thought to myself. You allowed that fucker to drain every ounce of happiness, confidence, and self-esteem you owned. How could I have been so desperate, so foolish to long for a man like him?

"God, please, just please let me get over him," I prayed aloud. No matter how much truth I faced, or how much I was in touch with reality, the truth was that I still loved him, and I just wanted to get over him.

Chapter Two

Lynn

I pulled into my drive, exhausted. My ovens were on their last leg, and improvements on my fifth-hand bakery, Fire and Icing, were long overdue. In a prime location on the south side of Chicago, on the corner near a busy bus line, I had to upgrade and do some renovations, but time and money were always an issue: the timing was always bad, and I didn't want to take on any financial burden. I mean, the bakery was doing well, but it had only just recently started to turn a profit. After three years of busting my ass, I was finally seeing some revenue, and if I wanted to keep it that way, I knew I'd have to shut down the shop and get the repairs and upgrades done.

I was not expecting to see Chez's car in my driveway. We hadn't talked in four days, and Lord knows, I didn't want to see his ugly-ass face. I hurried inside to see what he wanted and why he had come to my house without calling first.

"Chez," I called out.

"In here," he called from his office—well, what used to be his office.

I headed that way, and when I walked in, there were boxes everywhere. "Packing your things, huh?"

"Yes, my place was done sooner than the contractor expected, and I can move in now."

I smiled. Sounding casual, I said, "That's great."

"It certainly is. I will be back in flight next week, and my schedule is going to be kinda heavy, so I won't be able to get as much done as I want."

"Well, if you leave me your key, I'll be happy to move whatever I can," I offered. Seconds later I was wondering why I had offered and why, when I was around him, I wanted to prove that I was a great woman and that he was giving up the best. I was always in "Impress Chez" mode, just hoping he'd see what everyone else saw in me and take me in his strong arms and love me back.

"You'd do that for me?"

Fronting like I was 100 percent down with the breakup, I smiled brightly and said, "Of course.

The sooner I can get all your things out of my house, the sooner I can start living."

"I understand, and since we are both of the same accord about this, I spoke to Jimmy about drawing up our papers."

My eyes bulged. That was a gut punch. Square in the middle of my abdomen. I knew that would be next, but so soon? He had already spoken to his attorney.

I blinked and turned on fake Lynn again and smiled. "Good. The sooner the better, right?"

I didn't mean any of what I was saying. Deep down my heart was screaming, *Just love me, fool. Go to therapy, take a Viagra, get acupuncture, and just fix your sexual issues. I can deal with no flowers, no pet names, and a lack of romantic dinners. I just wanted to be held and fucked to sleep at night.*

"My thoughts exactly." He smiled. "I'm glad that we are doing this like civil adults," he added.

"Me too." I half smiled.

"For the record, Lynn, I do love you, but I can't force the exchanges or the romantic fairy tale you are looking for. I'm not that guy."

"Look, Chez, it's a done deal. I know there is someone on your level of love, and there is someone out there on mine. I know you love me, Chez, but I just want more. I'm forty-one, and I have a lot of life left and a lot of love to give to a man who wants what I have to offer."

"Lynn, you are a good woman."

I agreed. "Hell, I know I am."

He laughed. "I'm sorry that I didn't live up to your expectations of a husband."

Moving over to help him, I said, "I'm sorry too."

I helped out a bit, then made my way to the kitchen to cook dinner. We ate, talked about a few great moments in our marriage, and then I helped him load all we could into his car. Since he needed more than what would fit, we loaded my Tahoe, and I followed him to his place. The building was nice enough. It was still under construction and was lacking landscaping, but it was nice. We unloaded the cars, and he gave me the spare key, and I agreed to bring over whatever I could manage while he was away.

When I got home, I felt a little better. Although I loved him and wished we could have made it, it didn't happen, so I took off my wedding ring and smiled, instead of crying, when I put it away. I went downstairs for a glass of red. I was in the mood to do something that would enable me to focus on change and not loss.

I grabbed my stainless mixing bowl, some flour, eggs, and sugar and was relieved I had butter. Baking or cooking always made me feel good, so I'd make cupcakes and leave them on a couple of neighbors' porches in the morning. After whipping up four dozen, I packaged them all and then headed up to my bedroom.

It felt super cold in the room. I was used to Chez not being there, but knowing he'd never return made that night the longest night I'd ever had.

Chapter Three

Lynn

"Oh, please. No, please," I cried.

My favorite oven, also the largest one, hadn't heated up, and it had been on for more than twenty minutes. It had finally crashed, and I knew I'd have to shut down the shop early, because my other ovens couldn't handle the workload.

"Do you want me to refrigerate this batter, Ms. Lynn?" Mariah asked.

"Yes," I said sadly. I had a ton of things that should have been in the oven already, and my morning was already shot.

"I can start the apple fritters in this oven, ma'am," she said.

"Yes, go ahead, Mariah. We just won't open until seven, instead of six."

I headed to my office, sad, willing myself not to break out in tears. I went online to look for repair shops, but I knew there was no repairing Satan. I had named that oven Satan because it heated up like a good oven should, and I was not happy with it dying on me. "Lord, I have to get this place up to par," I said aloud.

After a few sighs, I went out and helped Mariah and Al, and we opened at seven and closed at two, because the smaller ovens couldn't perform fast enough.

"So are we opening tomorrow?" Al asked.

"Nah. You two are going to have a couple of weeks off. I got to get a new oven, and while that's happening, I'll make some upgrades back here. I'm going to find someone to get us up and running again."

"Two weeks," Mariah sighed.

"Yes, but paid. I'd never do you two like that."

"Aw, thanks, Ms. Lynn," Mariah said.

I smiled. "Don't mention it."

I headed home and walked in to find Chez's boxes. Dealing with the bakery, I had forgot that I had to make another drop-off. After loading the boxes in my SUV, I went upstairs and showered and changed. I figured I'd call my girlfriend Kenya and ask her to have a drink with me after I dropped off the boxes, so I put on makeup and threw a few curls in my hair. Yes, I had let myself go during my lonesome marriage with Chester, but I couldn't lose it all in one day, so I had to work with what I had. Satisfied with my maxi dress and sandals, I thought a few bangles and oversize earrings would dress up my outfit. I was aiming for a cocktail look, not a walk in the park look.

Pleased with my ensemble, I showered my mocha skin with body spray and headed out. When I got to Chez's building, I got out to unload the boxes. After my second trip, I took a quick break because I didn't want to sweat.

On my way back to get another bunch of boxes, a stranger asked, "Do you need any help?"

I was about to say, "No. I got this," but I turned to see one of the sexiest men I'd ever seen in my life. I did a quick head-to-toe scan, and yes, he was by far the sexiest. "Sure. Thank you." I smiled.

He followed me out and helped me unload the rest of the boxes.

"Thanks so much . . ." I said when the chore was completed. I paused, because I didn't know his name.

Smiling, he said, "William Daniels." He extended his hand.

We shook. His grip was firm, and I immediately wondered, *Could he give a good massage?* I told my inner voice to keep quiet and then introduced myself.

"Lynniah Bryant."

"Bryant, Bryant . . . Are you Chester's sister?"

I laughed. "No . . . I'm his wife."

His smile faded. "Oh, I'm sorry. I thought he was moving in alone. Nice to meet you."

"No, no, no. He *is* moving in alone. He and I are no longer together. We are getting a divorce. I was just helping him out. You know, clearing out his things from my home," I said with the quickness. I wanted this man's number.

"Oh, oh, okay. Well, sorry to hear that. I know divorce is hard."

"Not really." I made a face, scrunching my nose. "This one is kind of a walk in the park. We both agree on parting ways."

"I guess that does make it easier than average."

"Yes, and I'd love to take you for a beer. I mean, I really do appreciate you helping me out." My stomach was in knots. I'd never asked someone so beautiful out before, and he might not be into big girls. Damn! What was I thinking?

"I'd love to, but I'm on this tight deadline, and my day isn't done yet."

"I see. Letting a big girl down easy," I joked and then wanted to slap myself for saying something so stupid. The last thing I needed was for him to think I was insecure about the way I looked.

"No." He smiled brightly. "I actually like what I see, all of it. It's just that duty calls. We are almost done here, and the sooner I'm done with this contract, the better."

"So you're with the company that is doing all the work around here?" I needed a card pronto. My place was falling apart.

"Yes. I'm actually the owner."

"Get out. And you're out in the field?"

"Yes, this is my baby, so I'm a hands-on type of guy."

You can put your hands on me, all over me. Damn, baby. You can reconstruct my body if you like, I thought. Unable to keep my tongue in my mouth, because he looked so delicious, I licked my glossed lips, bit down on the corner of my lip, and then said, "Wow. I'm in need of a hands-on type of man . . . I mean, contractor." I hurried to correct myself. "I own a bakery, and I've put repairs off as long as I can. Do you have a card?"

"I do." He went into his back pocket and retrieved his wallet. After taking a card out of his wallet, he handed it to me. "And if you're willing to take a rain check on that drink, I'll be done by seven."

"Seven sounds great." I glanced at the card. "Is this your cell on the card?"

"Yes, it is." He gave me a look that made me think he wanted to say more about himself, but he said, "I must get back to it. The clock is ticking."

"No problem, William. I'll call you around seven."

"Great. And call me Will."

"Only if you call me Lynn." I smiled. Hell, I wanted him to call me baby, honey, sexy. *Hell . . . just call me.*

"Lynn it is. I'll see you later, beautiful."

I froze. I blinked ten times and snapped back. I hadn't had a compliment in so long, I had forgotten what that was like. "Later." I smiled, and he was off.

I looked down at the card again and then locked Chester's door. I headed to my vehicle, and as soon as I got inside it, I called Kenya and told her about my change of plans. I updated her on the miracle that had just taken place, and she squealed with me during my entire ride home.

Once I was back home, I went inside and started from scratch. Yes, I changed my hair and makeup and put on something different.

Around five after seven, I made the call, and he picked up.

"Hi, Will. This is Lynn."

"Hi, beautiful. I was just thinking of you. I was hoping you'd call."

"I said I would."

"You did."

"So are you still up for that drink?"

"I am, but can we push it forward a little? I'm actually just leaving the site, and I'd like to shower and change."

"Okay. That won't be a problem. I will text you my address. Just give me a heads-up when you're on your way."

"Sounds great," he said, and then we hung up.

I danced in place. I knew it was too soon to start naming our children, but I hoped he had potential. Hell, folks might think it was too soon, but I'd been lonely for years. Hadn't had sex in over a year. It was time.

I went for a glass of wine, then grabbed my Kindle to kill a little time. An hour later I got the alert that he was on his way. Twenty minutes after that, I was being helped into his Audi.

"Where to?" he asked.

"Wherever you wanna take me."

He pulled out of my drive, and I sat back and enjoyed the ride.

Chapter Four

Lynn

Laughing and enjoying his company, I felt like a woman again. Will and I did some heavy flirting, and before long he was on my side of the round booth. He made it a point to caress my face, my arm. He seemed to be the affectionate type, the type I liked.

"Can I get you guys anything else?" our server interrupted.

Will looked at me. "Would you like another?"

"Yes. Only because you're driving." I giggled like a teen.

"Another chardonnay for the lady and a coffee for me."

"Yes, sir," our server said.

I scrunched my nose. "Ewww, coffee."

"What's wrong with coffee?" He raised a brow.

"Nothing." I laughed and then said, "Coffee breath is not sexy."

"Aw, coffee breath. Damn. So I should get my kiss now, then?" He leaned in.

Excited and a little surprised, I swallowed hard. I just looked at him, and then his lips gently touched mine. A couple of tender pecks and then a nice soft tongue, with the residue of his steak dinner and the cheesecake we'd shared for dessert.

The kiss was so good, so sensual, that I forgot where we were. I allowed him to devour my mouth until the server cleared her throat.

"Chardonnay for you, ma'am, and coffee for you, sir."

"Should I send this back?" He smiled a sexy smile.

"Nah, baby. Enjoy your coffee. Coffee breath or not, you will be getting another kiss tonight," I said in a raspy voice. He had taken my breath away.

"Anything else?" our server asked.

"No. Just the check please," Will answered.

Gazing at him, I bit down on the corner of my lip again, because he was gorgeous. Deep, dark eyes, long lashes, and silky smooth chocolate skin. His beard was nicely trimmed, and it framed his masculine jawline perfectly. Nice low haircut, lined with a straight edge, one would think, because it was just that tight.

I sipped my drink and watched him add cream and sugar to his coffee.

He brought my eyes back to his luscious lips when he said, "So this bakery, how bad is it?"

"It's kinda bad. Kitchen needs an overhaul, and I need someone ASAP, because I don't want to be closed for too long."

"Well, I'm, like, a week away from finishing this current project. We have another contract coming up at the end of this month, so if it's not too bad, I may be able to squeeze you in."

You can squeeze all of me. "That would be great. We can go by after, and you can take a look around."

"That sounds like a plan."

The server was back. "Here you are, sir. When you're ready, just give me a wave, and I'll be back."

"Thanks," I said and reached for the bill.

He placed a hand over my hand. "No. Don't even think of looking at that."

"I will. This is on me. Remember, I invited you out to say thanks for lugging those boxes for me."

"That was my pleasure, and you will not take care of this." He tried to take the bill from me, but I refused to let go.

"Listen, Will, you'll have plenty of chances to treat me, but tonight it's my treat."

"Wow. I made the second date list."

"Oh, you did." I smiled.

He stole another kiss. "That's good to know."

We finished up and headed to my bakery. We did a walk-through. Then Will told me to hold tight, and he went out to his car. I ran to the bathroom to do a quick mirror check and freshen up my lips. When I came out, he was back, and he had a clipboard and a measuring tape.

"What's all this?" I asked.

"This is a clipboard, this is a tape measure, and this right here is a pencil," he joked.

"Ha-ha. I know what those things are." I chuckled. "I'd like to know what you're doing."

"I want to take a few quick measurements, and when I go home tonight, I'll browse around and see what I can get delivered the fastest for you. I have a couple of guys who would love to get in some overtime hours, and I can have a night crew here, so you don't have to be shut down too long."

"You'd do that for me?" I wasn't smiling at this point. I really wasn't used to a man being so nice to me.

"Yes."

"But why? You don't know me, Will."

"But I want to get to know you, and plus, I'm just a nice guy."

I then smiled brightly. "Yes, you are."

"Come on. Follow me. You can help me out."

"Okay."

I followed him into the kitchen and held the tape measure for him, and he jotted down numbers that made absolutely no sense to me. An hour later it was after midnight. I didn't have work the next morning, but I didn't want to keep him up all night. We took a seat at a table, and I sat quietly until he finished doing his thing.

"So, if I order your ovens, it may take a week, give or take a day, for them to arrive. In that time we can demo the kitchen, and I will sketch out a plan for you that may offer a better flow. The layout is just about perfect now, but I have some ideas that you may like that will make your process flow even better. I say if we start in the next couple of days, we can have you open in about three weeks, just before my next contract."

"Will, that would be awesome, but the big question is, how much is all of that going to cost me?"

"Well, I'll get you some prices in a couple of days. I have a few connections where I can save you some expense, and as a guy who is digging you, I can give you that potentially mine rate."

"Oh, how many women have you given that rate to?"

"None. Never had a woman who needed construction."

"I see. Well, I hope we can come to a reasonable agreement."

"I'm sure we will."

We stared each other down. God, I wanted to kiss him, touch him, and ride him. Damn. I just wanted him.

Breaking the silence, I said, "It's late, Will. I don't want to keep you out too late."

"You are good." He stood. He moved closer to me and stood over me. "You are a beautiful woman, Lynn. Tell me the truth. Why didn't your husband want to keep you around?"

I swallowed hard. That was the last question I had thought he'd ask. "Well, Chester just couldn't handle a woman like me."

Tracing my collarbone, he asked, "What type of woman are you?"

"I'm sexy, I'm sensual, affectionate, and I believe that love needs to be expressed in actions and in words. I was too hot for Chez. Too needy. Too much physical work."

"Well, I want to see and get to know all of you. All these things you just said about yourself, I want to see her."

"Okay," I whispered.

He planted another one on me, and my nipples went stiff. I wanted him to be all over me.

I wanted to spread my legs and let his hands travel up my thighs and stroke my clit. I pulled away.

"Will, we should go. I mean, this right here . . ." I gave him a slight push. "Baby, you are turning me on."

"You don't want to be turned on?"

"I do. Trust me, I do, but not here, not like this."

"You are right, beautiful. Let me get you home."

I stood. I went to turn out the lights and set the alarm system, and then we headed back to my house. He held my hand the entire ride and got out to walk me to the door. We kissed, and I said good night. He headed to his car and then paused.

"Oh." He turned back to me. "You and your crew should definitely get a few boxes and pack up your kitchen. We are going to need it to be empty to start."

"Sure thing."

We exchanged our final good nights, and then I stood in my foyer, with my back resting against the door, for a few moments, before I floated up to my bedroom. I had showered and was snuggling under my goose-down comforter when he texted me. I was naked and wished I could lure

him back to my place to do things to me that I
had dreamt Chez would do. As late as it was, we
texted for a while and exchanged selfies. The
next morning, bright and early, I sent another
text.

Good morning, Will.

Two minutes later I received a reply.

I'm glad you texted me. I was still sleeping.

Seriously, don't u have 2 b at work in,
like, 20 mins?

Yes . . . I'll hit you back when I arrive.

K ☺.

Thirty minutes later I got another text.

I made it. Missed breakfast, but I'll live.

I sent a reply.

Sorry, babe.

I was dressed and ready to get to work, but
before heading to my bakery with the boxes that
were left over from Chez's move, I went by and
surprised Will with coffee and a blueberry bagel.
When I made it to Chez's complex, I asked a
couple of uniformed workers for Will, and they
pointed me in the right direction. I tapped on the
trailer door and a baritone voice said, "Come in."
I walked in, and Will smiled.

"Good morning." He stood, came around his desk, and then greeted me with a soft kiss.

"Good morning. I'm heading over to the bakery to get started on the packing. I just wanted to bring you some food since you missed breakfast."

"I know, right? Thank God you texted when you did, because I'd probably still be sleeping."

"Well, I'm glad I did."

"Me too."

I smiled as brightly as my cheeks would allow. "I'll let you get to work, and I'll see you later."

"Yes. And tonight I'll grab some carryout. You come over to my place. We can take a look online at a few ovens and appliances, and I'll get the specs and the choices to my partner, and then we'll go from there."

"Sounds good."

"Great. I will text you my address a little later."

"Okay, that will work." I gave him a kiss and headed to the bakery.

Chapter Five

Lynn

After what seemed like days instead of hours, Mariah, Al, and I had almost half the kitchen done. They left for the day, and I did a walk-through. I decided I wanted to upgrade the entire bakery. I mean, the walls could use a fresh coat of paint; new tables and chairs were in order; and upon examining the floors, I came to the conclusion that wood would be nice.

The tiles were still in great shape, if you asked me, but the grout lines screamed out for a serious scrub. Not wanting to tackle that backbreaking task, I decided I'd mention the front area of the restaurant to Will that night. It wasn't as urgent as the kitchen, but it was in need of a serious face-lift, so maybe later on down the line he could transform my place into an upscale space. Upgrading the FIRE AND ICING sign would make a strong statement too.

After walking around and jotting down notes to share with Will, I headed home. As soon as I got inside, I ran a bath, and as I soaked, I imagined all the things Will could do to make my body quiver. "Oh, Will," I whispered. I relaxed and let my fingers roam to my special area. The warm water became my lubricant as I did quick circles over my bulb. A vision of Will and his hardened dick in my mouth, stroking me and pleasing me, invaded my sexual fantasies all at once. I was so aroused, my mind jumped from scene to scene: him kissing, sucking, fucking, squirting, nibbling, and stroking.

I was not able to put a cap on my thoughts, and that last image of him exploding on my tits made my love come down. I came hard and good and I shook and I yelled out. I called out Will's name, as if he were in the same room with me, but I was alone with my own imagination.

"Aahhh, aahhh, aahhh," I moaned and exhaled.

That was the most intense orgasm I'd experienced alone, and I knew it had to do with Will. I had pleasured myself tons of times, but never had my body quickened like that.

"Will, if you're not the one, at least fuck me out of my mind," I said aloud and then got out of the tub. As I dried my skin, I took a second look at myself in the mirror. I didn't like what I saw, but for the very first time, I didn't hate it, either.

I turned to the right and then to the left, examining my rolls and dimples, wondering whether Will would still be interested after seeing my nakedness. Would he still think I was beautiful?

"You should join the gym," I said to my reflection. "No. We should stop eating at the bakery."

I stood eyeing myself from head to toe, and then I snapped out of it. "You are who you are, Lynn. Yes, with rolls and dimples. If a man can have you as you are, that is the man you should be with." With that, I moisturized my skin with my shea butter products. Took my time with my makeup and my hair. The hair angels were on my side that night, because my locks fell into place perfectly.

I headed to Will's place, smelling good and looking delicious. It was early, but my cat purred, and tonight I knew I'd open wide if he tried.

I pulled in front of Will's house, but before getting out of the car, I gave myself one last pep talk. "You are beautiful. You are sexy. You are gorgeous. This is not Chez." I opened the car door, climbed out, and walked up the slate walkway. The landscaping was beautiful, and as I looked around, I realized that Will's home was the prettiest one on the block. I mean, the neighbors had nice houses, but the stucco, pavers, flowers, and bushes at Will's house, not to mention the red door, made quite a statement.

"He really needs to help me spruce up my place," I mumbled. I rang the bell. Seconds later he opened the door for me.

"Wow. You look amazing. I mean, I'd rather take you out," he said.

I stood there, waiting for him to allow me to enter. "Thank you, Will. I know I'm a little over-dressed." I knew I had glammed up a little too much. I just wanted to look good for him.

"No, you are perfect. Come on in."

I walked in, and his place was so beautifully decorated, my eyes darted from wall to wall. "You have a beautiful place."

"Thank you. You can have a seat. I got some greasy carryout, but I'm going to run up and change and take you to dinner."

"No. Will, I'm fine with whatever you ordered."

"Yes, but I'm not. I mean, you are stunning, and I have to take you out and show you off."

I laughed. I didn't mean to.

"What's funny?"

"Okay, okay, okay. Will, let's just get real right now. I know I'm not ugly, but please don't say things like that to me. I mean, I know I'm a big girl. I know I can stand to hit the gym, lay off the red velvet, and not indulge in cubed cheese every time I enjoy a glass of wine. So please, stop." After my outburst, I realized I was acting like that insecure fat chick, which I didn't want to be.

Nervously I sat on the sofa, because I felt awkward standing there. I felt like a huge eyesore.

"Wait, baby. Lynn, baby." He chuckled. "I happen to like what I see. I'm feeling you, and you are sexy. You are beautiful, and I know you're not slim or in a size five, but, baby, you look sexy as hell to me. People like what they like, and I happen to like women who are full figured. I don't have a problems with guts, rolls, stretch marks, or dimples. There is no perfect woman out there. She could be fit but could have an ugly attitude, slim but can't carry on a conversation. You are beautiful to me, Lynn. I'm not feeding you no lines. I am interested in you."

He came closer to me and reached for me. He pulled me up from the sofa. "I want all of you," he said before pushing his tongue into my mouth. Our tongues did the tangle, and my spot moistened. I wanted to disrobe and beg him to have me, but I kept it together.

Pulling away, I said, "I'm not insecure, Will. I know I'm beautiful. I love me, but men, people, look at plus-size women and see fat. They don't admire our beautiful features or even allow themselves to get to know us. They just often judge and look at us, me . . . like I'm disgusting."

I went on. "After the weight, Chez stop coming into my bed. He'd never say it or admit it, but I knew. I used to be on his arm at company events, and he'd drag me to a sports event and hold my hand in public." I looked down. I didn't want to visit Chez Lane.

"Listen, Chez was an idiot. Look at you, Lynn. I'm glad he's already shown you what half of a man is like. That makes my job of showing you what a real man is like even easier. Real men love women and can be with a woman regardless of her size. I mean, we all have our tastes, standards, and preferences. There is absolutely nothing wrong with having a preference, but you can't know what you don't like unless you've tried it. I'm not Chez, Lynn, and now, as sexy as you look, I want to take you out. I want everyone to see the beautiful woman who agreed to accompany me to dinner tonight."

I looked down, but his words were warm, and they penetrated me. "Well, go and change. I want everyone to see the sexy man whom I let take me out for dinner tonight."

"That's my girl. Have a seat. I'll get you a glass of wine. Remotes are here. You can turn on the tube, listen to music, whatever you'd like." He was off and back in a flash with a chilled glass of white.

I gladly accepted, and then he gave me a reassuring kiss. Wanting to do more to him than kiss, I pulled away.

"You should go get dressed."

"Yes, I should."

I watched him back away and disappear behind a wall, beyond which, I assumed, was a staircase leading to the upstairs. I sipped and reached for one of the remotes. It took me only a few moments to figure out how to get to the music channels on his paid programming. I was familiar with Direct TV, because I, too, was a subscriber, so it was easy to get to the channel I normally listened to. After I pressed a few more buttons, sounds floated out of his speakers, and I smiled at myself for figuring out his system without asking.

I finished my glass of wine and headed into the kitchen to pour another. His floor plan was open, so I had eyed him when he fixed my first glass. As I went, I took a closer look at his place, admiring the details and the craftsmanship of the space, and I wondered if it was original and had been refinished or if he had added the details himself.

As I ran my hand over the wood of a built-in, he cleared his throat.

"Your place is amazing. Is this original?"

"Nah. Everything is new. This was my mom's house, and when she died, I moved in and gutted the entire house myself. It took almost three years, but every spare moment of my time went into this place."

"You rehabbed this place alone?"

"For the most part, yes. Some things, like the beams in the ceiling, the plumbing, and some electrical work, I had friends do, but for the most part, everything, including the paint, was all me."

"Well, you have impeccable taste. I mean, everything just matches so well."

"Thanks. My mom was an interior designer. She married my stepdad when I was ten. He owned the construction company I own now. They met on a job." He smiled as he thought back. "I was a terrible kid, was in and out of trouble, but Ray still tried to take me under his wing. When I was still enough to listen, he taught me the business. When I got some act right in me, I had already been in and out of juvie and had caused a lot of tears to my moms and Ray, but they still didn't give up on me."

"Wow. You don't seem like the type to have had a rough childhood."

"Well, I did. When my pops died, I was mad at the world. Didn't listen, started skipping school, but by the grace of God, I got it together. I went back to school at eighteen, got my GED, got my contractor's license, and was on the straight and narrow, until . . ." He paused.

"What?" I asked. I wanted him to finish what he was saying.

"I . . . I . . . I . . . ," he stuttered. "Listen, I have to be honest. I went to prison for two years."

My heart stopped. He was an ex-con. "Prison!" My eyes widened. "What'd you do?"

"I drove a car from a robbery. I was out with a few friends. Didn't know they had robbed the store, and the clerk had written down my plates. A few hours later, the cops were at our door, and I was under arrest. Of course, no one believed that I had had no idea Fred and Donte had robbed the joint, so I got five years. Was paroled, and now I'm here. No more parole, but I have a record."

"Wow," I said, shocked. The man standing before me was no criminal—at least I felt he wasn't—so I didn't run. I walked over to him.

"I'm glad you told me."

"I planned to tell you, but I didn't think it would be this soon."

"Well, I'm glad. I mean, it's easier to move forward with the facts."

"True. I can assure you that that is all in my past. I'm a man, not the boy I was when I made horrible decisions and allowed the wrong people to be in my circle."

"I'm sure. You've change for the better, as far as I can tell."

"I have." He smiled.

"Are there any other secrets?"

"No, but I do have allergies to pet hair."

I laughed. "Well, my place is pet free."

We laughed, and then he pulled me into his arms. "You are the most interesting woman I've met in a very long time. I mean, I don't know where this is going, but I hope we go far."

"You know that already?"

"It doesn't take long to know that someone makes you feel good, and you make me feel good, and I really enjoy spending time with you." He kissed me.

"I enjoy spending time with you too."

He covered my lips with his, his tongue found its way to mine, and we did the tangle. My nipples hardened, and my spot tingled, and I wanted more than a kiss from Will.

When his kiss ran down my neck, I didn't stop him. I let him continue to tease me with his lips and tongue. All the while, he caressed my back and palmed my ass.

"Aren't you hungry?" I panted.

"For you," he returned.

"What are you saying?" I wanted to be clear about what he wanted.

"I want to taste you, and then I promise I will take you to dinner."

"Okay," I agreed quickly. I was horny as hell, so he didn't have to do a lot of convincing.

I followed him up to his bedroom, and we undressed so fast, I figured we didn't want the other to back out.

"Lie down," he whispered.

I climbed onto his bed, and he started with my lips and kissed me all the way down to my soft spot. It throbbed and ached to be touched, licked, and sucked, something that hadn't happened in ages.

"Aahhh," I moaned as soon as his lips touched my lower set of lips. My clit was already swollen. I was longing for him to suck on my bulb.

"Open up, baby," he said, and I opened wider for him. I felt a soft, warm breeze as he blew on me. I moaned louder when he went in on me. I gripped the comforter as his tongue gently caressed my enlarged clit. His tongue was soft and gentle, so I grabbed his head to press his tongue against my body, and he then licked harder and sucked on my lips and then gently sucked my clit. I guess he knew that the lighter was better there, because he pleased my center better than anyone had before him.

I massaged my own breasts with my free hand, because I refused to stop touching his head. I rubbed it, massaged it, and pushed him in closer when I wanted him to do it harder.

Pinching my nipples, I could no longer contain myself. I exploded, and I felt my opening contracting. I felt my love juices run down my center, and I knew that I had left a wet spot on his sheets.

"Oh, baby. Oh, baby," I whispered, out of breath. "That was so good, baby. So good."

He stood, and the sight of his erection made my eyes dance and my mouth water. I didn't know how to ask him if I could suck his dick, so I decided to just do it. I slid off the bed and got in his face and kissed him. I tasted myself on his lips, and I tasted good. I smiled and kissed him down his chest and then went into a squat. I expected him to say, "No thanks," but who in the hell was I kidding? I'd never met a man who didn't want head.

I stroked him softly before licking the tip, and then I went to work. I sucked and slurped, pulled and jerked, and let his moans and his body language cheer me on.

Not long after the oral pleasure began, he said. "Wait, baby. I'm there." He pulled back. I reached for him, and he tried to keep his erection from me, but I caressed his thighs and balls, he gave me control again. Two jerks later, I had his love juices on my breasts. He groaned until he was done and then leaned in and kissed me. "Baby, that felt so good. Damn!"

"Glad you liked it."

"I did." He reached for my hand. "Come on. Let's get cleaned up."

I followed him into an amazing master bathroom. He started the shower, and it was massive. We both got in.

"Will, I'm in love with your house. I mean, this shower is, like, the size of my walk-in closet."

"Yes. I took space away from the spare room next door. It is now my office, with no closet. We're in the old closet now." He laughed.

"Your work is incredible. I can't wait to see what you do to my bakery."

"I have some ideas, but right now I only want to talk about you." He embraced me from behind as the water hit our naked skin.

"Oh, yeah?" I smiled.

He kissed my neck. "Yes. I know that we had plans to go to dinner, and we still have time for that, but I can't leave before I feel the inside of your walls."

"Nah. Um, you have to feed me first, baby. I mean, I thought I was coming for dinner. I mean, I had a snack before, but I want real food."

He laughed. "Okay, okay. But after dinner, will you come back to my place?"

"Yes. We still have work to do. Don't forget about the bakery business."

"I haven't. We will get to that. I promise. Tonight just let me enjoy you."

"Okay."

I like him. I really like him!

Chapter Six

Lynn

"Wake up, sleepyhead," he said. I felt a soft kiss on my cheek, but I didn't want to open my eyes.

I was still on a high from the night we had shared together. Dinner, soft music, delicious wine, and the cherry on top, the lovemaking. Will had done things to my body that I'd never experienced before, and I guessed his line of work was the reason for his strength, because he'd lifted me up a few times with ease, tossing and turning my plump body. I'd seen strippers do that to big girls, but I'd never had anything like that done to me.

I knew that if I moved, I'd be in agony. No way was my body not going to be sore after the night he'd given me.

"Do I have to?" I whined.

"Yes. I want to make sure you eat breakfast before you start your day."

"Baby, I don't want to move."

"I'm sure, but I have a deadline, and you have to make sure your place is empty and ready to start the demo in a couple of days, so we have no time to waste, my love."

I opened my eyes after I heard that word. I knew he didn't say, "I love you," but I hadn't heard that word coming from a man's mouth in a very long time, so it was a foreign experience. I turned over to see him gazing at me.

I smiled. "Okay. I'll get up, but I hope you know how to make omelets, because I worked up an appetite last night."

"I do, and waffles and steak. Trust me, baby, I'm going to send you off right."

"So dick is also on the menu?"

"If that's what you want." He kissed my forehead.

I pulled him on top of me, and only the sheet separated our skin. "Yes, but I need to gargle."

"Yes, baby, you do," he teased.

I swatted his arm. I knew my breath might have been humming a funky tune. "Don't move," I playful instructed, wagging a finger at him.

I moved from under his hard, warm body and headed into the bathroom. There on the granite vanity was a set of towels and a toothbrush.

After relieving my bladder and doing a few nice wipes with the wipes he had on a little table near the throne, I did a finger test and decided I was okay for a round before a shower.

I snatched up the toothbrush, grabbed the Crest from his sink, and used the other sink to freshen my breath. I reached for the facecloth to get the crust out of my eyes and clean my face. Afterward, I fingered my hair. It was still cute, because his sheets were satin, so they hadn't done much damage to my hairdo. Flat, but still cute. With my finger, I took a swipe of the ChapStick from the tube he had on the sink and rubbed it into my lips. Then I went back to bed and joined him, and after a minimal amount of foreplay, he was pleasuring my insides again.

I was sore, but that didn't stop me from allowing him to push my legs over my head. He pounded and pumped, pushed and pulled, and even though I was close, my core refused to allow me relief. I pushed him back a little and spread my legs to have access to my bulb, and he stroked my tunnel and I stroked my clit.

"Yes, baby, yes," I moaned.

His eyes locked on mine, and when he grabbed my tits, I released. My body jerked and quivered, and I let out a loud sound of pleasure. It was good, so, so good, and I secretly wanted Will to be mine forever.

"Damn, girl. You are going to kill me. Your body is amazing, and I want this every morning and every night."

"I'm willing to give it to you."

He collapsed on the side of me. "I'm going to need that in writing."

"Baby, I'll sign anything. Hell, I'll sign over my life for this every morning."

We were quiet. I could not believe I had said that.

He broke the silence after a moment. "I like you, Lynn Bryant, and I am interested in you. I'd like for us to be exclusive. I mean, I know it's early, but my gut tells me that you're someone who I may not want to let get away."

"Listen to your gut, Mr. Daniels, because my gut is saying the same thing."

We smiled at each other and held each other's gaze for what felt like ages.

Will was the first to speak. "You lie here and let me shower, and then I'll head down and make breakfast."

"Okay," I agreed. I wanted to go back to sleep, but I knew I had to make moves that day and get some things done so that I wouldn't be out of business for too long.

He got up, and I watched his sexy chocolate ass go into the bathroom. When I heard the water running, I had a teenage fit in his bed. It was one of those fits of excitement, though I held in my squeals. I had settled for too long, and the past few years with Chez had been so unhappy. Now that time was over. I wanted more than ever to be divorced, so I could move on with my life.

I closed my eyes and dozed off. The smell of food woke me, and I got my lazy ass up and went in the shower. After showering, I put on the robe that was hanging on the door, and I headed downstairs. To my pleasant surprise, there was a spread of food on the island. Waffles, omelets, sausage, bacon, fruit, and carafes of cranberry juice and orange juice.

"Have a seat, baby."

"You cooked all this? Chez never cooked for me. No, wait. Once, for my birthday. He called himself serving me breakfast in bed, but he ate all of it before I came out of the bathroom." I laughed to myself. Chez was definitely a zero compared to this lovemaking hero in an apron, who had prepared breakfast for me.

"Well, let's not talk about our exes. It's about me and you," he said and leaned in to kiss me.

I sat at the island, and a couple of minutes later he joined me there. We ate and chatted, and then I headed home to change. He headed to work.

***

Hours later I showed up with lunch for him. When I was leaving, I ran into Chez, the last face I wanted to see.

"Lynn," he called out.

"Chez," I replied.

"What are you doing here?"

"I came to, um . . ." While I hesitated, Will ran out with my keys.

"Baby, you forgot these," he said, and then I figured he noticed Chez.

"Baby?" Chez's brows furrowed. "What's going on, Lynn?"

"Chez, this is Will. Will—"

Chez cut me off. "I know who he is. How do you know him?" he asked in his baritone voice.

"Baby, I'll call you later," I said to Will and took my keys. He gave me a nod and then gave me and Chez some privacy. "Listen, I came by here with your boxes the other day, and Will helped me out, and now . . ."

"What now? You're fucking him?"

"Hold on, Chez. Don't even."

"Don't even what? I'm calling it like I see it."

"You know what? I don't owe you shit, a'ight. Not even an explanation. You and I are done, so boom. I'll see you later." I walked away.

He yelled after me. "Lynn, get your ass back over here!"

I stopped in my tracks and turned to him. "Who in the hell do you think you are talking to, Chester? You cannot possibly be concerned with what or who I'm doing, so don't pretend to care."

"Fine. I knew you were hoeing around."

I laughed. "Think what you wanna think. Good day, Chez."

I hurried to my SUV and pulled away. A few moments later, my phone started to ring non-stop. It was Chez.

Damn!

I stood in the mirror, thinking and admiring myself at the same time. I was not the average woman, but I had a lot going for me, and I didn't mean this in a conceited way at all. I knew my eyes, my high cheekbones, and my winning smile were my best features. I had always been told I was beautiful, gorgeous, and pretty, even breathtaking. Back before the pounds, I'd had to fight men off with a stick, and then I'd met Chez. In the beginning he'd told me how perfect I was and that I was his type and an ideal mate. He'd said I possessed the look and the heart of the woman he knew he'd one day marry.

He wasn't a spontaneous romantic guy, but he had had his moments when he made me feel so special. Not long after the marriage had started, however, was when it all stopped. The compliments, the sex, the dinner dates, and the lazy afternoons on the couch, watching movies all day. We'd enjoyed pool, cards, dominos, and sports, but that had been just like two friends hanging out and doing something fun, not a husband and wife thing. There'd been nothing intimate or romantic about it. He'd been away most of the time because he was a pilot, and I'd known that us being apart a lot came with the territory, but I had thought he'd be happy to be home when he was, but that hadn't been the case.

In my opinion, everything but me had made him happy. Sports, video games, the news, movies he knew I didn't want to watch, just everything but me. We used to go out, but then we'd turned into an "order in" couple. I'd asked him tons of times if it was my weight, he had assured me it wasn't, but I hadn't believed him. I still didn't know. It was too late even to begin to think about it anymore.

I got up from my seat at the vanity. "It's done," I said out loud, and then the doorbell rang.

I looked at the digital clock on my nightstand and wondered why Will was so early. I didn't expect him for another hour.

My hair and my makeup were done, but I was still in my underwear. I grabbed my robe, slipped it on, and hurried downstairs. I did a quick peek through the peephole and saw it was Chez. "What in the hell is he doing here?" I said aloud to myself.

I opened the door. "Can I help you?"

"Hey, can I come in?"

"Yes, but you can't stay long. I'm expecting someone."

"Who? William Daniels?" he asked as he took two steps inside and closed the door. "You might as well go up and wash all that paint off your face, because he's not coming."

"Excuse me?"

"I had a little chat with him and told him that he needed to stay away."

"You didn't."

"I did," he said with a smirk on his face. "You and I are still married, and I don't think it's wise for my wife to be galloping around town with another man."

"Chez, please. You know you couldn't care less who I'm with. What? You're jealous? No, no. Did you realize you love me and want me? Oh, no. Do you want to, all of a sudden, work this out? What . . . ? Tell me, Chez. Why, after all the no love you've shown me over the years, would you care for a moment who I see?"

His jaw tightened, and I was really confused at that moment. He knew he wasn't in love with me, and I knew he knew we were a done deal.

"I've told you over and over again that I love you, Lynn."

"Yes, that's what your lips have said a hundred times over, but you don't treat me like a wife, Chez. We fell into this friend mode, baby, and it wasn't me, because I tried everything I could to turn you on, to put some fire in this cold ass marriage, but you didn't want me, Chez. So please don't try to sabotage things with Will and me. He's not you, and he treats me like a woman. I feel alive with him, and I'm not going to stop seeing him, so please stay out of it. I'm sure you'll be flying the friendly skies in a day or so, so just act like you have no idea what I'm doing and who I'm doing it with. I'm over you, Chez."

He stood there, looking at me, with no words. His eyes glossed over. "That fast, huh?"

My brows vaulted. I couldn't believe my ears. "What do you mean, Chez?"

"We broke up a minute ago, and already . . ." He paused. "Already you're seeing someone new."

"We physically parted long before that. It's been days, weeks, months since you checked out of this marriage, so please don't pretend otherwise. And don't come up in here acting like you care, Chez, because I know you don't love me."

He didn't speak for a few moments. He just stood there looking at me.

"Chez," I said.

"I do love you, Lynn, and I'm sorry I couldn't love you the way you deserve to be loved. Call your friend and talk to him. I'm sure he won't let me stop him from being with you." He turned to face the door. He put his hand on the knob and then said, "By the way, you look stunning, and I hope he makes you happy." He opened the door and left.

"Me too," I whispered as I closed and locked the door.

I turned to head back upstairs, and then I ran up when I heard my cell phone ringing. It was Will, so I hurried to answer. "Will, baby, I'm so sorry about Chez."

"Hello to you too, sweetheart."

I smiled. "Oh, hi," I gushed. I sat on my chaise. "Listen, baby, please don't let Chez scare you. He's all talk. He's not a threat."

"I'm not afraid of Chez, Lynn. I don't scare easily. I'm not concerned with him. I just want to make sure that you're okay with us. I want to know if you are certain you're ready to move on, and I need your word that there is nothing between you two anymore. I mean, the last thing I need is to fall for a woman who is on the fence. Is this divorce really happening? Is there a chance that you and your husband will reconcile?"

I heard the urgency in his voice and acknowledged to myself that his questions were legit. I totally understood his position. I took a deep breath and tried to sound as convincing and as honest as I could. "Will, baby, I can guarantee you that there is nothing left to reconcile between Chez and me. We were done long before we split, and I love him, yes, but not the way a woman should love a man she desires or wants to be with. He and I are over, and there is no going back, Will. Chez and I had already decided that even before I met you. This tantrum he's having right now is because he didn't expect me to move on so fast, but it has absolutely nothing to do with him wanting me back. You have nothing to worry about. I'm all in."

"All in?"

"All in. You've awakened things inside of me that I'd forgotten existed. Making love to you last night was full of the passion and fire I've longed for forever, and this is the road I want to travel on. I mean, you've done something to me in a matter of days that neither of my husbands was able to do in years."

"Husbands?"

"Yes. Chez is my second marriage."

"Really?"

"Yes. Is that a problem?" My brow arched.

"No, no, no, not at all. It's just a little surprising that two let you get away."

I laughed. "Yes, they both did, and the ones in between."

"Well, I plan to be around for a while. So far there isn't one thing I can say I don't like about you."

"Give it a couple more weeks, and then let's revisit this conversation."

"What? Really? What are you hiding? What evil ways have you kept hidden from me?"

"None that I know of. How about you come over like we planned and we can talk when you get here?"

"Sounds good. I'll be there soon."

We hung up, and I went to get dressed.

Chapter Seven

Lynn

My kitchen was a disaster. The demo had started, and I was super excited. Will had assured me that the kitchen would be functioning in two weeks and that he and his guys could knock out the front area in a matter of a weekend. He had an efficient team that seemed loyal, and when I had the final numbers for the project, I was blown away.

"No, Will. This can't be right. I mean, I know we are, like, involved, but I know this is way too low."

"Lynn, my guys are doing this for half price for me, as long as we have plenty of beer and wings. I'm not even taking a cut, and a lot of the items you picked out, I did some hunting and got you a better deal. Come on. You still have money to invest in paint, lighting, and furni-

ture for the front, and I heard you talk about a new FIRE AND ICING sign, so this is the damage, baby."

I looked at the final number, and it was fifteen grand less than I had thought it would be, so I hugged his neck tight. "Baby, I'll sling a hammer. I will do whatever you need. Just teach me, and I will do it."

He smiled. "I will. Since my other contract is complete, you and I can work during the day, and my guys can come by in the evenings, when they are done with whatever they are working on."

"So your crew works for other companies?"

"No, but during their downtime, they do their thing, like home projects or drinking or whatever they want to do during the day. Some of them will be in and out during the day, if they like, but I asked them for evening help, and that's all I've asked for. Half the pay. I can't ask for much more, but my guys are good, and I promise we'll have you up and running on time, baby."

I smiled at him and then gave him a soft kiss. That night I cooked for him. Gave him a bath, a massage, and head all night long. He begged to slide inside of me, but I said, "Baby, tonight it's all about you."

He said, "If that's the deal, open up."

And I did. I let him have his way. The next day I didn't want to move. We slept in late, made love again, ate, got it in again, and then met the evening crew and worked.

That was a week and an half ago, and my kitchen finally looked like a kitchen, and Will and I started on the dining area. Will predicted we'd be done with everything in a couple of days, but that was just positive thinking, I reasoned.

But Will was right. The last two days of the renovation, he made me stay away. I was counting down the minutes to the reveal, and he didn't let me down.

"Oh, my God, baby. It's amazing," I said when I met him at the bakery once the work was complete. "It turned out better than I could have ever imagined." I was shocked and overjoyed. He had even given the bathroom a face-lift. The place was beautiful. I mean, it was like a dream. "Will, baby," I said, wiping my eyes. "You did this for me? Baby, this is . . ." I paused. "I'm speechless."

"You really like it?"

I just wrapped my arms around his neck and decided to let the tears of joy flow. "I love it. You are the sweetest man I've met in my life."

"Am I?"

"Yes," I said, drying my face. I moved around the space, touching everything. "The purple is just beautiful, and the glass cases are so elegant. Will, I mean . . . How, baby? You've outdone yourself. I knew it would be nice, but this is above and beyond what I expected."

"I'm glad you're happy."

"Oh, baby, I'm . . . I'm . . ." I stuttered. "Come and let me bake something for you."

"Right now?"

"Yes. You've showed off your skills, so now I want to show off mine, and I'm dying to turn on my new oven."

"Okay. Lead the way."

He followed me into the kitchen. It took me a minute to get all the ingredients together for my signature red velvet cake, because everything had a new home, but once I had everything I needed, I fired up my brand-new oven and began to mix all the right things in my mixing bowl to blow his socks off. We normally did red velvet cupcakes, but my man deserved a cake. Once the three layers were in the oven, Will ran to the store two doors down for a bottle of wine. He was back in a flash with the wine, a corkscrew, and two glasses, which I washed with a quickness.

We talked laughed and sipped, and the aroma of red velvet cake graced the entire bakery. He joined me as I made the icing, and I gave him a taste from my finger. His smile was confirmation that it was perfect. Out of the oven to the cooling station went the cake layers, and I cleaned the prep area while we listened to Will's phone play R & B from Pandora. He showed me a few of his moves, and I took off my apron and slow danced with him to Avant and Keke's "You & I." I was falling fast, and I didn't want to stop. Hell, I wouldn't know how to if I did want to.

"Time to frost the cake," I said after he gave me a deep kiss. His lips were so delicious, and I loved kissing him.

"Can I help?"

"Of course." I took the first layer of three from the cooling rack and put it in place to be frosted. I was excited to use my frosting spinner. I started it, and he laughed.

"So that's what that's for," he noted.

"Yes, and I am so glad to have one now."

"I bet."

He stood behind me. I spooned a generous amount of icing on the center and took my spreading spatula and put it in place. I pressed the pedal with my foot to spin the cake, as I held my spatula in place. I smoothed and he put his finger on the side to remove some of the icing I had added.

"Baby, stop it. . . . You said you'd help."

"I did, but I meant that I'd help myself to this delicious frosting," he quipped.

I laughed at him. "Listen, go refill my glass and sit so I can finish this."

"As you wish."

I finished the cake, cut him a slice, handed it to him with a fork, and waited for his reaction.

"Baby, this is the best cake I've ever tasted in my life."

"Don't lie."

"No, I'm serious. I'm dying to try all your desserts."

"Thanks, Will. My place turned out beautiful."

"You're welcome."

We kissed. I wanted him. It was time to go. "Baby, my place or yours? Because I'm ready."

"Ready for what?" he joked.

"Don't play. I'm ready to scream."

"Yours is closer."

"My place it is."

Chapter Eight

Lynn

Six months had passed, and we were insepa-rable. Will was my match, my mate, my heart, my love, my joy, my source of happiness. He was romantic, sensitive, loving, and spontaneous, and he was a beast in the bedroom. He had learned that I was a big, needy baby, and he was okay with that. He was okay with the fact that I required a lot of attention, and he wasn't afraid or too busy to give it to me. He enjoyed being with me as much as I enjoyed being with him, and we were in love. Well, I figured we were. No one had said it yet. I had come close a zillion times, but I had vowed I'd never say it first to a man again.

"Are you still working?" I asked him on the phone one night. The new project he was work-ing on had him working later and later.

"Yes, baby. I'm so sorry. These city codes and inspectors are slowing this process down completely, but the owners still want us to hit this deadline, and it's a bunch of weight on your man's shoulders, babe."

"I know, Will. I just miss you so much. My bed is starting to be cold."

"I know, baby, but please bear with me. You know it's work." He paused. "Dude, where are your safety goggles and hard hat?" he yelled. I knew he was talking to a worker.

"Baby, I'll let you get back to work. I'm at your place, so I'll see you later."

"I'll try not to wake you."

"Okay. Bye." I wanted to say, "I love you," but I didn't again.

I snuggled under the covers and tried to get some sleep. Unlike Will, I ran a bakery, so I was at my workplace by 4:00 a.m. For that reason, I didn't burn the midnight oil during the week and instead got some shut-eye. I tossed and turned on this night, and finally, I decided to get up. It was 8:20 p.m., and I missed my baby. I knew he'd crawl into the bed after midnight, and I'd have to get out of the bed by 3:00 a.m., and I needed more than a kiss on this night. I needed dick. That would be the only way I'd fall asleep.

I slipped on my yoga pants, my tennis shoes, and his Bears hoodie. I grabbed my phone and headed downstairs. I went into the kitchen and got his dinner, which was in a Ziploc container, popped it in the microwave, and prayed that it would still be warm after my thirty-minute drive to his work site. Yes, I was ghetto at heart, because I grabbed the wine, a corkscrew, and two red Solo cups. I put all that, plus napkins, a small bowl of salad, and salad dressing, in a paper Olive Garden bag that I took from my stash of restaurant bags, which Will had begged me to toss, and then I was off.

I drove, hoping I'd give him a sweet surprise and not an unpleasant one. I knew how meticulous and precise Will was when it came to work, so I hoped he wouldn't frown at me for showing up.

"I'm looking for Will," I said to one of the workers as I got out of my car.

"He's in the trailer." He pointed to a trailer about twenty-five yards away.

"Thanks."

I retrieved the Olive Garden bag from the passenger seat and hurried in that direction. Before I could make it to the two short steps in front of the trailer door, a woman walked out. She looked like a model. Tall, slim. *Damn that . . .* She was petite, with a body I had never owned, even when I was at my slimmest. She was gorgeous hands down, and for the first time in our relationship, I felt insecure and jealous.

"Hi," she said as she walked by me, and I paused to watch her head to a dark BMW.

"Hello," I whispered, and I knew she didn't hear me, because my voice had abandoned me. I stood still for a moment, and she drove away. I debated whether I should just leave. As soon as I decided to walk away, the trailer door swung open, and it was Will. He spotted me.

"Baby, hey." He smiled.

I tried to detect if his smile was fake.

"Hey, baby," I said nervously.

He approached me quickly and kissed me. "I didn't know you were coming by, bae. What's all this?"

"Your dinner." I tried to say it with a straight face. I didn't want to look upset or pissed because I had seen a drop-dead gorgeous woman walk out of his trailer.

"Thank God, honey. I'm starving. I have to do a quick check. Go inside."

"Yes." I nodded, and he was off.

Okay, Lynn, maybe it was nothing. Don't get crazy, I told myself as I walked to the trailer. Once inside, I surveyed the area. His desk was too cluttered for them to have done it there, but Will did have arm strength, so they could have done it against the wall. I did a check of the trash, looking for condoms, and when I saw there were none, my heart started to beat even harder. *Please, God, tell me he didn't do her without protection.* I was going out of my mind.

Moments later he was back. He started to unload the Olive Garden bag, which I'd placed on his desk. "Baby, thank you, because your man is starving. I'm so hungry, I can eat a horse."

Folding my arms across my breasts, I tilted my head. "Are you sure that's all you're hungry for?" It just jumped out of my mouth.

"Huh?" He looked puzzled.

Crazy had come out. I hadn't wanted her to, but I was jealous, and I wanted the truth. "The big-titty chick with the small waist, in the blue dress and heels, who I saw walking out of here when I arrived."

He paused. "Baby, that's Yvonne. That is my partner's lady. He told her he was here at the site, and she came down looking for him, so relax. I'm with you, and you only." He kissed my forehead. "I'm not that guy, babe. I'm starving. I'm glad you're here, and I'm grateful for this meal," he said, ignoring my jealous pouting. He helped himself to the dinner I'd brought for him. "If you'd walked in here five minutes earlier, I would have introduced you two, Lynn, so don't give me that face. I love you, babe. You're the only woman for me."

He'd said it. He'd said it first. He loved me.

I swallowed hard. "Okay. I'm sorry, Will. I just saw this gorgeous woman sashay out of here, and all sorts of things ran through my head."

"Well, check the mirror, baby. I got a gorgeous woman too." He sat and popped the lid on his microwaved food. He started eating, so I moved to open the wine.

"By the way, I love you too, Will." I smiled, and he smiled back at me.

"I know," he said.

"You know? How could you know?"

"By the way you've treated me over the past six months, baby. I mean, if neither one of us had ever said it, it wouldn't have mattered, because it's all in how we take care of each other. And don't stand there, acting as if you didn't already know too."

"I did, but I didn't want to be the first to say it," I confessed.

"Well, I'm not used to saying it. But it was time to let you know."

"Well, I'm happy about that news, and I love you back."

I handed him his drink and sat. He finished his meal, eating every morsel. When I was pouring our second cup of wine, there was a knock on the door.

"Come in," Will called.

"Boss, there is a problem," one of his workers explained.

Will stood. "Stay put," he told me.

I nodded. It was now 9:50 p.m., and I should have been asleep. I sat and waited, and twenty minutes later he was back.

"Is everything okay?" I asked.

"Yes, but I'll be here for a while." He locked the door. "Take off your clothes."

"Baby, someone will hear us."

"Listen," he said, and I did.

All I heard was noise. Construction noise.

"Now, take those off," he insisted. "I need some before my sack bursts."

I stood and took off my bottoms.

"The hoodie too," he instructed. "You know I want to see your pretty titties."

I did what I was told. There was no space on his desk, but the other desk was free and clear.

"Come over here."

I did what he said.

"Do you have condoms?" I asked.

"No," he answered before going down on me.

In the back of my mind, I wondered what the hell we were doing. We always, always used condoms. "Baby, I don't know. We don't have condoms."

"Whatever happens, happens, Lynn. I'm all in," he said and made his way back up to my lips. He pushed my thighs farther apart, and then he slid inside of me.

I closed my eyes and allowed my man to pleasure me without the plastic. He felt new, good, and I loved feeling his flesh inside of me. "Aah, aah, aah," I moaned as he pumped harder.

"Your pussy is so good, baby. You're gonna make me cum. I'm going to explode in this wet pussy," he cried, closing his eyes. That look he always had when he was inside of me was on his face, and it was a look of enjoyment.

When he opened his eyes, though, the expression on his face started to change, and his soft words grew louder, and his hips moved faster, and he pushed deeper. I was going out of my mind with pleasure as his organ slid in and out of me, giving my walls a rhythmic massage.

My spot got wetter, my walls contracted tighter, and we were now one in this dingy trailer he had claimed as an office.

"Will, baby, I'm going to cum, baby. I'm going to cum all over your dick, baby," I yelled.

My body was experiencing a new level with him, and when I exploded, I felt my muscles spasm. He countered with his own explosion. We kissed deeply as our fluids mixed. I was on a high. "Drunk in love," as Bey would say, and I only wanted this man. I wanted only him, and I worshipped him at that moment.

"I love you," I breathed in his ear.

"I love you too, baby," he said and pushed his tongue into my mouth so deep, I couldn't help but suck it.

I was his, and I had claimed him as mine, even if he felt differently. I had made my own declaration of what we were, and that was inseparable. No way I'd ever let him go.

Chapter Nine

Lynn

"So do you think you and Will may get married?" Yvonne asked.

She and I were in the kitchen alone, while Will and his partner, Lance, were watching the game. Lance and Will were thick as thieves, and Lance ran the company with Will. The fact that Lance was Will's best friend made it impossible for me to avoid Yvonne.

Not that I hated her—no, that was too strong a word—but I truly didn't like her much. Now, I might have been a bit harsh because I wasn't accustomed to her kind—you know, the kind who lived off their looks and not their brains. I wondered what she'd do for money if she was in an accident that destroyed her perfect face. She wasn't a black blonde, far from it, but she was definitely a professional gold digger.

She was classy. I'd give her that, because everything from her fake hair to her lashes, contacts, and nails were top-notch, but I had a thing against legal prostitutes.

Stirring my homemade mac and cheese in the extra-large bowl, I replied, "I don't know, Yvonne. I mean, it's only been a year. We're good, but we have never discussed marriage." I hated Will had invited them, but since I was a sucker for the kitchen, I had greens cooking, chicken baking, potato salad chilling and sweet potatoes on keep warm. I was no stranger to cooking, so I didn't make a big stink about having them over.

"Well, I say persuade that ass. Lance thought I'd keep waiting on this diamond, and I told his ass either he'd make this official or I'd find another sponsor, and *bam*!" she yelled, throwing her five-carat diamond in my face.

"Well, I don't believe in ultimatums anymore, Yvonne. He wants to because he wants to, not because I make him choose."

She shook her head. "I know you're a lot older than I am," she said with no shame. I assumed I had this young madam by ten, maybe twelve years, but this heifer had just called me old. "But you have a lot to learn. Lance is not only fine as hell, but he is also paid, and Will is going to be as rich as Lance is someday, so I suggest you get in now."

I raised a brow. "*Someday*? Lance and Will are equal partners, Yvonne. Will makes just as much as Lance does," I said.

The expression on her face said she had spoken too much, and she quickly replied, "Yeah, you're right." She stood up from the island. "Now, which way is the bathroom again?" she asked.

I stopped stirring. "Down the hall, third door on the left."

I was now curious about what was really going on. I mean, Will lived well, and I had just thought Lance was flashy rather than wealthier. I poured my mac and cheese into the glass dish I'd set out, then put it in the oven. By the time Miss Fancy came back, I was cleaning up my prep area.

"So is there anything I can help with, Lynn? I'm not much of a cook, but I can make bomb-ass Kool-Aid."

I chuckled. "No. Dinner will be ready soon. We can go in and join the guys. I cannot mix Kool-Aid with this wine." I gave her a fake smile.

Beauty, no brains. Can't cook. Probably don't clean. And if I have to guess, her sex is probably a three. Shit, she had nothing on me.

"Whose winning, bae?" I asked Will when I sat down close to him on our huge sectional in the family room. That room was the most used because it was the only room we entertained ourselves and guests in.

"Chicago, baby. Up by seven, but the fourth quarter just started, so you know how it goes."

"I know. Do you want another beer, baby?" I said.

"That would be awesome," he replied.

I got up, and then I heard Lance say, "Um, Yvonne, I'd like another beer too."

"Yo' legs work," she snapped.

"Don't worry, Lance. I'll get it," I said and reached for his empty bottle.

"Thank you, Lynn. This one right here ain't good for shit but spending my money," Lance joked.

"Man, please. I please that dick, though," she returned.

My eyes widened, although I was not surprised that this came out of her mouth. I just shook my head and went into the kitchen. I did a quick peek at my mac and cheese and stirred my greens. Potato salad was chilling in the fridge, and the sweet potatoes were done. All we were waiting on was the baked chicken breasts and the mac and cheese. Will had double ovens now, thanks to me, because I did all the cooking. As soon as I had said I needed another oven, he and two of his crew members had had one installed within four days.

He was sexy, talented, and loving. I honestly hoped marriage was in our future. I grabbed two beers from the refrigerator and joined the others.

"Here you go, Lance," I said before handing him a beer.

"Thanks, Lynn."

I flopped down next to Will, and before I could hand off his beer, he was up on his feet, cheering, because Chicago had scored. The Bears were up by two touchdowns against Green Bay, our rival team, and Will was happy. He finally calmed down, and I handed him his beer.

An hour after the game was over—it ended with a Chicago victory—we were at the table, eating. I always shook my head at some of the things Yvonne said, but I normally ignored her remarks, because she wasn't too swift. I was overjoyed when we walked them to the door and said good night.

Before long Will and I headed upstairs. I went into the bathroom, and when I came out, Will was in bed, surfing the channels.

"Baby," I said, and he turned to me. I knew I should stay out of it, but I had to ask.

"Yeah?" he replied.

"How well . . . or let me say . . . How much control does Lance have in your company?"

"What do you mean?"

I went over and sat near him on the bed. "I just mean, what does he do differently from you?"

"Other than he can't swing a hammer?" He laughed.

"Yes, I guess. I mean, how often do you look at the numbers?"

"Well, babe, to be honest, Lance handles that side of it. I have too much construction and actual manual labor going on to even look at that stuff."

"Maybe you should," I suggested.

His brow arched. "Come on, babe. Lance has been my boy since fifth grade. He is on the up-and-up."

"I know, but it's strange how his house is three times as big as yours. He has, like, four vehicles."

"He likes to floss."

"Okay." I paused and breathed deeply. "I know you're not as flashy as he is, and, baby, please, I'm not trying to stir up any trouble, but your company is worth millions. The work I see you do, baby . . . come on. No way he's living ten times better when you two are equal partners. I mean, just look into it."

"Where is this coming from, Lynn? I mean, are you jealous of the bullshit he laces Yvonne with? I mean, if you want me to buy you some bling, I can. I have lots of money to buy you or give you anything, love. Even a larger house, a fancier car. I just don't splurge like Lance. Remember, I chose this home. This was my parents' home."

I could tell I was rubbing him the wrong way. "Will, baby, you know that's not who I am. Yvonne just said something to me in the kitchen that raised a red flag, and I love you too much not to mention it."

"What did she say?"

"She made a comment about you becoming as wealthy as Lance one day, as if Lance made so much more than you. So all I'm saying is, check it out, baby. See what's going on in that office. You are so smart, Will, and talented, and you can turn a ghetto into paradise if you touch it. You work too hard, baby, and if there is something going on in that office that you're unaware of, you need to check it out. I mean, being flashy is one thing, but I just want you to double-check that it's flashiness and not thievery."

He nodded and then put his head down. I touched his face.

"I'm sorry, Will. If I'm overstepping, please forgive me."

"You're not, and I hear where you are coming from. The truth is . . . ," he whispered.

"What? What is it, baby? Talk to me. You can tell me anything." I was concerned because his shoulders were slumped low.

"First, I want you to know that I trust Lance with my life, and I know he's on the up-and-up, and given where we came from, I know in my heart he'd never do me in. And . . . ," he said, trailing off. He turned his gaze to the muted television.

"Baby, talk to me. If you trust him and you're okay, I'll leave it alone. I'm sorry I said anything."

"It's not that, babe." He dropped his head even lower.

"Will?"

"Lance does the finance end of it all because I . . . I . . . I can't read," He mumbled.

"Will, baby, what did you say?"

"I can't read, Lynn. I know numbers—yes. I can measure, most time eye it, and know how much I'll need. I can do anything hands on, but I can't comprehend paperwork, contracts, or the legal stuff. Lance and I grew up together, but when I went to prison, he went to college. So that's my secret."

I touched his face again. "Baby, it's okay. There is absolutely nothing to be ashamed of, because you're brilliant. What you do, not just for me, but for the millions of clients, is noteworthy. You are a master at construction. Lance may not be doing anything underhanded, and I'm sorry for even bringing it up."

I went on. "But I got you, baby. I will help you. I am not here to ruin your friendship or cause any trouble. I just know what you're worth, and if he is taking advantage because he knows you can't understand, he needs to be stopped. I just have your best interests at heart, my love." My eyes welled up. I knew it was hard for him to share that with me, but I was his ride or die chick, if that was the accurate way of saying it. Just like that gold-digging ass Yvonne was Team Lance, I was Team Will.

"So what do I do?" Will asked.

"Honestly, babe, I don't have a clue where we should start, but I will help you, Will. I love you, baby, and it's not about greed. It's about honesty and doing what's right. You are so good at what you do, and you don't deserve to be cheated, especially by someone you love and trust."

He didn't say anything for a few moments. I then got scared. I didn't want him to think I was trying to control his business.

"Marry me," he finally said.

I blinked rapidly. With those words, my body was launched into orbit, or so it seemed. I pulled myself back into that moment, still blinking like I had some kind of allergy. "I'm sorry?" I said.

"You heard me, Lynn. Marry me."

I swallowed hard. "Yes," I whispered.

My world begin to flash in front of my eyes. I could not process one thought; my mind was all over the place. He grabbed my face and kissed me deeply. Quickly, the room began to heat up, and it felt like a match or flame was on my face, because my face got so hot. There were no more words, only the sounds of our moans as we pleasured each other all through the night.

I made it to the bakery the next morning, exhausted as hell, and couldn't wait until closing. I had accepted the marriage proposal of the century, and when he came home, he laced my finger properly with eight carats of white and purple diamonds.

Yvonne, eat your heart out, bitch.

Part Two

Chapter Ten

Lynn

It had been two quiet weeks since I'd approached Will about investigating Lance, and he hadn't said a word to me about going forward, so I decided to leave it alone. It bothered me and pressed on my nerves like an unruly child, but I let it go.

"Bae, do you want fish or chicken?" I yelled up the stairs.

"Why are you cooking?" he asked from the top of the stairs. "You know tonight is Yvonne's birthday party. You're supposed to be getting dressed."

"Oh, shit, baby. I completely forgot. My dress is at my house, so I have to go home to get dressed."

He looked at his watch. "Seriously, Lynn. I mean, you knew about this."

"I know, and I have no idea how it slipped my mind. Look, I'll race home, and you can pick me up. I promise I'll be ready in no time."

"Hurry up," he scolded as I went for my keys and purse.

I rushed out, rushed home, and took a bird-bath. I had gotten my weekly beauty treatments the day before, so all I had to do was make up my face. By the time Will made it over to get me, I was dressed and ready.

"Baby, you look breathtaking."

"Thank you, handsome." I put my arm in his, and we headed out to the party.

When we made it to our destination, my eyes bulged. The party was at a resort on the outskirts of Chicago, and it had a casino theme. It was a serious party at a party venue of the century. You'd think it was their wedding.

"Baby, this cannot be her party," I told Will as we sat in the car.

"It is."

"Oh, my God, Will. I mean, this is like a . . ." I said, trailing off. The valet opened my door and helped me out of the car. Will grabbed my hand. "This had to cost a fortune," I said, hoping I'd get him to take up investigating Lance.

"You're right. This is more of a . . . Shit, I don't know. Definitely not the average party."

We walked in. Champagne flutes were readily available, and servers were offering up delectables. I held on tight to my man because there were tons of gorgeous gals everywhere and none that looked like me.

"Lynn, Will, you made it." I knew that voice.

"Yvonne, this is certainly a party." I said.

"Yes. What Yvonne wants is what Yvonne gets," she returned, then placed a couple of kisses on our cheeks. "Come, come, come. Lance and I have been waiting for you two."

We followed her through the crowded room to a grand table, where two seats near her and Lance had been saved for Will and me. We enjoyed the music, the champagne and the birthday wishes that were given by several of Yvonne's family members. After a couple of drinks, I was ready to eat. The appetizers were so delicious, but I wanted some real food. I was happy when the servers came around. They offered, chicken, fish or steak and I chose the steak.

"Baby, this is sooo good," I said. Finally the main course, and I was in food heaven.

"It is." Will said and put his fork down. He leaned in closer to me. "And so I tried to avoid the conversation we had a couple of weeks ago, and I hate to admit it, Lynn, but it's time. This here"—he waved a hand in the air—"this had to be a couple hundred grand. I mean, they refill my glass before it is empty."

I knew it was killing him. "I'm sorry, Will." I rubbed his thigh.

"Don't be, baby. It just has to be done. Whether the outcome is positive or negative, I have to face the truth."

"I'm with you all the way, Will. You won't have to do this alone, my love."

"I know, and I love you for looking out for me, baby. And with you, I feel so free. There are no more secrets. But I'm all exposed, and I feel like a fool."

"Why?"

"Because if things are not in order, it's my own fault."

"Baby, stop, okay? It's not Team *You* anymore. It's Team Us, and we are going to get to the bottom of whatever it is. And for your sake, bae, I hope I'm wrong."

He looked around. "There are fifteen fucking ice sculptures in the image of Yvonne, babe. I doubt that you're wrong," he said. He wrapped his arm around me, and I moved in close to him and kissed his neck.

"No matter what, I got your back," I assured him.

"No matter what?"

"Yep. No matter what," I said, and just then Lance tapped his glass.

The soft music that was playing stopped, and Lance gave his undying love speech for Yvonne and wished her a happy birthday. A few of her size-zero friends spoke, extending their birthday wishes, and then the DJ got it going.

Will and I drank so much at the party, we got a room at the resort instead of going home. That night we passed out without lovemaking because the overflow of champagne had done us in.

I thanked God that I didn't open the bakery on Sundays, because Will and I could not move the next day. After devouring a room service breakfast, we called down to the front desk and extended our stay for another night because we were still too exhausted to leave. I made sure my bakery staff could open for me that Monday morning, and then Will and I enjoyed the rest of our day and evening naked, with room service, a jetted tub, and lovemaking.

Eyes shut, enjoying our intimate bath, Will kissed my head and then said, "Once we're married, can we have a baby?"

Surprised, I paused and thought for a second before answering. "We're not young anymore, Will."

"I know, but we're not old, either."

"You're right, my love, but I just thought now, at this age, I'd find my soul mate, and I did, and we'd just enjoy each other," I said and then blew at the bubbles under my chin. We were in the tub again, relaxing and sipping more champagne.

"I thought that too, but I look at you, Lynn, and I want so much from you and from us, and I would love for us to make a baby, at least one. A little person we can just love and spoil and cherish together. I keep thinking of this little girl with your face, my personality, mixed with her own little finesse." He paused. "I don't know, Lynn. It's just that I love you so much, and I want to share everything humanly possible with you, so I just had to ask."

"Ask what?"

"I want you to stop taking the pill."

"Wait a minute. How can you ask me something like that, Will? I mean, after we are married, I'd consider it, but before marriage, I don't know."

"So let's get married now."

My ears had to be playing tricks on me. "Let's do what now?"

"Get married. I mean, we practically live together, and there is no reason to wait. We can live in my house or yours—your choice, baby—and sell one. All I know is I want to be with you, Lynn. I'd never thought I'd be blessed with someone like you. You're gorgeous for one, smart, ambitious, sexy, and on top of that, you can cook and bake your ass off. I mean, your red velvet is the best in this world," he joked.

I laughed. "Stop it, Will. I mean, I adore you too, but I don't want this to be a hasty thing."

"It's not." His tone was serious. "I want to marry you, Lynn. Let's just do it. Time is moving, and I want to spend the rest of my days with you, and I want to be a dad. Can you give me a baby?"

"Yes." It just came out. Although I had some hang-ups and uncertainties, I was caught up in his web. I was at his command. I loved him, and I wanted whatever he wanted. I'd give him ten babies if I could.

"Then it's settled. Can you take off a few days from work?"

"Well, I guess I can."

"I want to take you to Vegas. Let's do it Vegas style. We can leave from here, Lynn. No packing required. Whatever you need, we can buy."

I looked over my shoulder at him. "You're serious?"

"Yes. Dead serious."

I contemplated this idea for a moment and then yelled, "Vegas, here we come!" Glowing and basking in a sense of adventure, spontaneity, and chance, I planted a wet kiss on the back of his hand. This man had done the unthinkable to me, and I swore, I had no control when I was with Will. He was so good to me, and he loved me hard and strong, and I couldn't ask him for more, because my heart was happy with him.

"Now, I hope you got your debit card," he joked.

I hit him playfully. "For you, baby, I do."

"Don't worry. I got us. And when we come home, we will get to the bottom of what is really going on here in Chicago with my company and my business partner."

I agreed. "Yes, baby, we will."

Chapter Eleven

Lynn

Once we were back in Chicago, I was still on a high. I hadn't told anyone about exchanging vows with Will, and I wondered how everyone would react once I announced I was married.

I quickly gathered a few items at my house to take to Will's place, and before leaving, I took a moment to call my mom. She was pissed that I had gone to Vegas, but she had already met Will, had instantly loved him like I did, and after an hour of scolding, she prayed with me on the line for God to bless our marriage.

After getting my mom, the super Christian, who had reminded me it was better to marry than to burn, off the line, I dialed my girlfriend Kenya to tell her and learned she had good news too.

Since Will and I were in bliss, I had failed to answer her calls when I was in Vegas.

"Oh, my God, Kenya. Congrats," I said. She had informed me that her longtime boyfriend, Joseph, had finally gone down on one knee and had asked her to be his wife.

It had taken him only six years, but I had never once shared with her that I thought he was stringing her along.

"Never did I think he'd do it, L. And my ring . . . it is so gorgeous. I mean, it is way more beautiful than I could imagine. Joseph did good. I mean, I cannot stop staring down at this beautiful ring. I mean, I can't believe that he asked. I mean, I'm so elated, so happy, so excited."

"I so understand. When you see this rock my Will laced my finger with, you just might cum as hard as I did last night." I laughed; Kenya didn't.

"Watch your mouth, girl. I got you on speaker."

"Then freakin' take me off of speaker," I retorted and then heard what sounded like a phone being picked up.

"Okay. Anyway, I'm looking forward to seeing your ring, and I do hope this one loves you better than that last husband of yours." Kenya paused, as if she was taking a puff of a cigarette. "I mean, you fought like a champ to stay as long as you did."

"Hey, this is Will we are talking about. He adores me, girl, and you know that he is ten times the man Chez proclaimed to be. And now that we are married, I finally feel like I got it right. I mean, he married me as I am. A big and beautiful woman. He sexes me as if I was light as a feather, and to be loved by someone so caring, so romantic, so selfless is, like, surreal. Chez fucked up my self-esteem, had me blaming myself for things going south, but Will . . ." I paused.

Five seconds went by, and the right words came to me. "Will has just shown me what real love is about, and how real love is supposed to be, Kenya. I mean, for a long time I thought I knew. I mean, for a moment I really thought that love had to hurt to be real, but I now know better."

"Well, Chez is somewhere now wishing he'd done right by you. I know no other woman is doing half the shit you did for him. I mean, a clean home, cooking two or three meals a day when he was in town, something I'd never do."

I laughed and then teased, "That is why Joseph took so long to pop the question."

She laughed with me. "Shit, you're probably right. I'm not domesticated. I know how to make reservations and budget my money so my house-keeper will always return twice a week. Hell, I can't help that my mama raised me this way.

Clean a toilet? Shit, no thank you. I'll suck your dick all night long, but damn your laundry," she joked.

I laughed so hard.

"No, I'm serious, and I'm so glad Joseph is a six-figure brother, because he already know."

"Hey, I know that's right," I said. "I'm not mad at'cha, sis. I just have never been comfortable with sharing my kitchen, nor can I allow some woman to wash my man's boxers. Now, a cleaning lady . . . ? I think this year I'll spring for one, but she cannot be some slim, attractive chick. I trust Will, but I'd never serve up temptation on a platter in my house."

"Speak on it. Trust, my two cleaning ladies are not a threat. They are old enough to be both of our mothers, and Estelle is mean as hell. If you walk on wet floors, that is your ass. Norma bosses you around like she gave birth to ya, so I don't have anything to worry about."

I giggled. "Well, you'll have to ask them for a recommendation. I will be putting my house on the market soon and moving to Will's."

"Really? You're giving up your palace?"

"Yes. There are too many Chez memories here. Too many memories of how marriage is not supposed to be. Plus, Will's place is super gorgeous, and he's already revamped the kitchen for me, and, girl, I have three ovens, eight burn-ers, a grill, and let's just say cooking is never a chore at his place."

"That means there is a dinner invite for Joseph and me in the works to celebrate your marriage and my engagement."

I took the hint. "As a matter of fact, there is. Let me decide on a good night with Will and get back to you."

"Okay, love. I must go now. A judge is never off. I have several search warrant requests on my desk as we speak, and if I want to put the bad guys away, I need to get to signing."

"You mean rubber stamping?" I teased.

"Yeah, that." She laughed. "Still takes arm strength."

"Okay. Bye, girl. And again congrats. I will call you later, after I talk to Will."

"Okay, darling, and please put red velvet on the menu. Your red velvet is to die for."

"So says my husband." I snickered. We hung up, and I immediately dialed Will.

"Hey, you," he sang.

"Hey, husband." I had a huge, uncontrollable smile on my face. I smiled so hard, I knew my face should hurt or become stuck.

"Yes, my wife? What can I do you for? I am in the middle of something right now, baby."

"Oh, okay." My smile diminished. "Nothing big. I can talk to you later, my love."

"No. I have a couple of moments now, but only that. The city is down here, and they are combing my project like they are searching for a cure for cancer."

"Aw, baby, I'm sorry. I just wanted to tell you that Kenya got engaged while we were in Vegas, and I want to have a dinner for her and her fiancé at the house. I know this project is behind schedule because of our trip, so I wanted to know when you think you'll be free. Maybe invite Lance and Yvonne, a couple of your employees. I want it to be a little celebration."

"Well, I can say a Sunday will work. I know my Saturdays will be full, but no matter how far behind schedule a project gets, my love, Sunday is a day we don't slang a hammer."

"Okay, love. Not this Sunday, but the following one. Kenya is going to be so thrilled."

"I'm sure. Babe, I gotta go."

"Okay, baby. And that thing with Lance . . ." I had tried to squeeze the topic in, but the line had disconnected. "Hello?" I repeated three times, and then I tossed my phone and went back to gathering things from my house. It had been only a week since I'd said, "I do," and we'd been home only four days, and so there had been no talk of the issue with Lance.

I knew I was out of line. . . . *Maybe* I was out of line. I took stock of the entire situation. Lance might have made a lot of money, and Will and I hadn't sat down and opened bank accounts just yet, but I still thought it strange that Lance was living like he was Jay Z and my man was living like Trey Songz. Trey Songz was popular and was doing well, of course, but we all knew that Jay Z's money was a lot longer than his was.

I made it to my new home, and after unloading my truck, I saw it was still early enough to shop for dinner. Since my bakery was open as early as the roosters crowed, we closed by three, leaving me time in the late afternoon to run errands. Now I hurried out to get some fresh fish, clams, wild rice, and veggies from the market. Since I got in a lot earlier than Will, dinner was and probably would always be my chore. Will made a mean, hearty breakfast for me on Sunday mornings at my place or his, so being his dinner maid made me happy.

Hours later I looked at the clock and wondered what was keeping my husband. It was close to eight, and I was ready to greet him with wine, food, and lovemaking. Hating that I couldn't keep late nights because I had the bakery, I decided not to call him. I left the food on very low on the stove and put the white wine back into the fridge.

I closed my robe, which hid my sexy satin nightie, and got on the sofa. Grabbed the remote, and within minutes I had dozed off.

Sometime later I felt a soft kiss.

"Baby," he whispered.

I opened my eyes. "Will, baby," I said, blinking.

"I'm sorry I'm late, baby. The city gave me hell, and there was a lot of electrical work that had to be redone."

I yawned, covering my mouth. "It's okay, baby. What time is it?"

"Close to eleven."

"Damn. That late? I cooked. I hope nothing dried out." I rose and headed to the kitchen.

"Me too, because I'm starving."

As I went into the kitchen, I thanked God that I had made another trip there to turn everything completely off before dozing.

"Go on up and shower, baby, and I'll get your dinner," I told him.

He paused and came close. "It's not always like this, baby." He kissed my shoulder.

"Will, bae, I know. Work is work, and I'd never complain about your duties at work. I know what I signed up for."

"That's my girl. I love you."

"I love you too. Now go. Dinner will be served when you are cleaned up."

My husband dashed up the stairs, and I set about reheating our dinner. I knew I'd be crying in the a.m., but I didn't mind. I made a decision at that moment to find a person to open the bakery in the mornings, or to promote one of my employees and have him or her do that task, so that I could relax and not think about opening. So my new husband and I could have late nights together, if we had to. Hell, Chez had always been away, but now I had a husband who came home every night and who was in love with me, so I had to make some changes.

Chapter Twelve

Will

I sat at my desk in my office, staring into space. I wondered how to begin to investigate my friend. Lance and I went way back, boys from the hood, and I knew he had a history, but, hell, so did I. But I had to admit I was living a BMW lifestyle, while he liked an Aston Martin lifestyle.

I mean, I had the finer things and could afford top-notch things, but I'd never throw my wife a party like the one he had thrown for Yvonne. Not that I couldn't afford it. I just thought it was not smart. When I added up all the vacations he went on, versus me barely having a moment to breathe, it was clear that the numbers weren't adding up.

As hard as it was, I made that call—the call that I had thought for a few seconds should not be made. But Lynn's voice had replayed over and over in my head. "Baby, it never hurts to just check. I mean, just check. If there is nothing, there's nothing," she'd said.

"Hey, Royce. This is Will. How are you, bro?" Royce was my accountant, and I also considered him a friend.

"Well, I'm doing well, Will. What's up? How is the married life? I hope you guys got my and Tamia's gift."

"We did, as a matter of fact, and thanks. Marriage so far is wonderful. I mean, Lynn is a breath of fresh air, the best thing that could have ever happened to me."

"I hear ya. . . . Tamia is like my lifeline, and I couldn't imagine life without her."

"I now know what you mean, man."

"So what prompted this call? I mean, we meet only twice a year, and we are nowhere near review or tax time."

"I know, and I normally would have never called. I'd let you and Lance do what y'all do. I know you two have been keeping this company running without a hitch, and you know since the numbers and the business side are foreign to me, I barely stop to survey what's going on."

"True, but whatever you wanna know, I'll be happy to tell you or show you. Your records are up to date. Is there something wrong?"

"No, well, no . . . Well, let's just put it this way. . . . Lance has been splurging a bit more and more lately, and I just want to make sure he's still on the straight and narrow. I mean, this is my business, and my pops worked too hard for me to fuck up and lose it, you know, so I think I should see more of the financial parts, more than just the labor."

"Well, you are the boss, and whatever you want, I will be happy to show you, explain, and provide for you. I mean, your company has quadrupled since you and Lance took over."

"Quadrupled?" I questioned. I knew we had increased our profits, but *quadrupled* was a term that I wasn't aware of. But thinking back, I knew he was about right.

"Yes, plus some. I'll be happy to go over every number with you, Will. I mean, at midyear and year-end, I e-mail you the numbers too. I had no idea you had questions."

This was a kick in the head. Not being able to read and comprehend the facts was my reason for not even opening those e-mails, and now that I had Lynn to help me, I'd have to go back and let her read and explain the reports to me.

"I know, but I have been so busy and have let Lance handle that. You know I'm a hands-on man," I said, making an excuse. Truth was, I wouldn't know what I was reading.

"That I know, so I'll go ahead and forward you the e-mails from the past five years, since you've been my client, and if there are any questions, just please don't hesitate," he said.

"Thanks. That will help, and I will give you a call if there is anything that I don't understand."

"Great. And congrats again on your new marriage. I'm happy for you, man."

"Thanks. Take care and send Tamia a hello."

"Will do."

Chapter Thirteen

Will

I stood to leave and head home, but Yvonne walked into my office just then.

"Hey, how are you?" I asked, shocked. Lance always worked at the office, never on site, so what she was doing there, I had no idea.

"I'm fantastic. Are you on your way out?"

"As a matter of fact, I am."

"Well, I'm glad I caught you." She smiled brightly and then took a seat. "First, I wanted to say that I am glad you and Lynn came out to my birthday celebration. It was, like, the best party I've ever had in my life."

"I bet," I smirked.

"It was, but now I have to plan something for Lance. His birthday is in a couple of months, and since you're his best friend, I figured you could be my party-planning partner."

"Aw, Yvonne, I'd love to, but I think you should get with Lynn on that. She'd be better than me."

"Nooo," she whined. "Secretly, I know your wife is not too fond of me. Most women aren't, so I'm not mad at her. However, you're Lance's best friend, and in order for this to be the party of the century, you and I will have to work side by side to make this happen."

Unwillingly I agreed. "Okay, Yvonne. Whatever you need."

She hopped up and down like a bunny. "Yay!" she squealed. "I will come by your house maybe Saturday morning with a list of ideas, and we can get this party started."

"Okay. But I have to work this Saturday, so it has to be early, like before nine."

"I'm there. I just want to keep this on the low. I've never been able to surprise him, so I really want this to be special."

"Hey, I'll be happy to help." I stood, and I walked her to the door. I had a funny feeling, because I was about to help plan a party for a man who I was also going to investigate due to the possibility that he was stealing from me.

I headed home, feeling like maybe I was making a mistake. I mean, Lance had made some serious money, and I had never pried, so he could have had great investments and other things going on in his world. With that, I started to second-guess my decision, and I started to wonder why Lynn was so concerned about this when we lived well.

I walked into the house. Whatever she was cooking smelled divine. I made my way to the kitchen, where I found Lynn.

"I talked to Royce. He's going to send over all the numbers for the past five years," I said as I opened the fridge for a beer.

"Okay, and I'm sure you have absolutely nothing to worry about."

I was silent for a moment. She sounded supportive and loving, but that didn't help how I felt about being a grown-up idiot. If Lance had been stealing from me, it only served me right for being a dumb ass and for never going back to school.

"Baby, I feel so stupid," I confessed.

"Will, baby, don't say that. You are brilliant. You build homes, businesses, and corporate offices from the ground up with your knowledge and skills, so damn a book. You are more brilliant than a man who has ten degrees. At the end of the day, not many can do what you do, so please, don't insult yourself. Hell, don't insult me. I married a brilliant man, and school doesn't make a man. You are self-made and damn good at what you do, so please, bae, don't."

I listened, but my head still hung low. "How did I not see it?"

"You just trusted someone, baby. We all do. I trusted Chez, but he let me down. And we don't know yet about Lance. Let's get proof before we go down this road, okay?"

She was right. "Okay. I'm going to go up and shower. What's for dinner?"

"Smothered chicken, rice, veggies, and a side of good loving afterward."

"All I want on my plate is the side of good loving, please, for now." I smiled, readjusting my dick in my Dickies. It instantly swelled at the thought of being inside of her.

"How about saving that for dessert? The chicken, rice, and veggies will give you energy, and then she will give you pleasure." She point toward her treasure.

"That is a better idea. I love you, woman, and you better know it."

"I do, and I love you too, man. You better know it."

I smiled. "I do. I'll be back down in a little while. Fix me a drink, would ya?"

"What my baby wants is what he gets."

I kissed her and then headed up the steps and showered. After a nice dinner, we settled on the sofa, and we didn't dare speak about Lance and his possible misappropriation of funds. We talked about making love and making babies. We decided we'd work on making a baby while we worked on ascertaining Lance's loyalty to me and our friendship and to my company.

Chapter Fourteen

Will

"Yvonne, you're here," I said when I opened the front door.

"I said bright and early." She walked in without an invite. She headed for the kitchen, stopped at the island, tossed her designer bag onto a stool, and then handed me a large OJ and a Dunkin' Donuts bag.

"Thanks. I honestly forgot you were coming."

"Well, you may want to take advantage of the apps in your phone. Even I know there is an appointment app," she scolded and took a seat. She pulled out a list. "Okay, first things first. Themes. Now, I know Lance is a sports guy and he loves cars, but I'm at a loss when it comes to choosing one."

I took a swig of the juice, and it was a little bitter. But I wasn't rude, so I drank it, anyway, and then fished around in the bag and took out a hot

breakfast sandwich. I was glad she was thought-
ful enough to show up with breakfast, because
she was messing with my timeline.

"Yvonne, are you sure you can't do this with
my wife? I mean, Lynn is very capable of helping
you."

"But you're his best friend, not Lynn," she
snapped.

"You're right, so my suggestion will be sports."

"Bulls or Bears?"

"Bears."

"Indoor or out?"

"Out. That way we can do some touch football
and grilling. You should consider park space.
Have a half field drawn out and have, like, a tail-
gate theme."

"Oh, my fucking God. You are brilliant," she
said, her eyes bright.

"Get with some barbecue restaurant and see
what it will cost to have them set up different
food stations. We can have kegs, contests and
giveaways, sports trivia. It could be awesome."

"Okay, I will do a lot of shopping and then get
back to you with the figures."

Pause! "Come again?"

"Will, you know I'm not working, and Lance
deserves a party. I mean, he's your best friend.
Surely, you can fund it if I plan it right," she said,

looking like an innocent eight-year-old little girl. At that moment I saw how she had Lance wrapped around her finger.

"Okay, well, let me ask this. What kind of budget are you looking at?"

"Ten grand."

I almost spit out the orange juice. "Ten grand? Lance is my best friend, not my wife."

"Come on, Will. That is the cheapest. I mean, we are trying to do a lot of stuff."

"Yvonne, Lance doesn't even know enough people to invite."

"I know, but I'll be inviting my friends, and you saw the turnout at my party."

She had a point. There had been a slew of people there.

"Six," I offered.

"Eight," she countered.

"Seven. And that's my final offer."

"Done," she agreed. She hopped up and ran over to squeeze my neck. "Thank you, Will. Lance is going to be so happy. You're awesome."

"Yeah, I know."'

"I'll be in touch," she said, grabbing her things. She hurried to the door.

I downed the OJ and headed upstairs to finish getting ready for work. I pondered how I had just agreed to spend seven grand on a party for a man who I thought was stealing funds from me. Lynn was going to flip her lid.

"Damn!" I said to myself and wondered how I'd tell her.

When I got to work, I started to feel a little funny. My stomach was cramping so bad that I could no longer ignore the discomfort, so I handed my assistant my clipboard and headed home. Unable to deal with the pain, I forced myself to vomit but hardly got any relief. I went for the phone and called Lynn, and she was home within thirty minutes.

"What did you eat?" she asked me as I lay in bed.

Clenching the covers, I replied, "Dunkin' Donuts. I had a breakfast sandwich and orange juice."

She felt my head. "Well, you're burning up. It may be a virus, baby. Let me get you some soup and tea, and we have Alka-Seltzer. That should help."

"Okay." I frowned. I hadn't experienced a stomachache this bad ever in my life.

A few minutes later she came back with the stomach medicine, and she brought up a bucket.

"Drink this, baby. I've been in situations where I vomited within minutes after drinking it, so here is a bucket. I'm going to go downstairs and make some soup for you."

"Thank you, baby," I whispered, taking quick sips. I wanted to down the Alka-Seltzer so I could have some relief.

After twenty minutes or so, Lynn was back. I hadn't vomited, and the Alka-Seltzer had given me a little relief. Not as much as I would have liked.

She fed me a few spoonfuls of the soup, and I just wanted to go to sleep.

"Here, baby. Try some more soup first."

I nodded but wanted to say no. I managed two more spoons and lay there and thanked God when I felt myself finally drifting off to sleep.

I woke up sometime that night and was feeling so much better. Whatever had hit me had hit me hard. I went into the bathroom, looked in the mirror, and was happy to see that my color had returned. That bug had sure hit me out of nowhere.

I climbed back in bed.

"Baby, how are you feeling?" Lynn asked when she walked into the room.

"Better. That bug whipped your man's ass today, baby."

"I know. I'm so glad you're feeling better."

"Me too."

"Okay. Good night, baby," she said.

I kissed the side of her head. "Good night."

Chapter Fifteen

Will

The next day, when I got to the office, I was grateful to be feeling better. At lunch I was going to head to a sandwich shop nearby, but Lance and Yvonne walked in.

"What brings you to the site?" I asked, my brow furrowed. "You know you don't like getting your hands dirty."

"The guys told me how sick you were yesterday, so Yvonne thought it would be good to come check on you and bring you some lunch. Lynn said it was best to get you something light, so we got you some soup and orange juice. Yvonne talked me into it, because I was like, 'He's a man, not a baby.'"

We all laughed.

"That's right, but I appreciate it." I reached for the bag.

"No. Let me," Yvonne offered. She put every-thing on my desk, and Lance and I sat. She handed me a bowl and then Lance, and she gave us each a cup of juice.

"Thanks," I said. I carefully pulled back the lid on the soup, and it smelled good.

"So how's the married life? I mean, how are things at home with Lynn?" Lance asked.

"It's great. I don't have one complaint. I mean, she is amazing, and I'm going to have to start hitting the gym soon, because that woman can cook."

"I wish this one here could."

"Hey, I can cook," Yvonne protested.

"Baby, setting the oven to four-fifty and set-ting a timer for a premade meal from the freezer is hardly what you can call cooking."

"Well, I have other skills," she teased.

"Well, a cooking class or two wouldn't kill you," Lance replied.

He and I laughed.

"Maybe Lynn could give me a few pointers," Yvonne mused.

"Ask her. I'm sure she'd do it," I told her.

"Call her," she ordered, pointing at my phone.

I picked the phone up, dialed Lynn, and put it on speaker.

"Hello?"

"Baby, hey."

"Hey. What's going on?"

"I got you on speaker," I said quickly. I knew Lynn. She'd probably say, "Hell naw!" when she heard Yvonne's request. "Lance and Yvonne are here, and Yvonne wants to know if you could give her a couple of cooking lessons."

"Sure I could."

In the back of my mind, I knew she'd have a few words for me for putting her on the spot.

"That would be fantastic." Yvonne beamed.

"Yes, thank you, Lynn. This woman thinks microwave dinners means she cooks," Lance interjected.

We all laughed.

"But I told him, Lynn, I have other skills," Yvonne added.

We continue to laugh and chat a bit. By the time Lynn got off the phone, she and Yvonne had planned to meet the very next day for the first cooking lesson.

I finished out my day, and when I headed home, my stomach started to tug at me again. Praying it wouldn't be like the night before, I pulled into a service station, parked, and grabbed the Alka-Seltzer. After taking one with bottled water, I pulled out of the service station and hurried home. Before long I curled up in a ball on my bed. That was it. I was going to the doctor first thing the next morning.

As I had figured, it was a virus. I got an anti-nausea medication, my doctor and headed to work. I took my meds and was feeling better. When I got home that day, I wasn't expecting to see Yvonne's car. I walked into the house, and the aroma of something good was in the air, so I headed straight to the kitchen.

"Oh, my goodness. Would you look at this?" I said, taking out my phone. Yvonne in the kitchen, in an apron. I'm putting this on Facebook," I said and snapped a picture.

"Don't play with me, Will. Don't nobody need to know that I'm trying to be a little domesticated." Yvonne tossed an oven mitt at me.

"Hey, baby," Lynn said.

I walked over to greet her properly with a kiss. "Hey, gorgeous. You teaching this one how to cook?"

"Yep, I am." She smiled.

"Well, let me get out of you ladies' way. I'm going up to shower."

"And you better not post that pic, Will. I'm not playing."

"I won't today, but I'll hold on to it for later. I'm sure I'll be able to blackmail you with it."

"Whatever," Yvonne returned.

We laughed, and then I ran on upstairs to shower. I was anxious for dinner, because it smelled divine.

Chapter Sixteen

Lynn

"I'm going to go and change," I said. Yvonne was a klutz in the kitchen. She had knocked over the pitcher of lemonade, and some of it had splashed on me.

"I'm so sorry, Lynn," she said, apologizing again.

"It's okay. Just keep an eye on dinner for me. I won't be long." I headed up the steps, shaking my head. This girl was remedial.

Yvonne

"Hey," I whispered.

"Hey."

"Listen, I don't have long. She finally left me alone."

"Did you plant the stuff, Yvonne?" Lance asked.

"Yes, finally. I put it in her spice cabinet."

"Good girl."

"Lance, I don't know about this. I mean, we could go to jail if we're caught." I was nervous.

"We won't. Now, don't bitch up on me, baby. I can't keep falsifying employees on the payroll, Yvonne. We have to take him out, if you want it all, baby. You can't back out now. He is a stupid-ass, illiterate fool, but he is with Lynn, and she is as sharp as a knife."

"I know, baby, but any other way but this . . ." I was having second thoughts.

"Yvonne, this is the only way. He dies, she goes to jail, and the company and all the money are ours, baby. Now come on. Put your game face on. We are going to have everything if we stick to the plan."

"Lance, but I—"

"No buts, Yvonne. We've already started, and we can't turn back now. All we have to do is keep slipping that shit in his food and drinks and, *boom*, when he dies, they will search his house, and Lynn will be put behind bars. It's so easy, baby, so come on. Two months tops . . . I mean, we can't give him as much as the last time. We have to kill him slowly, so he won't end up in the hospital, where they will figure out that he's being poisoned. Once we've weakened him, we hit him with the fatal dose."

I just stood and listened to him, biting down on the corner of my lip. The shit we were using was something that they normally ordered in the business, so no one would suspect Lance.

"Yvonne, baby?"

"Yes? I'm here, Lance."

"Come on, baby. You can do this. We are going to live like a king and a queen when this is done."

"I hear you," I whispered.

"Okay, now get your sexy ass home. I have a surprise for you."

My expression went from one of gloom to a bright smile. "What is it, baby? Tell me."

"Nope. It's a surprise."

"I can't wait."

"So wrap up that fake-ass lesson and get home. After this is all said and done, you'll never have to spend a day in the kitchen, baby. We will have staff to do everything for us. You won't have to lift a pretty manicured finger."

"I hope you're right."

"Have I ever been wrong?"

"No, baby. Never. I gotta go. Lynn is on her way back down."

"Okay. I love you, and this is going to work, baby."

"I hope so," I said and hung up.

"So is dinner still eatable?" Lynn asked after entering the kitchen.

"I guess. I just stood here," I said.

Lynn walked over to check on things.

"Listen, Lynn, this has been fun," I said, taking off my apron, "but I should head home."

"You're not going to take a plate for you and Lance? I mean, even though it was a bumpy ride, you did help cook."

I smiled, because the food did smell good. "Okay. I'll wait for a couple of plates. Lance needs to taste the fruits of my labor."

We laughed.

"I know that's right," Lynn said.

"Lynn, let me ask you something."

"Go ahead."

"It's about Will."

She paused. "What about Will?"

"You guys are okay, right? I mean, I know it's not my place, but you two are doing okay, yes?"

"Of course. Why would you think otherwise? I mean, not too long ago we got married. And we never argue. We are closer than I've ever been to any man, so I don't know what you mean."

"You're right, so forget I even said anything," I said. I was supposed to bring up this topic earlier, but I hadn't wanted to sound fake. The

plan was to create friction, as it would be help-
ful when making a case against Lynn when the
police searched her house.

"No. You brought it up, so what's going on? Is
there something I should know?"

"Well, it's not any of my business, but Will
was over the other night, and I overheard him
and Lance talking about you guys, and he was
just saying that married life was a bit different
for him, and that he was still trying to adjust to
having to report to a person every second of the
day, and that already the sex has slowed down."

Dumbfounded, Lynn opened her mouth to
reply, but no words came out.

"Listen, Lynn, I didn't want to say anything,
but you know how it is. We sisters have to stick
together, and I'm only saying this as a friend.
Please don't mention it to Will, because if you
do, Will will know I told you, and then he'll tell
Lance. I'm just looking out . . ."

"Listen, I'm sure it's nothing, and I know the
sex has kinda slowed down, but our lovemaking
is just as good," Lynn said calmly. "As a matter
of fact, it's better, but men are visual, and maybe
I'm becoming a little boring. I mean, my mornings are super early, and some projects keep Will
late, but I'm not blowing up his phone or any-

thing. I mean, I call him a lot, sometimes just to hear his voice, but reporting to me? I had no idea Will felt that way."

"Hey, with men you never know. I mean, you can be throwing down your best moves in the bedroom, be looking gorgeous as hell, like myself, every day, but they still could stray or not appreciate us for what we do. Just please don't mention it to Will. I don't want any scoldings from Lance about running my mouth or sticking my nose in where it don't belong, but I thought it was the right thing to do." I paused. "I mean, I'm taking cooking lessons, cooking lessons for my man, because I'm trying to keep him," I joked playfully, but Lynn didn't laugh with me.

She remained serious and calm.

"Look, I'm sorry," I said.

"No, no, no, Yvonne. I'm good. Thanks. I know what I'll be doing tonight, after dinner." She sipped her wine with a wondering look in her eyes.

I was curious. "What's that?"

"Well, it damn sure won't be a movie on the sofa. Just when he thinks it's time to cuddle close on the sofa with the remote, I'm going to give him something he can feel." Her look of defeat was replaced with a smile. She went to her pantry, grabbed a couple to-go cartons, and fixed my and Lance's plate with a bright smile, all the while humming a tune. She packed up some food and handed it to me. Assuring me that our conversation would stay between us, she walked me out.

As soon as I got in the car, I called Lance with an update.

Chapter Seventeen

Lynn

I sat across the table from Will, playing with my food. What Yvonne had said weighed heavily on my mind. How could he have shared that with Lance and not with me? I mean, I had had no clue that he felt bored and smothered. I mean, we hadn't been married more than eight months, and I didn't think the thrill was gone. I mean, we got it in whenever we could, sometimes in his office or in my office at the bakery. I knew we had drive-by sex, but I had thought that turned him on.

"Lynn?"

I heard Will's voice. "Huh? Yes?" I answered.

"Baby, are you okay? I called you, like, three times. What's on your mind?"

"I'm sorry, baby. I was just thinking. I . . . I . . . I . . . I . . . ," I stuttered.

"Are you done? I mean, you're just playing with your food, baby."

"Yes. I'm sorry. My mind was somewhere else."

"Like where?" He stood and took my plate.

"Nothing, babe." I stood quickly. "I can get that. Go and sit on the sofa, and I'll join you in a minute."

He stopped me and grabbed my arm. "No. What's going on? We don't have secrets from each other. I know that look. When it was time to decide on the finishing touches for the bakery and when we went shopping for the new ovens for our kitchen, you'd stared at your choices with that same expression, so out with it," he demanded.

I sighed.

"Lynn," he said, pressing.

I looked down. He lifted my face by my chin.

"Baby, talk to me. What's on your mind? As long as we've been married, as long as we've eaten at that table, you've never, ever been this quiet."

"Okay, okay, okay, but please don't go back to Lance with this."

"What? What is it? Did he hit on you?"

"No, no, baby. Nothing like that."

"Then what?"

"When you were over at their house a few nights ago, Yvonne overheard you guys talking," I said, looking at him with furrowed brows, like he was supposed to say something.

"And?"

"She overheard you say that you were having trouble with having to check in with me and that already our lovemaking was pretty much gone."

"What?"

"Yvonne said she overheard—"

He cut me off. "I heard what you said, baby, but that is so not what I said or how I said it. Lance and I were chatting, and he was clowning me about being the first to get married. I joked with him about how strange it was to now be responsible for a person other than myself, and about how having to answer to or make plans with someone and make compromises was something new for me. But I said it was okay, because you and I have one heartbeat and our desires are the same. I did say we have resorted to quickies and lazy sex, but I was joking. We are good, baby. I love you. I love how we are and where we are at."

He went on. "It's all good, bae. I know you didn't want to drum up drama, but I can assure you that the conversation we had didn't have anything negative about you, our marriage, or our routine. Hell, I love getting head in my office and sexing you on your desk. I love every moment I share with you, whether it be face-to-face or on the phone. Baby, I am extremely happy with you. You are the most beautiful, sexy full-figured woman I've ever had the pleasure to touch, hold, and make love to. I know that our schedules prevent us from doing all the things we did in our honeymoon stage, baby, but I don't have one complaint."

I smiled brightly. "Bae, I knew she was exaggerating about the conversation. I knew it. I know you, and I know you'd talk to me, so I'm sorry for not just coming to you pronto. I'm sorry for not saying something right away. You are the sweetest man on the planet, Will. Before you, I had no idea that love and marriage could be this good. This sexy, this romantic, and this beautiful."

I stepped back and began to remove my clothes, and he kept his eyes locked on me. "I feel like the most beautiful woman in the world when I'm with you," I said and continued to undress. "I feel free, sexy, wanted, needed, and it's all because of you," I added, stepping out of my panties.

His man was at full attention as he surveyed the curves and rolls of my plus-size frame. I was smooth with my movements as I took a couple of steps closer to him to undress him.

"Baby, you are turning me on so much right now that I'm scared I'm going to explode the minute I slide inside of you."

"That's the thing. You can do that, because we have all night."

Within a few moments, I was giving him the sexiest and wettest blow job I'd ever given him. His back was against the dining room wall, and he watched my sexy, thick legs hold a squat position as I pleased my man.

He closed his eyes, but I begged him to watch.

"That will make it impossible for me not to nut all over the place. Seeing your beautiful face, your lustful mouth, and your naked curves makes me want to make a baby, buy out the mall, give up a kidney. Anything you need, I'd give it all!"

I slurped and sucked harder, making sucking sounds, as if his dick was better than the dinner I had prepared earlier.

"Yes, baby. I love you. I love all of you. You are the sexiest BBW, thick chick, full-figured woman, or whatever society uses these days to describe your curves."

He was sweet, because all the words he spoke were society's nice way of saying a woman was fat. *Fat* wasn't a sinful word; it was the truth. The soft bulges were fat, but society had turned that word into something so negative, people didn't want to be called it.

"Oh, Lynn, baby. You are so good, baby," he said, looking down at me.

I knew my performance was stellar that night, and he definitely let me know it.

"You are damn good at pleasing my dick, baby. . . . Let me taste you," he moaned.

"No. I want you to cum in my mouth," I said between slurps and licks.

"Do you, baby? Do you, baby?" he moaned. "I can cum in your mouth, baby," he said and grabbed my head with both hands. He worked his pelvis and then quickly pulled away. "I want to be inside of you. I want to give you a baby. I want my seeds inside of you. Lynn. I want a child. I want to take you upstairs and make love to you. I want to cum with you. Inside of you. I want us to make a baby."

I smiled. We had said over and over again that we would start trying, but he still hardly ever deposited inside of me, and I had never stopped taking the pill.

"Are we really ready to be parents?" I asked.

"I don't know about you, but I am," he answered.

"Well, let's take this upstairs."

He followed me, watching my voluptuous hips sway from side to side.

"I am under your spell, baby. Look at you. I love watching you walk. Men who can't appreciate all of this are just plain old crazy. Those fat-ass thighs are my safe haven when I penetrate you, baby. Holding on to you after the lovemaking makes it even better for me. I am in love, lust, and am mesmerized by you, woman. You are gorgeous from head to toe, and don't you forget it."

I turned to him, smiled, and then wrapped my arms around his neck. He kissed me gently.

"I won't. You are the best thing that has ever happened to me. And I'm not ashamed or embarrassed to be myself with you. Thank you for that, baby," I said.

He smiled. "No. Thank *you* for sharing your love with me." He kissed me again, and then we headed on up to bed.

Will

Awakened by the ringing doorbell, I managed to get out to bed. It was Saturday, and Lynn had already gone to the bakery. My first appointment was with Yvonne for party planning. I stepped into my boxers and then some sweats and grabbed a tee and put it on as I headed down the steps.

Someone was still ringing the hell out of my bell, so I yelled, "I'm coming."

I opened the door to a perky Yvonne, with a briefcase and breakfast.

"Rise and shine, Will. We have party planning." She walked in without being invited again, and I followed her into the kitchen and over to the island. "I got us some breakfast and some ideas," she said. She handed me a cup of orange juice, and I was so thirsty, I opened the lid and drank the juice straight down.

It was bitter. "Can you please stop bringing me this sugar-free OJ? I mean, I know you watch your figure and all, but I am a man, Yvonne, and I not only do construction, but I also work out. That bitter-ass juice tastes like crap."

"I will keep that in mind. But remember, you are not as young as you used to be, so you should take better care of yourself. All that sugar they put in juices nowadays ain't good for you, old man."

"Whatever. What's all this?" I asked and then opened up the McDonald's bag to see what she had brought for breakfast. Lynn and I had had a good night, and I was drained and starving. "Steak bagel. Yvonne, I hope you got me two," I said.

"I didn't, but you're welcome to mine," she said and sipped her juice. "Anyway, here is the theme, and here is the venue," she said.

As I ate my steak bagel, I half listened to all her extravagant plans and thought they were a bit much, but the glow in her eyes was like nothing was too good for Lance, and I then kind of got on board, because there was nothing too good for Lynn. I waited for her to add up the charges for what she had come up with so far, and then I wrote her a check.

Once she finally shut up and left, I went to pop the other steak bagel in the microwave and discovered that my wife had left me a plate of breakfast. I had had no idea she had cooked. I sat the bagel to the side and heated up my food, and then I sat in the family room and devoured the plate as if I hadn't eaten the first steak bagel.

I put my plate in the sink, went back to the sofa in the family room, and was suddenly overcome by severe cramps in my stomach again. Rushing to the first-floor bathroom, I vomited, hoping it would relieve the tight spasms in my abdomen, but it didn't give me any relief. After I put down the lid and rinsed my mouth, I had to hit the toilet again. This time I had to sit, as the violent stomach cramping was unbelievably painful. After twenty minutes on the can, I felt a little relief, but not enough to say I felt fine.

Remembering the meds I had from my last visit to the doctor, I took them and went to bed. I slept until my wife woke me, and that was five hours later.

Chapter Eighteen

Will

"Are you sure you don't want to go to the emergency room, baby? I mean, you don't look good."

"Lynn, I'll be fine, babe. Just whip me up some of that chicken soup you made the last time, and I will be fine. I think I need to lay off the greasy foods, babe, and the pork. I'm not as young as I used to be." I didn't want to argue, I just wanted to lay there in bed until I felt better and her soup and tea usually made me better.

"I know, bae, but I hate seeing you this way. You don't look fine to me, Will, and I would feel better if we just went to urgent care."

"Lynn, you know how I feel about doctors, and all they are going to give me is some more meds. Your soup is the only thing I need to get over this."

"Okay, baby. You stay put, and I'll be back up after I get it going. I'm going to shower really fast first. Do you need anything right now?"

"Naw, baby. Go and shower. I know you'll take care of me."

"Of course." She leaned in and kissed me.

"Lynn, I love you," I said. I had no idea what was going on, and I was afraid to find out. I just didn't want to be sick on my new bride. She deserved a life full of happiness, and if I was getting ill or if something was wrong, I didn't want to know. I didn't want to worry Lynn or burden her with taking care of me.

She smiled brightly at me. Her face was just as beautiful as a sunset, and it always warmed my insides. "I love you too, Will, with all my being," she said softly. "Now rest, baby, while I shower, and I will make you some homemade soup."

"Thank you."

She walked away, and I sobbed. Yes, I was a crying grown-ass man. I had been having too many stomach episodes lately, and my biggest fear was cancer. I had tried to ignore the gut-clenching episodes, and most of them I hadn't even shared with Lynn. I pretended to be fine, and I was terrified about finding out what was really wrong with me. Finding out would be owning up to it, and I was not ready.

Lynn

I stood under our rain shower and cried. I hadn't planned on getting my hair wet, but my husband being ill again scared the shit out of me, and I just couldn't focus on keeping my hair dry. I had no idea what was going on with him, and Will was so damn stubborn, he refused to go to the doctor. I was afraid it was something serious, and I didn't want to lose him. I wanted him to be helped, treated, and to live a long life with me. Why was he so hardheaded?

I had seen the pain in his eyes on occasion, and he pretended he was well, but I knew he wasn't. There had been nights when I cooked up a huge meal, one that I knew he'd beat me to the table to eat, but he'd showered and gone to sleep without dinner.

"Lord, please heal him. Whatever is going on with my husband, please fix it, Lord. Please open up his mind to medicine, so a doctor can help us with whatever he has going on with him, Lord. Please don't take him," I cried and prayed.

I got out of the shower, dried my skin, wrapped a towel around me, put leave-in conditioner in my hair, and moisturized my skin. After throwing on one of Will's oversize Chicago Bears T-shirts, I checked in on him before going

downstairs to make him some soup. I pulled a
chicken breast from the freezer, tossed it into a
pot, added water, put the pot on the stove, and
turned on the fire. I added a pinch of salt
and chicken broth to another pot. When it came
to a boil, I turned down the fire. Then I diced
some veggies, drained the thawed chicken and
diced it. After twenty minutes or so, I added
more broth and then my veggies and covered the
pot with a lid. The aroma was pleasant. While
the soup was cooking, I went up to check on
Will.

He looked like a different man. His hair needed
a cut. He normally did that on a Saturday, but
he was stuck in bed. And he was a little pale.
He didn't look like my Will. I blinked back the
tears as I sat on the edge of the bed. "Lord, God,
please," I prayed quietly, touching his face gently.

About twenty minutes later I got up and went
down and stirred the soup. I tasted it to make
sure the seasoning was perfect and the meat and
the veggies were tender. They were, so I then
added the noodles. The noodles were thin, so
they didn't need to cook long. After replacing
the lid on the pot, I went for a glass and the wine
cooler.

All I could think about was my husband's
health. I didn't want him to be bedridden or sick

or hurt or in discomfort. I drank two glasses
before preparing a serving tray for Will. I poured
him some green tea, grabbed some crackers and
put them on a saucer, and then filled my husband's favorite bowl with the homemade soup. I
was not in the mood to eat, but the aroma of the
soup was so fabulous, I put a little in a bowl to
cool for myself. Then loaded everything on the
serving tray and went up to feed him. Hating
to wake him, I set the tray on the dresser and
kissed him.

"Baby, I got your soup. You wanna sit up for
me?"

He opened his lids. "It's ready?"

"Yes. I am going to feed it to you."

"Aw, bae, I can do it. I'm not disabled," he
protested, sitting up.

"I know, but I want to take care of you, baby,
so please, this will go a lot smoother if you don't
argue."

"Okay," he said.

I smiled at him. "Do you know how much I
love you?" I said. My eyes watered, and I didn't
want to go there. I thought the wine had spurred
my emotions.

"Just as much as I love you," he answered.

"Will, I know you don't do doctors, but, baby,
I'm terrified. I don't want this to be bigger than

what we are guessing it is. I want to know why, all of a sudden, my stallion is sick, so for me, can you please see the doctor? If it's nothing, it's nothing, but if it's something, Will, we need to know."

His eyes shifted to the covers. He was silent.

Then I couldn't help it. A tear fell and then another and then another. "Will," I whispered.

"I'll go," he said, giving in. "For you to have peace of mind, baby, I'll go."

I leaned in and kissed him and then rested my head on his chest. He held me. I loved being in his arms. "I can't lose you, Will."

"I know, baby, but please don't worry. Please. I didn't want to go, because if it is something, our lives are going to convert to this 'Will is sick' life, and I don't want that."

"I know, my love, but whatever is going on could be prevented, so please."

He kissed my head. "Baby, I will."

With that, I lifted my head and kissed my husband, and then I got up and got his tray. I fed him, and within an hour or so, he was back to his normal self.

"It was your soup, baby. I told you I was fine," he said.

"Well, my soup is just plain ole home cooking, not a remedy. I still want you to see someone."

"Baby, I'm fine."

"Will."

"Okay, okay. If I have another episode, I promise."

I didn't agree with waiting for another episode, but I said okay. My husband then danced with me in our family room to show me how much better he was, and then we dressed and went out to dinner and took in a late movie.

That night he was deep inside of me, and he was getting the job done. My core was doing somersaults as he stroked me to multiple orgasms. I was in bliss, and we both decided to take a couple of days off. Not returning to work until Wednesday, we finished out the week without a hiccup or an episode, and I felt that God had answered my prayers, because my husband was just fine.

Since the bakery had been doing so well since the renovations, I decided to scale back my hours and stay home more and care for my man. He hadn't had an episode for a week and a couple of days and I thought it was because I was able to make breakfast for us, take him lunch, and have his dinner ready for him every night I was home. I still employed a housekeeper for deep cleaning and laundry, chores that I simply hated doing, and she came over once a week.

Cooking being my favorite task, I wondered why I was too lazy to get out of bed that morning to fix my husband's breakfast.

"Lynn, baby, you're still in bed."

My head popped up. "Huh? What?"

"You said you were going down to make breakfast when I went to shower, yet I'm dressed, and there are no bacon, eggs, and toast."

"I'm so sorry, Will. I mean, I sat up, but I wanted five more minutes in bed, and I must have dozed off."

"It's okay. I'm meeting with Yvonne this morning to finalize this party mess, and I'm sure she'll have some breakfast with her. She always does."

"Okay, and I'm sorry, baby. I am just super tired."

"Go back to bed." He kissed my forehead. "Get some rest, and I'll see you later." He smiled.

As soon as he was on the other side of the door, I was fast asleep again.

Chapter Nineteen

Lynn

I was awakened by the phone. Not wanting to answer, I let it ring, and then five seconds later it rang out again. I opened one eye and saw that it was a little after 11:00 a.m. I reached for my phone, looked at the screen, and saw it was an unrecognizable number, but I went ahead and answered.

Groggy, and not trying to hide my irritation over being awaken out of my sleep, I said, "Hello."

"Hello. I'm trying to reach Mrs. Daniels."

I let out an annoyed breath. "This is she."

"Mrs. Daniels, this is Dr. Patterson I'm calling from the University of Chicago Medical Center."

I hopped up, and my heart raced. "Yes, yes! How can I help you?"

"Your husband came into the hospital a little while ago with violent stomach pains and cramping. Since he said this is not his first episode, we are going to run a few tests, but I suggest you come down here."

"Sure, sure. I'm on my way."

I dashed into the shower and brushed my teeth. I had no time to fuss with my hair, so I grabbed one of Will's caps. Then I rushed over to the hospital. When I got there, Will was resting in his room. They had already admitted him. I didn't want to wake him, so I went to find his doctor. I caught up with him at the nurses' station, and we discussed Will's condition.

"So, Dr. Patterson, did you figure out what's wrong with him? I mean, these stomach pains and episodes have started to come more frequently," I said.

"Well, it could be a number of things. We are doing the standard tests, but I wanted to know if you wanted to send his samples over to our toxicology lab."

"Why? What does that mean? Why would I have to do that?"

"It's just a precaution. Just in case."

"In case what, Doctor? What are you suggesting?"

"Are you and your husband having any marital problems?"

"No. Not that that is any of your business."

"I didn't mean to offend, Mrs. Daniels. I just want to rule out any possibilities."

"Well, we're fine, and that won't be necessary. You can speak to Will yourself when he's awake."

"I have spoken to him and asked about submitting his samples, and he declined."

"Well, there it is."

He nodded. "Very well. I will be in to discuss his results as soon as I have them."

"You do that," I said and rolled my eyes.

The nerve of him to even suggest or imply that I did something to my husband, I thought. The notion was absurd. I went back in to check on Will. His eyes were slits, but they were open.

"Baby, how are you feeling?" I caressed his face.

"Better. What did the doctor say? You know I hate hospitals, and I'm ready to go home and rest in my own bed."

"I know, baby, but something is going on, and we have to find out what. I mean, you were healthy as a horse up until a couple of months ago, and the episodes are starting to happen more frequently."

"I know. It could be a number of things, Lynn. I work construction, and we go into houses that have mold, asbestos, and all kinds of things. Plus, we work with so many chemicals."

"I know, baby, and I'm worried."

"Hey." He smiled at me. "Don't worry, pretty lady. I'm not checking out just yet. The doctors will figure it out."

"I know," I said with a faint smile. I believed Will and knew he was right, but I was terrified. I sat with my husband a couple more hours, and then finally the doctor came in.

"Well, there was nothing that we could see, but I do recommend a toxicology test, just to rule out everything," Dr. Patterson said.

"We're good on that, Doctor. I told you I have no enemies, and my wife would never do anything to hurt me," Will said.

The look on Dr. Patterson's face showed he was surprised that Will would repeat what he had suggested, which was that I'd tried to hurt him.

"Now, can I and my beautiful wife get out of here?" Will asked.

"Yes, Mr. Daniels. They are processing your paperwork as we speak. Here is a prescription for an antacid. Take Imodium if the diarrhea returns. Take care of yourself, and if you need me for anything, you know you can call me," Dr. Patterson said with a kind smile.

I knew he meant no harm. He was just looking out for his patient.

"Will do, Doc."

After Will dressed and was released, we headed home. He went upstairs, while I made him some soup and a light salad and poured some tea and added some lemon.

After he ate and had a nap, he came down to join me. I was on my hands and knees, scrubbing the kitchen floor. Yes, I was domesticated, but I cleaned deeper when I was stressed, afraid, or worried.

"Baby," I heard him say. "What are you doing?"

"Cleaning the floor."

"I can see that, but why are you on your hands and knees? We have, like, a steam mop and a Swiffer and all that jazz."

"I know, but I'm . . . I'm . . ." I said, trailing off. I tossed the rag into the bucket.

"What is it?"

"I'm worried about you, Will. Maybe we should do that toxicology test. Maybe something at work is making you sick, and we need to figure out what it is."

"Come here." He reached out his hands and help me up from the floor. "I've been doing this all my adult life, Lynn, so don't worry."

My eyes welled up with tears. "I can't just not worry. You're the love of my life and the best thing to have happened to me, and if I were to lose—"

He cut me off. "Shhh! Baby, don't worry. I'm fine, and if I have another episode, I promise I will do it."

"You promise?"

"Yes, baby, I promise," he said and kissed me deeply.

I loved his kisses and his touch. There was a fire constantly burning deep down inside of me for Will, and I was ready for him to take my body again.

We undressed right there in the kitchen. After we were both naked, he hoisted me up onto our kitchen island. My husband was so strong and resilient that he effortlessly lifted my full-figured frame up onto the cool surface. During our lovemaking sessions, he'd flip and toss me as if I were a size three, and every time it was over, I'd be breathless. He'd explore every inch of me, and I loved making love to him. He always took his time to make sure I was pleasured, and I hadn't ever been with any lover like him.

He made me feel sexy, even though my rolls were exposed, my stretch marks were visible, and everything jiggled when he pumped me to ecstasy. I'd sometimes stare at his eight-pack abs, his defined arms and shoulders, and his chiseled chest and wonder how I got so lucky to have someone so sexy, so fine, and so fit when I was plus size. That he looked beyond my physical makeup and saw me for the woman who I was and still labeled me as sexy made him all the more special to me.

Now, on the kitchen island, I purred at the touch of his fingertips caressing my bulb. It was so swollen for him. Climaxing for me was always so smooth with Will, because he had learned how to please me and what made me feel good early on in our relationship. Each time felt better than the last.

"Yes, baby, I like that," I moaned.

He wrapped his strong arms around my thighs and pulled my body closer to his mouth, and before long my bottom half was off the island, meeting his mouth, and I was shaking from the tingling in my core. I had cum, and I felt my walls contract. Though I was out of breath, I was ready for even more. I wanted him. I wanted to make his dick cum just as he had made me.

"Let me taste you, baby. Let me make you cum," I moaned and reached out my hands for him. He pulled me up and helped me off the island. He took me by my hand, and I followed him into our family room. He grabbed the throw on the back of the sofa and then laid it on the cushions before he sat. He grabbed his rod and began to stroke it, and I watched it grow larger in his fist, and my mouth watered.

Eyeing his head and noticing how smooth and shiny it was, I couldn't wait to taste him. I got down on my knees in front of him, and within moments I was bobbing my head up and down while he massaged my scalp. He moaned as I teased the tip and planted wet kisses on his shaft. I was in a zone, and all I wanted him to do was explode inside of my mouth.

"Cum for me," I begged between slurps. "I wanna taste you too," I hissed. I stroked hard and faster, and it shot out onto my face and almost got my eye. "Baby, I wanted to taste it," I pouted.

"I know, but it just erupted," he said.

I laughed. He laughed with me. I got up and went for a paper towel, and I wet it. I cleaned my face and rejoined my husband on the sofa. I pulled the throw over more of the cushions and then rested in his arms. We were quiet. He gently stroked my skin, and I felt safe in his arms.

"You are my everything," he said, breaking the silence.

"You are also my everything."

"I've been thinking about what we talked about with Lance and the money. I have the e-mails from our accountant, and to be honest with you, Lynn, I'm scared to even find out."

"Why, baby? I mean, if he is stealing from the company, he isn't loyal or a friend."

"I know, but who then will I hire? Who will I ever be able to trust without knowing how to read?"

"Me," I said and looked up at him.

"You, baby? But you bake. You have a business of your own to run."

"I can do both." I sat up to look at him. "A person who will steal from you isn't a person you need working for you, Will. I told you I got your back. I will help you. I can teach you the business side. We can do this together."

"How about I just demote him instead and give you his position? You know, I'll still give him his annual salary, but all this investigating him isn't what I want to do, Lynn. That's not how I want to treat my friend. Lance, as crazy as he is, has been there for me, for my folks, and I just don't want to investigate him, Lynn. Once he's demoted, you can make it so he has no access to the important stuff, right? Like, you are so smart, baby. I know you can change passwords and update software and just get things in order, right?"

His eyes glossed over, and I understood that this was a tough decision for my husband to make, but I had his back all the way.

"Yes. We can get a tech to come in and help us install a new program, a new system, and do things our way and keep Lance out of the financial side."

"Good. I mean, he could still be my equal partner, but I don't want him having any books or financial access. After we see how he lives on his salary alone, if he is stealing, we'll have our answer. I mean, it will show its own ugly head, right?"

"Yes. Just know that if he is stealing, he is going to be furious at the idea of me coming on board."

"Well, technically, it is still my company, and his position is not legally documented. It was verbal, so he won't have a choice."

I swallowed hard. I thought the investigation would have been easier. Catching him red-handed would have left no room for animosity, as Lance would have been tossed out of the company. I knew this new approach would cause problems once Lance got the news about it.

After a few moments of silence, my husband lifted my chin and gave me a passionate kiss. We made love and called it a night.

By doctor's orders, Will didn't go into work for two days, but I worked at the bakery, training Mariah to be a full-time manager and showing her the ropes, including how to make deposits, order products, and do the reports. I put her in charge of hiring two new employees. I felt I had made a great decision to help my husband full-time. I was just nervous about meeting with Lance. I knew he'd have an issue with his demotion, and I knew he'd blame me.

For some strange reason, old friends always blamed the new girlfriend, boyfriend, spouse, or lover for changes that their best friend or old friend made, not realizing that their friend had a mind of his or her own. Now, I'd admit that some partners did have an undue influence, but that was mostly when their intentions were ill and selfish, but in this case my intentions were good. I was genuinely looking out for the most important person in my life, and that was Will.

Chapter Twenty

Lynn

"Come again!" Lance said, standing from the chair on the other side of my desk.

"I've decided to bring Lynn aboard to handle our accounting and management. You will now be her assistant and in charge of ordering and budgeting our contracts. You will still do the estimates and keep our budgets on target, so we don't go over, but Lynn will be in charge of payroll, accounts payable and receivable, and expenses."

"Why? I mean, am I not doing a great job? I mean, this company is excelling because of my ability to keep things running like clockwork. And we are partners!" Lance yelled.

"I know, Lance, but Lynn is my wife and now also a partner in this company. It's my company, Lance, and I'm not taking away your title. I'm just rearranging your responsibilities."

Lance's jaw tightened. "What's this about? Huh? Will, I've been loyal to you all these years, and now your little wife controls our company?" Veins were popping out everywhere on Lance, and I knew he was furious about the news.

"Now hold on, Lance. I didn't fire you, nor did I remove you as a partner. That hasn't changed. I just want to restructure some things, man. It's nothing personal. Yes, I know you think my wife had something to do with the change, but she didn't. I asked her to come on board because I want her here. Since she is now my wife, she has to learn this business too. This is my company, and after the legal papers are complete, it will be hers as well. All I am doing is shifting responsibilities. I'm not cutting your pay, and you will still have a partnership in this. But since it's my company to begin with, I and my family will always come first."

Lance stood. "I get it, boss," he said with anger and then vacated the room.

"That didn't go too well," I said. I sat on the sofa near the window and tried my best to not say a word. I wanted to jump in with my two cents, but I was happy I allowed Will to handle it.

"I know, but it's better than a full-blown investigation, with me possibly finding out the worst and not only firing him but also sending him to prison," Will said. "You don't have the slightest idea of what prison is like, Lynn. He'll get over this. He'll be okay."

I stood and walked into my husband's arms. "Are you sure?"

"I'm sure."

I smiled. "Well, can you show me to my new office?"

"Yes. Follow me." We walked down the hall to an office that had Will's name on the nameplate.

"But, baby, this is your office," I said.

"An office I've used only maybe five times since I started. My office is always in the trailer at a job site, so now this is your office. There is nothing in the drawers. If so, I haven't used it in years, so you can trash it. And I need you to call in a tech from the software company we use to help you with the important things, because I know Lance isn't going to be happy to train you. I'm sure a tech can tell you what is what. There should be a roster in that pile right there on the desk with every number you need. I have to get to the site. Can you manage everything from here? I mean, if you need help, Sarah, my assistant, is out front. She can help you out. She's worked here longer than me and Lance."

"I think I can handle things, but I'm going to need the company card, because I needs some plants, an iPod dock, a splash of color. I mean, you've seen my office at the bakery."

"Yes," he said, digging into his back pocket to retrieve his wallet. "Listen, if you see the paint you like, don't get it. We have a corporate account for paint. Just get the swatch, and my guys will have the paint done in no time for you." He handed me the card.

I kissed him. "Thank you, baby, and you're making the right decision. You have a heart, and with that you allowed him to stay without even checking up on him, so if he's on some BS, he will eventually be grateful."

"I hope so," he said and pulled me close.

"I love you."

"I love you too."

Chapter Twenty-one

Yvonne

"We have to do it now!" Lance yelled into the phone.

I was at the salon, getting my weekly regimen, and I didn't want to hear any more plots about poisoning Will and sending Lynn to jail. I had never had a set of honest friends in my life; most were backbiting bitches or disrespectful men who didn't care that my friend was their girlfriend or spouse. Lynn was kind to me, and Will had never treated me like a whore. He had always had respect for me and had never crossed any lines.

"Calm down, Lance, and stop yelling in my ear. I'm at the salon, and folks can hear you," I warned.

He lowered his voice. "We have to do something now, like, right now. He gave Lynn my position."

I was shocked. "He fired you? Lance, he has to know what's been going on. To fire you out of the blue—"

"He didn't fire me. I still have my position."

"Then I'm confused."

"He gave the accounting and the books to Lynn."

"What? Why would he do that? I told you that you were too flashy, Lance. He has to know," I said, hurrying outside to have some privacy. I had a hair full of rollers, but I didn't care.

"I don't think he's onto me, Yvonne, because not only would Will have fired me, but he also would have stepped to me with fists. We grew up together. Will would take our issue to the streets."

"Okay. Then why do you think he did it?"

"He went on and on about family and how, now that they're married, Lynn's part owner of the company. Since he is legally the primary owner, he is processing paperwork to add her name to the company, something we've never legally gotten around to. But I know if he was dead and she went to prison, everything would come to me. They have no children."

"So what's our next move?"

"The poison. You have to arrange another cooking lesson with Lynn. Offer to take Will his plate, and hit him with a dose. I mean, a deadly dose, Yvonne. If they get into my records and dig, they are going to find something, and I can't let that happen."

"Lance, I really don't want to do this. Please don't make me do this."

"We have no other choice. If they find out about all the thousands of dollars I took, Yvonne, I will go to jail, and the lifestyle you're living will be gone. We can't live like we want to live unless they are out of the picture. This construction business is a gold mine. So many are renovating and upgrading their homes, we are making money hand over fist, and I want it all!"

I said nothing. I wanted it all too, but the idea of killing Will haunted me. Taking a life for money had sounded good in the beginning, but now that it was actually going to happen, I was terrified.

"Yvonne, you want this, don't you?"

I tried to speak. "I do, but . . . I . . ."

"No buts, Yvonne. You can't back out now. There is no turning back."

I hesitated. "Okay. I'll call Lynn."

"That's my girl. I'm going to head back to the office and try to cover my tracks. See if I can put my transactions on my pen drive so I can cover my ass."

"Yes, you do that."

"Yvonne?"

I was quiet.

"Yvonne. You can do this, baby. We are going to live well once this is over. I love you."

"I love you too." I hung up.

I slowly dialed Lynn's number.

"Yvonne, hi," she sang.

"Hey, Lynn. How are you?"

"Good. Just picking out some accessories for my new office."

"Yes. Congrats. Lance told me."

"I bet, and I'm sorry. I know he was angry."

"Yes, he was, but I talked to him. He's okay."

"I hope. . . . I know he and Will have been friends since forever, so I know he thinks that my coming on board was my idea, but it was Will's."

"I already explained to him that that is how business goes. I told him that Will has every right to put his wife wherever he chooses, and after we talked, he understood. That brings me to the reason I'm calling. I mean, I want to cheer him up and make the air clear between us, so I was hoping we could come over one night this week. You and I can cook up something good, and we can all have a few drinks and talk about it, to let Lance know that he's still a part of the business and that he still has a future there, even though you and Will have decided to make changes."

"That would be a great idea, because we don't want things to get awkward. I mean, we are sorta like family," Lynn said.

I agreed. "We are, so let's cook our men up a feast and drink and have a good time," I added.

"Friday night will be good for me."

"Awesome," I said and then tried to get an update on work. "So how is your first day?"

"Well, just made a few phone calls. I have to have a tech come in and teach me the software, because I know Lance is a little sore about it, but the tech won't be in until Friday, so I'm just out shopping for office stuff, you know, to give my office that cozy feminine touch. It's so stark and cold."

"Well, I'm just about done at the salon. How about I meet you? I mean, I can't cook, but I have a good eye for decorating."

"Sure. I'm headed to IKEA. Just give me a buzz when you're done."

"Will do."

I hung up and went back inside the salon and was so grateful it was time to sit in the chair and finish up. Afterward, I called Lance when I got in the car and told him that it would be a couple of days before the tech showed, but he informed me that his passwords had been locked and he couldn't unlock them until Friday, and so he urged me to move the dinner up to Thursday. I said I'd try, but I didn't want to make Lynn suspicious.

Half an hour later I met up with Lynn at IKEA. After a day of shopping and taking some of the things to the office, I said, "Oh, shoot. Lynn. I forgot, Friday is our girls' night out, and I'm the host this month. Is it possible to move our dinner up? Thursday would work better."

"Of course. No problem. I mean, I didn't want to drink and stay up late on a work night, but Thursday will be fine," she agreed.

"Thursday it is, then" I said and clinked my glass against hers.

I had insisted that a mini fridge and wine cooler were musts for her office, and it had taken no convincing for her to agree, so we had grabbed a few bottles before heading back to her office and unloading the stuff. We had cracked open a bottle and had poured two glasses before we began placing the trinkets and plants around the office, all the while listening to Pandora on the wireless speaker I had talked her into getting.

"You know, iPod docks are history," I had said and laughed when we were in the store. "More sound comes out of these babies right here." I'd pointed to the wireless speaker. "Connect with Bluetooth, and jam to your playlist, Spotify, or Pandora all day long."

She had agreed and had added the wireless speaker to her cart.

We drank the wine, laughed, and decorated, and by the time we called it quits, all the room needed was a coat of paint.

"All this work and we are going to have to move everything for the painters," Lynn said.

"Oh, no, baby. They use airbrushes nowadays. I've seen it done on the sites. They will move everything to the center of the room, cover it all, spray, and within hours your office will be right back to normal."

"Really?"

"Yes, really."

She smirked. "Sounds good to me."

We said our good-byes.

I headed home, and as soon as I walked through the door, Lance went into full "Kill Will" mode.

Fuck! Fuck! Fuck! How was I going to get out of this?

Chapter Twenty-two

Yvonne

"Dinner was delicious," Will said. His plate was clean.

"Well, we must applaud Yvonne, because all I did was supervise," Lynn said.

"Baby, you did this?" Lance asked.

"Yes. I followed the recipe that Lynn wrote out for me, and she just watched and only helped a little." I was proud. I had cooked a roast, homemade mac and cheese, cabbage, sweet potatoes, and homemade corn bread.

"Baby, you did well. Can you refill our glasses?" Lance asked.

I stood and took his and Will's glass. My smile faded, because I didn't want to give Will another dose, but Lance made me. I went into the kitchen trembling, looking over my shoulder every second, hoping no one would walk in on me. I made them both another vodka, cran, and orange juice and added a pinch of the powder to Will's drink. This was round two, and I was so nervous, my hands shook when I picked up the glasses to return back to the living room.

"Are you okay?" Lynn's voice frightened me. I was so glad that I had slipped the vile back into my front pocket before she entered.

"I'm fine." I turned to her, swirling both glasses in my hands, as if I was trying to mix the contents.

"Are you sure? You seem uneasy. I mean, dinner was great, so you can relax now."

I let out a sigh, like that was really the problem. "Thank God. I was so nervous, Lynn. I mean, this cooking thing is hard."

"I know, but once you grow to love it, it will come so easy."

"I hope so. And I noticed you didn't drink with me tonight. I mean, I've been killing the Riesling alone."

She smiled. "Let's take the guys their drinks, and I'll tell you why," she said.

I followed behind her. I was sure to give the drink in my right hand to Will and the one in my left hand to Lance. I sat, but Lynn remained standing.

"Okay, guys. I have an announcement," she said.

All eyes landed on her.

"I have news," she went on.

"You're not coming on board as a partner and taking my position," Lance joked.

I swatted his arm, but we all laughed.

"No. I am going to be a part of my husband's company, and I'm also going to be my husband's baby's mother."

The room went silent.

Will looked at her. "Say it again," he said.

"I'm going to be your child's mother, Will. We are pregnant," she said.

He leaped from his chair and embraced her so tightly. My eyes welled up as I watched them hold each other, exchange love and emotions. I then looked at Will's drink and wanted to tell him what I had done, but the look I got from Lance said, "You better not say a word." I stood and ran over to hug the couple. I was excited for Lynn. She had the life I wanted. A moment ago money and things were all that mattered to me, but I instantly wanted what she and Will had.

"This is cause for champagne, not vodka," I said and snatched up Will's glass and went over to Lance's. I could read his body language and facial expression. He did not want me to abort the plan. "I know you have champagne in this house!" I yelled, heading toward the kitchen.

Will and Lynn continued to embrace, but Lance stormed into the kitchen as I poured their drinks down the drain.

"What in the hell are you doing?" he whispered angrily.

"Not tonight," I whispered back. "She's pregnant, Lance. Pregnant. I can't do this to them. It's not right. We live comfortably. I'm not feeling it anymore. I can't do it."

"You better," he was about to say, but just then Will walked in.

"Check the liquor cabinet for champagne, Yvonne," Will said. He went to a cabinet and took out four champagne glasses, and before I could get the champagne, Lynn walked into the kitchen.

"Baby, no, I can't drink," she told him.

"We are celebrating. One glass, one toast will not hurt our baby, I promise you." He kissed her softly. I gazed at them, and then my eyes landed on an infuriated Lance, so I turned and went for the champagne.

"Put the bottle in the wine cooler. In fifteen minutes we will toast. For now I just want to dance with my wife," Will said and then pulled Lynn into the family room.

I stood there awkwardly and avoided eye contact with my lover. There was no denying he was pissed.

Will turned on the music, and Jill Scott and Anthony Hamilton's "So in Love" blared from the speakers. Will and Lynn danced, with bright smiles, and I grabbed Lance's hand.

He was resistant, and then I whispered, "If you act this way, they are going to know something's up."

He nodded, smiled, and we went to dance with the happy soon-to-be parents. After three or maybe four fun up-tempo jams, we moved back into the kitchen, where we popped the cork on the champagne bottle and had a toast to celebrate Will and Lynn's baby news.

Chapter Twenty-three

Lynn

"Are you sure you're ready to hear this?" I asked Will. The tech had come and gone, but not before giving me the information that I needed to pass on to Will, which was, to my surprise, clean.

"Yes, I'm ready."

We sat at my new office desk, and I opened the computer file with first couple of years of company earnings and reports. They looked normal, and nothing raised a brow. However, by 2011, things looked a bit different. I assumed this because Will was no longer nodding and saying okay to the things I read to him.

"Wait. Stop there. Go back. Explain this right here again to me please," he said.

I scrolled up. "Where?"

"Right there." He pointed. Nothing seemed strange to me, so I waited for him to say something, but he simply took over the mouse.

"Son of a bitch," he said.

"What is it, Will?"

I had combed through the files, and everything had looked in order to me. I didn't have any suspicions at all. The numbers had seemed to be right, so my theory of Lance stealing was just that, a theory.

"Do you see these four names here?"

"Yes." I nodded.

"They left the company a couple of years ago."

"Left? You mean they are still getting a check, when they no longer work for you?"

"Exactly."

We took a closer look.

"Well, it shows they all made at least forty-eight thousand dollars last year and close to that the year before. That times four is close to two hundred grand last year alone, Will."

"Let me see the year before again, and explain it to me one more time, baby, so I can be clear," he said.

When we reviewed it again, Will identified those four names again, plus the names of three others who had stopped working for the company a year ago. My heart stopped. That meant my suspicions had been right. Lance was stealing.

"So he's paying men who no longer work here? This makes no sense," I said.

"Unless he's cashing their checks."

"Hold on," I said, opening up a new tab. I typed in the payroll-processing program and signed in. I went to the profiles of each of the employees we were examining and saw that a direct deposit had been set up for four of them, but the account was the same for all four, and the other three from the year prior all shared a different account. "So this is how he does it. I bet you any amount of money that these account numbers belong to Lance," I said.

"How can we find out?"

"I don't know, but this is enough to confront him."

"No, baby, it isn't. This could be something that HR did, so we have to have proof that Lance is taking this money and not someone else. He is stealing thousands from my company, and I don't know how I missed this for so long," he said.

I knew Will loved Lance like a brother, and I truly didn't want him to be the culprit.

"Listen, baby, don't blame yourself, okay? We just have to get to the bottom of this and quickly, without alerting him."

"This sorry son of a bitch. Does he know how much trouble he may have caused for these men? I'm sure they don't know that their names are still in the system. The IRS could be after them right now."

"Damn. You're right," I said. "Let's just call the police, Will. I'm sure they can figure out the details," I suggested.

Will's eyes watered, and he rubbed his head.

"Baby, it's going to be okay. He won't get away with this."

"I know, Lynn, but I just feel so stupid. I mean, I trusted Lance, and he'd do this me? To my company? This motherfucker is laughing it up at my expense, and I'm so fucking mad right now, I want to go and beat the shit out of him."

"Baby, calm down. That is not the answer. We just have to go to the police. Tell them what we found and let them handle it. We are having our first baby, Will, and we can't handle things on our own. Let the legal system handle Lance. If you go off on a crazy rampage, that won't help. You are going to have to relax and let the police handle this."

"I'd rather whip his ass, and then we go to the police."

"And I'll be visiting you in a cell right next to his. We've figured it out, so let's just do it the right way. For our baby's sake."

He nodded. "Okay. In the morning I will handle it. Right now I need a drink to digest this all.

Because I'm so mad and angry, I could beat him senseless. If he walked through that door, I can't promise you that I'd keep my cool."

By then he was pacing the floor. I got up and stood in front of him.

"Will, it's going to be okay. I know it hurts, and I know you feel used and cheated, but it will be okay." I pulled him close and gave him a couple of soft, wet kisses to soothe him. "I'll take you home and take care of you, baby. We will tackle this Lance issue tomorrow, okay? I love you, and I can't lose you over some man rage, so calm down for me and the baby. We will get him, love. I promise. Evildoers don't reign forever."

"I know, but it's like they win and we suffer."

In my heart I knew my husband's words were true, but I didn't want to agree with that. I just caressed his face and then hugged his neck tighter. There was a possibility we'd get some of the money back, if Lance still had some left in those accounts, and whatever his property was worth, we'd sue for that too. The last thing that popped into my head before we left the office was Yvonne. I was sure she had played a part, and I was going to find out what it was.

Chapter Twenty-four

Will

The next morning I got up and headed into the bathroom to shower. Lynn wanted to go to the police department with me, but I had convinced her to stay at home. She had given me a hard time, but I had told her I wanted to handle it on my own. When I got in my car, I had so many thoughts going through my mind, and all I wanted to do was beat the shit out of Lance, so instead of going to the police, I headed to his house.

I sat in his driveway and wondered whether it was a good idea to confront him before going to the authorities and without proof that he was the perpetrator, but I just had to see him face-to-face. To see his expression when I told him about my suspicions. I wanted to see if he got nervous. Would he admit what he had done or what? I just wanted to know, so I got out of the car and went up to the door. I rubbed my palms together, took a deep breath, and then rang the bell.

Moments later Yvonne was standing before me.

"Will, did we have a meeting scheduled that I forgot about?"

"No. I'm here to see Lance."

"Well, he's not here. He's out on his morning run."

"Is it all right if I wait?"

"Sure. Come on in. He should be back soon."

"Thanks." I entered the house and followed her into the family room.

"Have a seat. Can I get you anything?"

"Nah. I'm good."

"You sure? I made some mimosas this morning, and my mimosas are kick ass."

"No. I'm good for now."

She headed into the kitchen and came back with a glass. She sat, and we talked small talk about me being a father and plenty about Lance's party. The party I no longer wanted to fund. He had stolen thousands, so I didn't owe him shit.

I was just about to take Yvonne up on her mimosa offer when Lance walked in.

"Will, man, what's up? I thought that was your car outside. To what do I owe this honor before ten a.m.?"

"I just need to discuss a little business."

"On a Saturday?"

"Yes. Is now not a good time?"

"It is, but please spare me ten minutes to shower."

"Go ahead," I told him. I could smell the workout on him.

"All right. I'll be back down in a few minutes."

"Take your time."

I had all the time he needed, because I wanted to get to the bottom of this.

"Yvonne," he called out.

"Yes?" she said when she reentered the room from the kitchen.

"Come up and grab me something to change into."

"What's wrong with yo' hands?" she asked with attitude.

"Yvonne, damn. Why can't you do one thing that I ask you?" he griped.

"Fine, Negro. This is why I can't be a housewife. Too many responsibilities."

"You don't say that when your ass wanna shop," Lance retorted. I heard him arguing as they both proceeded up the stairs.

I tried to relax and keep my cool, but I was all over the place. My mind was racing. Thoughts were spinning in my head, and I then wished I had taken Yvonne up on that drink offer. After a couple of drinks, I would have been more relaxed.

I got up, went over to the liquor counter, and poured myself a shot of tequila. After hitting two more shots, I shook off my nerves and told myself that I was ready to hear the truth.

Yvonne

"He knows," I whispered in the bathroom.

"No. He has no idea."

"I know he knows," I continued. I was scared to death that Will had come to say that he knew that Lance and I had been trying to kill him.

"Yvonne, calm down, baby. Calm down. If he thought for one second that we were trying to kill him, he wouldn't be calm and sitting on the sofa. He would have flipped this house upside down by now."

"Then why is he here? Will has never just shown up without calling or on a Saturday morning."

He removed his clothes, calm and cool, and I was about to pass out.

"Baby, stop, okay? I know Will. He's not this calm over shit, so if it was something bad, the mood would be hostile. So relax. He's probably here to tell me he made a mistake bringing Lynn on board. Couples can't work together. He's probably here to try to get me to help him get rid of her, without her suspecting he wanted her gone."

"You think that's all it is?"

He turned on the water in the shower. "Trust me, I know my friend. I've known him for a long time. If he had something ill on his mind, he would not be that pleasant right now."

"So I shouldn't worry?"

He tested the water and then stepped into the shower. "No. As a matter of fact, go down and make us a couple of drinks, and you know what to do."

"No, Lance, not now, not in our house. If I give him a dose and he has any pains, aches, or anything, he will know."

"No he won't. Baby, we are so close to having it all, and I'm tired of waiting, so please just do what I tell me and trust me."

I stood there and just stared at him. I had a mind to go down and tell Will what Lance was making me do. I was so scared, and Lance was so at ease, and that scared me too. I then wondered whether he would eventually do me the same way. I mean, after we got married and I became entitled to half of his assets, he might take me out.

"Lance, baby, I don't know about this."

He looked at me. "I knew you'd bitch up. I knew you wasn't down for me."

"I am, Lance, but I'm just terrified. Giving him the poison in our house puts us at risk, so I say no, Lance. It's not wise."

"Fine. Just go downstairs, you crazy bitch. I knew I should have done this alone."

My eyes bulged. "Lance, how can you talk to me that way? I've always done everything you've told me, but you're not using your head, Lance."

"You think you're smarter than me?" he said in anger. "You acting all scared and shit, but you're not scared when you're spending my money. Yeah, yeah. When your ass wanna go on shopping sprees and shit, you are okay with everything I say," he roared, and I hoped Will couldn't hear us. Our house was huge, and I was sure he couldn't hear our conversation, but I was so scared he would, I just gave in and told Lance I'd go down and do what he said.

"Thought so. Tell Will I'll be down in ten."

Chapter Twenty-five

Will

I took the glass that Lance was handing me, even though I had already had a couple of shots of tequila. I'd never been a soft man, or a raging bull, either, but I'd been raised to handle my business and to take care of those who crossed me, even if I had to handle them with my fists.

He took a sip of his drink and then asked, "So what business is so important that you had to come by on a Saturday?"

I took a drink, let out a breath, and didn't hint at the issue or beat around the bush. I got right to it. "Have you been stealing from me?" My face was serious. There was not a hint of sarcasm or comedy in my voice, so when he laughed, I took offense.

"Stealing? What, me?" He chuckled. "Really? You come to my house and ask me that?"

"Yes, and I want the truth."

"No. That is crazy. Why would I steal from the company? I make good money. I have no reason to steal. Where would you get an idea like that?" He paused. "So now that your wife is filling my shoes, I'm a thief?"

"Don't, Lance. Don't. This has absolutely nothing to do with Lynn. This is about you and me and the thousands of dollars that are going out to employees who no longer work at our fucking company."

"Well, it's an oversight by HR. I didn't know we had employees on the payroll who were no longer working for us." His expression was sincere, yet I didn't believe him.

"So you do the books and you didn't notice that we had checks going out to men who left the company over a year ago?"

"Will, I work in the office, not at the site. How would I or how could I keep track of who's swinging a hammer? I don't know the crew like you do. I couldn't name or even call out the men who you have on-site. It's up to HR to delete them and update the system when they are no longer employed by the company. You know I'm not that stupid."

"I know you're not stupid, Lance. You are smart, and when you have complete access to our money and determine how it is spent, I find it hard to believe that this is an HR oversight."

He stood over me. "I'm not stealing."

I gulp down the rest of my drink and stood to meet his level. "You're not stealing?" I asked again.

"No!" he said in my face.

"Well, if I'm wrong, I apologize. I will get with HR on the matter."

"Yeah, you do that," he said, with his jaw clenched.

I headed for the door and then turned to face him. "I hope, for your sake, that you're telling me the truth. This is not over, and if I find out otherwise, I will handle you."

"Get out of my house."

"Gladly."

I left and went to my car. I climbed in and drove out of his circular driveway, but before I could make it to the police station, I had to pull into a gas station. My stomach pains had come back strong, and I was starting to think I had an ulcer and the stress was trying to kill me.

I went into the bathroom and tried to vomit, to no avail, and then I had to do personal business in a public restroom. Sweat poured from my face, and the pain was so sharp and violent, I had to call Lynn. This time the doctor could run any test at all, because the pain was unbearable.

"Baby, are you okay? Where are you? What happened?" Lynn said.

"I need you to come and get me," I cried through my grunting. I was in so much pain, I could barely speak. After telling her my location, I hung up and moaned like a woman in labor. It was so painful, I could hardly position myself to wipe my own ass. Whatever was going on with me, I wanted it cured.

I managed to make it back to my car, but I slumped over. Finally, I saw my wife pull up, and she had to help me into her SUV.

By the time we made it to the hospital, the pain was so excruciating, I couldn't walk. They had to wheel me in on a gurney. The doctors asked questions that neither I nor Lynn could answer, because I was in too much pain to talk, and all she knew was that I had called her for help.

After they tried to do a simple exam and were unsuccessful, they gave me something to put me to sleep and out of my misery.

Chapter Twenty-six

I stood over my husband, praying that he would recover. Whatever was happening to him was serious, and the doctors seemed to be dragging their damn feet when it came to answers. Even though I had given in and had allowed them to do the toxicology report, it would be weeks before we got answers.

I rubbed his face and held his hand and wanted him to open his eyes, and I also wanted him to rest. I wanted answers. I wanted to know what had happened between the time he left that morning to go to the authorities and his sudden onset of stomach pains. I needed to know what he had taken or had consumed, but he was in too much pain to tell me anything when I tried to talk to him.

"Mrs. Daniels?" the doctor said, snapping me out of my daze.

I turned to him. "Yes?"

"You should go home and get some rest. This medication we are giving your husband may have him out for a while."

"I just need some answers please. What could this be?" I pleaded.

"It could be a number of things, and without those test results, I can't give you a solid answer."

I nodded and then took a seat. "I'll stay a little longer with him. I want to be here if he wakes."

"Very well. As soon as I know something, so will you."

"Thank you."

I sat there and tried not to cry, but my hormones had me sobbing at commercials, so my husband lying sick in that bed made me cry puddles of tears. The tubes and the IV made my husband look as if he was dying.

Soon after I calmed myself down and stood to leave. I stepped close to Will.

"Will, I love you, and whatever it is that keeps making you sick, I am praying to God to heal you. You are the best man I've ever had in my life, so you have to get better for me and your baby. I can't imagine a life with you not in it with me, so please, baby, fight. We can change your diet. Anything you need, I will do," I said.

I was about to make my exit when Will's phone rang. It was Lance, so I answered. I hadn't called him, since we had our suspicions about him taking company funds, but he did need to know that Will was sick.

"Hello?"

"Lynn?" he said, surprised. I knew he would be.

"Yes."

"Where is Will? We need to talk."

"Will is back in the hospital, Lance, and the doctors don't know what's wrong with him."

"What? Why didn't you call me?" His voice indicated he was now in a panic.

"I wasn't thinking. I wasn't thinking. I'm so afraid this time. I've never seen him this bad. The last episodes were bad, but this one is . . ." I paused. "I don't know."

"Where are you?"

"At the University of Chicago."

"I'm on my way."

"No, Lance. He's sedated, and visiting hours will soon be over, I'm leaving now."

"Well, Yvonne and I can meet you at the house. You shouldn't be alone."

I didn't want to see Lance's face, and if he was guilty, I knew Yvonne knew, so I didn't want to see hers, either. "No. I'm going to Kenya's for the night. But I will be in touch." I hung up. I kissed my husband and headed to Kenya's.

Before I made it to my car, my phone was ringing. It was Yvonne, so I hit ignore. I called Kenya to alert her about what was going on and then asked about coming over. She welcomed me, and as soon as I walked into her arms, I began to cry again.

"Shhh. It's going to be all right. Your husband is strong, and he is going to recover from whatever it is he's been sick with. Don't worry, Lynn."

"I can't help but worry. Finally, God has given me the man of my dreams, someone who loves me with everything, only to take him away."

"He's not dying, darling."

"I don't know, Kenya. You didn't see him. My husband could barely walk. He was in so much pain, Kenya, and I couldn't do anything to help him. I felt so helpless and scared."

She walked me into the living room, and we sat.

"I know how you must feel, but I promise you, he is going to recover. You have to talk to him. Ask him what he ate. Where did he go?"

"I tried, but he was just in agonizing pain, and he couldn't answer. I'm sure he went to Lance's place. I mean, he was supposed to go to the police, but I—"

"Police?" she said, cutting me off. "The police? What's going on, Lynn?"

"For a few months Will and I had been suspicious of Lance. We believe he's been stealing from the company, and we may have found proof. Long story short, I work for Will now, and after accessing some accounting records, we found that there are employees still on the payroll who haven't work there in a while, and their pay is being direct deposited into the same account."

"What? That is crazy. How much money are we talking here?"

"Thousands, Kenya. Like these men grossed over forty thousand a year."

"Get the hell out of here. Are you serious?"

"Dead serious."

"Wait a minute. If he went to Lance's to confront him and then was rushed to the hospital, maybe Lance gave him something. I mean, he confronts him about stealing, and then he gets deathly ill. That don't add up."

The more Kenya spoke, the more it made sense, and my hands started shaking. My mind began to race. I had to go to the cops myself.

"Oh, my God, Kenya. I hope you're wrong, because I can't imagine Lance doing something to hurt Will physically. I mean, they've been friends since they were teens."

"That didn't stop Lance from thieving money from him. You said thousands, Lynn, and that's motive. He'd go to prison for sure."

"Stealing is one thing, but murder?"

"When people are desperate, Lynn, they'll do just about anything."

"Well, I have to go to the police with what we have. I need to get to Will's car. There is a file with proof of Lance embezzling money. Can you take me? We left it parked at the service station."

"Sure. Let's go."

We headed out, and as soon as we got in Kenya's car, I got a call from the hospital. The look on my face said it all, because what the doctor had said to me almost stopped my heart.

"What's wrong?" Kenya asked.

I took a few deep breaths and let out a sigh. The tears started to fill up my eyes, and it was like I couldn't open my mouth to say it. Finally, I managed to say, "We need to get to the hospital. Will has slipped into a coma."

"Oh, my God," Kenya said, also stunned by the news. "I'm so sorry." She reached over and squeezed my hand.

"If I lose him . . . I can't lose him," I cried.

She turned to me. "You won't. Let's just get there and let the doctor tell us what's going on."

"Just hurry. And I need to get to Will's car first. I have to get that folder."

"Okay."

Chapter Twenty-seven

We got to the hospital, and after the doctor updated me about my husband's condition, I didn't have to call the police, because they were waiting in the hall to speak with me. I guessed Will's doctor had called them.

"Mrs. Daniels, can we talk?" one of the officers asked.

"Sure," I said and then followed them to the lobby.

"Can you tell us what happened to your husband today?" the same officer asked. "The doctor is not sure yet, but he says that your husband has been treated before for the exact same symptoms, and these symptoms can be related to someone slowly being poisoned."

"Well, I didn't poison my husband. I love him, and I can't imagine my life without him. However, I know someone who might have."

"Go on."

I handed him the folder. "My husband and I found some evidence that Lance Morgan may have been stealing from my husband's company. Now, we can't say for sure. . . . My husband left the house this morning to go to the police department with this evidence, but as angry as he was, I believe he went instead to Lance's home to confront him. I later got a call from my husband saying he was in too much pain to drive, so I met him and brought him here. I tried talking to him about what happened, but he was in so much pain, he didn't tell me anything."

"What does this mean?" the officer asked, looking at the reports in the folder.

"These names that are circled are people who haven't worked for my husband's company in over a year, yet they are still getting a check every two weeks. Checks for these four are going into the exact same bank account, and these three share the same account number too. Unless all these workers are close family members or lovers, I doubt if they'd share the exact same account. Lance Morgan is the one who handled all the finances at the company and he has to be the one responsible for diverting all of these funds into these two accounts. I bet my life that these accounts belong to Lance."

"I see. So you think this Lance guy has made an attempt on your husband's life?"

"It's possible. I don't know what's going on. I am pregnant with our first child. My husband is my everything, and I'd never hurt him in any way. Will and I are so close, and if he was awake, he'd tell you the same thing. If Lance has tried to kill my husband, I want him to rot in prison." By then I couldn't hold back my tears.

"We can investigate this and let you know if this is enough to bring charges on him, but the easiest way is just to get a confession. That will make this process so much easier. However if any of this pans out, we can get the judge to order us to take the suspect into custody and the prosecutor will review the report and decide if the government can proceed with the case."

"Yes, but I really need to check on my husband before I go."

"Understandable." He handed me a card. "This is my information. Just ask for me when you get to the station, and we will help you get to the bottom of this."

"Thank you, sir."

"Does Lance Morgan know that your husband is here?"

"He does."

"Well, it may be wise to have a uniformed officer here."

"Do you think that is necessary? I mean, I don't want him to know that we are onto him or even suspect him. He still has access to the company's funds. I don't want him to leave town or the country."

"Well, we have an idea."

"Okay."

"Go and check on your husband and meet us at the station."

"Okay."

I did what I was instructed to do, and then Kenya took me to the police station. They asked her to leave, and then three officers took me into a little room and gave me instructions on what to do about Lance. I listened carefully and thought the plan was good. I hoped it would work.

"Are you sure you can do this?" one of the officers asked.

"Yes. I'm sure."

"This is just to buy a little time. Monday morning we can verify the accounts easily and then arrest him. But as for attempted murder, without proof, we won't be able to do anything until we investigate. Talk to your husband or get something that implicates Lance."

"I understand." I dialed Lance's number on my cell phone.

"Hello."

"Oh, thank God, Lance! I need you to come down to the police station. I've been arrested."

"Arrested?"

"Yes. They think I've been poisoning Will. Please, come down here."

"Oh, my God, that is crazy. I'm on my way."

We hung up. Thirty minutes later he was there. They brought him into the same interrogation room they took me in before.

"Thank you for coming, Lance. I don't know what's going on," I told him.

"What happened? Start from the beginning," he said and took a seat across from me like he was truly concerned.

"Well, today Will said he had to go out and handle some business. I thought it was work. Later he called, yelling in pain, and I went to pick him up and get him to the hospital. They stabilized him, and then, after I spoke to you, I went to Kenya's. Then I get a call saying that he had slipped into a coma, and I rushed back to the hospital. When I got there, there were two cops there, and they arrested me.

"The doctor had called the police because he did a toxicology report on Will weeks ago, when he was sick before, and it came back with traces of some type of poison, something I can't even pronounce. Lance, they think I've been poisoning him. The doctor said my husband may not pull through, and now they are blaming me." By now my face was drenched with tears. Listening to my own words had torn my heart apart. My husband not making it would kill me too.

"Relax, Lynn. It's okay. I will call our lawyer. Don't answer any more questions." He hugged me to comfort me, and I wanted him to take his thieving, murdering, lying hands off of me, but I had to pretend no one suspected him.

"I have my lawyer already. I called her before calling you. She should be here any minute."

Just then the female officer who was in on our plan walked in. She had changed into plain clothing. She introduced herself and asked Lance to leave the room so she and I could talk.

He agreed and stood. "Don't worry, Lynn. I know you're innocent. I know how much you love Will, and we are not going to let them do this to you. We are going to get to the bottom of this."

"Thanks, Lance. Please keep your phone on," I said.

"I will. You know I will." He pretended like he actually cared.

Lying bastard.

He addressed my "lawyer." "Um, miss? Do you know when she will be able to go home?"

"Hopefully tomorrow. Since she is pregnant, I will call in a favor. I'm sure we can go before the judge and enter a plea in the a.m., and she can go home on bail most likely. Will you be able to bail her out?"

"Yes. No doubt Will is like a brother to me, and he'd kill me if I didn't help his wife."

"Thanks, Lance," I said.

"You're welcome. Stay strong. This will be over soon."

He left, and then I let out a deep breath. "Do you think he bought it?"

"I hope so."

The other two officers walked in.

"What's next?" I asked.

"You go to a friend's or family member's house," one of the officers explained. "Be back here bright and early. We fake your bail, and then Monday morning we check out the bank account numbers. If his name is on those bank accounts, we have the evidence to arrest him for grand theft."

"And poisoning my husband?"

"Well, that case is not going to happen overnight," the same officer said. "We have to get the actual toxicology reports, get evidence that it was him, and that may take a while. Let's just pray that your husband wakes up soon and tells us what happened to him."

"God knows I hope he wakes up soon," I uttered.

The police took me to Kenya's house. After taking a bath, I just lay in bed and prayed and cried.

Chapter Twenty-eight

Lance

I popped open the bottle of champagne and filled our glasses. I had rushed home to celebrate with Yvonne. Earlier, after Will had left the house, I had gone to that bank, moved all my money, and closed those dummy accounts. I had been making plans to leave town, because I had believed it would be only a matter of time before the police pinned the money and the accounts on me. However, with Will now in a coma and Lynn being charged for poisoning him, there was no longer any reason to leave. I just had to get to the hospital and finish him off. I'd do it after Lynn made bail, so it would look like she did it.

"I told you this would work. Now that those two are out of the picture, we are going to live like we've always wanted," I told Yvonne. I reclined in my lazy boy, feeling good. I looked around thinking I'd miss that room, when I moved into my next place. The money I was going to walked away with caused for something more lavish.

"I didn't think this would ever be." Her face indicated that she didn't share the same excitement.

"Why the long face, Yvonne? This is what you wanted. I did all of this for you."

"I didn't want this. I didn't want Will dead, nor do I want Lynn to go to prison. This was your idea, and at first it did sound like a good one, but that was before I got to know them, Lance. Hanging out with them has changed it all, and now I'm terrified."

"Yvonne, snap out of it. You can't just jump ship when the shit hits the fan. You were all for it, and now that it's happening, I gotta know that you're still on my team. I gotta know that you are still with me." By then I was in her face. She couldn't just abandon ship. If she did, I'd have to find a way to get rid of her ass too.

Her eyes glossed over. "I'm still with you, Lance. I'm not going anywhere." A tear fell. "You're right. This is what I wanted, and you did it, baby. You made it happen."

She wrapped her arms around me. I kissed the top of her head and then handed her a glass. We celebrated, and that night the sex was amazing. She and I had won, and it felt pretty damn good.

The next morning Lynn made bail. I wrote the check and took her home. She was quiet in the car during the entire ride. When we got to her house, I got out and opened the car door for her. I helped her out and walked her to the front door.

"Thank you, Lance," she said once we were inside.

"You're welcome. Are you going to be okay alone?"

"Yes. I'm going to shower and then head to the hospital."

"Okay. I'll get Yvonne, and we'll meet you there."

"Okay."

"Hey, Lynn. Did Will mention anything to you about money missing or say he suspected me of stealing?"

She laughed. "No. Why?" She sat down on the sofa. "Will knows you'd never do that."

I let out a sigh of relief. I was glad he hadn't told her. "I know, right? This is the thing. There was a mix-up in HR, and yesterday, before Will went into the hospital, he came by and asked me about it, and I told him I'd take care of things first thing Monday morning."

"That's fine. I'm sure it's nothing. I went into work on Friday but didn't stay long, because, you know, morning sickness. Of course, if Will isn't better, you know I won't be in on Monday, so can you please just hold down the fort?"

I sat next to her and held her hand. "Of course I will. Don't worry, Lynn. I know you're innocent, and Will is going to pull through."

"Thank you, Lance. I don't know how I'd manage without you right now. I mean, I don't know the ropes yet, and Will needs me. I want to be there when he opens his eyes."

"So do I. Now I'm going to go, and I will meet you at the hospital."

"Okay."

I stood to leave and then headed outside. When I got in my car, I cranked my radio. I drove home, feeling like the self-made multi-millionaire that I was soon to become.

Chapter Twenty-nine

Lynn

The next day I was anxious to get to the hospital and check on Will. He was still doing the same as he was when I left the night before, and I was going out of my mind. I was overwhelmed with stress, and on top of it all, I was still having morning, afternoon, and evening sickness. I didn't know what was going to happen to my husband or my husband's business. I was on edge and afraid to death.

I sat in the hospital room for a few hours, talking to Will and hoping he'd open his eyes. I stepped out of his room for a moment to go eat, and just then my phone rang. It was the officer that was handling my case.

"Hello, hello," I said, anxious to hear from him.

"Mrs. Daniels, we have news."

"Okay."

"We verified that those bank accounts are in Lance Morgan's name. He closed those accounts on Saturday, but since the judge signed a subpoena for his records, we have enough to make an arrest."

"Oh, thank God." I let out a sigh of relief. "So when? When will you arrest him? Will he get bail?"

"Well, considering he has a motive to do something to your husband, we are going to request no bail," Officer Williams said. "We plan to question him, and we will look for any witness who can confirm that your husband was with him on Saturday, before he had another episode."

"Will that even work? I mean, what if no one knows or confirms it? I know in my heart that Lance is behind my husband becoming ill. I mean, they worked together. You must talk to his fiancée. She has to know something. I just don't want him to be released on bail. If there's no proof that he harmed Will and he's released on bail, he could leave town or, worse, come after me."

"Don't worry, Mrs. Daniels," Officer Williams assured me. "We have frozen his assets, his accounts, and if he is considered a flight risk, the judge will most likely rule in your favor."

"I'm now terrified, because I lied and told him I had no idea that Will suspected him of stealing, and he's going to know I told you, because Will is unconscious."

"Listen, I will make sure the prosecuting lawyer and the judge know all those details."

"Please, because I don't know what he is capable of."

"Don't worry, Mrs. Daniels."

"Please. I'm pregnant. My husband is lying in a coma."

"I know, Mrs. Daniels, but believe me, we will protect you and make sure he doesn't hurt you or your husband again."

"Thank you. Just please let me know as soon as you know something."

"You know I will."

I hung up, trembling. I didn't want Lance to come after me. He had looked me in the eyes, as if he had nothing to do with my husband becoming ill, and had pretended that the missing money was an HR error with the payroll. I was shaking as I dialed Kenya. After I explained what was about to go down, she rushed to the hospital to be with me.

***

Later that day, when Kenya and I got to my house to get me some clothes, I was surprised to see Yvonne's car parked outside. When I got out of the car, I thought there was going to be a battle, because they had arrested Lance, but as I got closer to Yvonne, I saw that her face was drenched with tears.

I quickly approached her. "Yvonne, I'm sorry. I know about the arrest."

"I'm so sorry, Lynn," she said, and we hugged.

"I hate that things ended like this, Yvonne, but Lance has been up to no good."

"I know. Can we go inside? I have something I need to talk to you about." She sniffled.

"Sure. Come on." I felt bad for her, because she looked a mess.

When we got inside, we went into the family room. We all sat, and I spoke up first.

"Did you know Lance was stealing from the company?"

"No," she answered and wiped her cheek.

"Yvonne, please don't lie to me. You know a man like Lance is not going to go out alone, and if you had any idea, he is going to take you down with him."

"I didn't know at first. I just thought Lance was doing well. He never once told me that he was taking more than he actually made . . . until recently, and I'm so sorry for what we did to Will."

"We did to Will . . ." I leaped up from the sofa. "What did you do?" I yelled. I took steps in her direction and towered over her. "What in the hell did you do to him?" I knew I was pregnant, but I balled up my fists, anyway. I was ready to beat her ass.

"He made me," she whispered.

"Made you what, Yvonne? Speak up! Tell me what happened to Will. He is in a coma, Yvonne, and my husband could die!" I was shaking at that point.

"I'll tell you everything, and I'm willing to testify, because I feel so horrible, and I am sorry. I didn't want to do it."

"Enough!" Kenya yelled. "Just tell us what you did. What did you give him?"

"I don't know. It was something, something that they use in construction all the time. That is how Lance had access to it. I honestly don't know what the powder was, but I put it in Will's juice a few times."

"A few? What's a few, Yvonne?" I asked, lowering my voice. I eased down on the sofa to give her my undivided attention, I wanted her to be honest and to tell me everything.

"A couple of the mornings we met to discuss Lance's party, I put a couple of pinches in Will's orange juice. Lance encouraged me to put more in it, but I never did, because I didn't want to hurt Will. The plan was to move Will out of the way so that Lance could take over the company."

I covered my mouth. "You guys were plotting to kill my husband." I had heard what she said, but never in a million years did I think someone would actually do that to me and my family.

"Lance was, yes. I only did what he told me to do, but I swear on my life that I never put enough in his glass that it was fatal. The other day, when I made their drinks, Lance came into the kitchen and added more to Will's glass. Then he threatened to kill me if I talked, Lynn, and I was too scared to say anything. Initially, the plan was simple, and I thought I could do it. But I started to see Will more, spend time with you, and after getting to know you two, you were no longer strangers to me, so I tried to back out, but Lance was persistent."

"Why didn't you just leave?" I asked.

"And go where? I have nothing and no one. I grew up with everything, and when my father died, my stepmother took everything from me. I lost my friends, and things didn't get better for me until I met Lance. He was able to provide the things I was accustomed to, and I didn't want to go back to having nothing. At first I went along with it. I saw Will only in passing, never said much to him, but then that changed. . . . So I'm sorry."

"You have to go to the station with me and tell them what you know," I insisted.

"I'll go to jail."

"Well, you should have thought of that before you tried to kill Will," Kenya shot at her.

Yvonne looked at me like she wanted me to save her, but I had nothing to say about that.

"Let's go. You are going to tell the police everything you've told me, and if my husband doesn't pull through, I swear that I will kill you myself. No jail will keep me from doing that," I thundered, knowing it was an empty threat, but I was hurt and furious at her for what she and Lance had done to my husband.

She stood.

I went to get my purse.

"There is one more thing," Yvonne said quietly.

"What?" I demanded.

She headed into my kitchen and quickly came back with a bottle that looked like a container of seasoning.

"What is that, and why did you take it from my kitchen?" I quizzed.

"This is proof."

"Come again?"

"Lance wanted to frame you for Will's murder."

The more Yvonne spoke, the angrier I became. "Let's go."

We left my house in one car, and when we got to the police station, I explained the situation and they handcuffed Yvonne. I felt bad for her, but worse for myself. My husband was the one who had lost the most in this, and even though Lance and Yvonne were going to be locked up for a long time, they'd still get to live.

Epilogue

Lance got the max, and in exchange for her cooperation, Yvonne got probation. It was unbelievable, but that was how the system worked. Every dime and all the other assets that Lance had were seized, and every dollar he had stolen that we had record of was returned to me. Yvonne took ownership of the house she and Lance had lived in, because the money and investments that Lance had acquired settled our debt. I was not sure if Yvonne had a nest egg, but I didn't care, because I had no more dealings with her.

Will wasn't brain dead, but after four months of praying and hoping, I was ready to let him be free. It killed me more each day to see him like that, so as hard as it was for me to let go, by my eighth month I made a decision to do so. I spoke with Will's doctor and decided on a date to let him go.

I was in the recliner next to his hospital bed, eating my famous red velvet cake, when I heard a scratchy voice ask, "Where is mine?"

I dropped my fork and looked at him. He was awake. I hopped up as fast as my oversize, pregnant body would allow me and ran for the doctor.

"He's awake! He's awake!" I yelled at the top of my lungs, and Dr. Patterson and two nurses rushed into the room.

They began to check his vitals, his reflexes, and to ask him questions. He didn't know he had been under for so many months, but he knew me, he knew his name, and when he looked at my stomach, his eyes bulged.

"I've been gone that long?" His voice was raspy.

"Yes," I answered.

He tried unsuccessfully to sit up, so I pressed a button on the bed so that he could sit upright.

"Listen, don't try any sudden moves, Mr. Daniels," the doctor warned. "We have to run a couple more tests. With some physical therapy, you have a great chance at a full recovery."

"Thank you, Dr. Patterson," Will said. "You've been so good to me, and I appreciate you."

"Just doing my job. Glad to have you back, Will. Take a few moments with your wife, and I'll be back soon to check on you."

Will nodded. As soon as they left the room, I hugged him so tight.

"I've missed you," he said.

"Baby, I've missed you too."

A week later Will was home. Things got back to normal for the most part, and it was just in time, because two weeks after he got home, I gave birth to a little girl. It was hell, but we made it, and I was the happiest woman on the planet.